# My Best Friend

Also by Laura Wilson

*A Little Death*

*Dying Voices*

# My Best Friend

## Laura Wilson

*Delacorte Press*

Published by
DELACORTE PRESS
Random House, Inc.
1540 Broadway
New York, New York 10036

*Book design by Virginia Norey*

Delacorte Press® is a registered trademark of Random House, Inc.,
and the colophon is a trademark of Random House, Inc.

LIBRARY OF CONGRESS CATALOGING IN PUBLICATION DATA
Wilson, Laura, 1964–
My best friend / Laura Wilson.
p.    cm.
ISBN 0-385-33579-2
1. England—Fiction    I. Title

PS3573.I4585 M9 2002        2001037187

813/.54 21

Manufactured in the United States of America
First published in 2001 by Orion Publishing Group, UK
Published simultaneously in Canada

January 2002

10  9  8  7  6  5  4  3  2  1
BVG

*To Tim Donnelly, who speeded up the process,*
*and to Freeway, who slowed it down*

## Acknowledgments

I am very grateful to Jane Barlow, Laura Darby, David and Claire Foster, Jane Gregory, Mo Hayder, Hazel Orme, Michael and Janet O'Sullivan, Lisanne Radice, Michael Rimmer, Edward Russell-Walling, Robert Russell-Walling, my parents June and William Wilson, and Jane Wood, for their encouragement, advice, and support. I am also grateful to the staff at the Mass-Observation Archive at the University of Sussex, a unique and wonderful historical resource.

I have taken some minor liberties with the geography of West London, Suffolk, and the Essex coast.

# My Best Friend

## Gerald

*It wasn't the first time* I'd come across a hand. I remember thinking at the time what a coincidence it was. Two hands. Mind you, it was wartime, so I should think that must have shortened the odds a bit. I'd been with Eric on the first occasion—one of the few times I can recall when he'd let me play with him. We were in the woods when we heard the plane explode. Flames everywhere—whoever was on board didn't stand a chance. We went to have a look, and I remember running—neither of us had seen a plane go down at close quarters before, and I was excited; we both were. We were hoping it was German, because German souvenirs were better for swaps than British ones, and in 1943 there wasn't much American stuff around, at least not where I lived. They were still building the new airfields. Lorries full of sand and stone rattled through our village all day, every day.

I must have been about three hundred yards away from the blaze when I saw the glove. Worn brown leather, lying on the grass, palm upward. The fingers were curled over like a violinist's and the moment I touched them I felt the solidness inside. The glove was still . . . well, *occupied*. I dropped it, wiped my hand on my shorts, and carried on running toward the plane. I can't say I thought anything more about it until I found the second one, a year later.

It was autumn and I was in the woods again, but by myself. I think I must have been playing soldiers, because I remember lying on my stomach behind a thick tree root, pretending I was shooting from behind a parapet. I wriggled forward a couple of feet to look over the top, and there it was, a couple of feet from my face. No glove, just pinkish-gray flesh, sticking out of a pile of leaves. Wrist bent, palm downward, and fingers spread out as if it were about to crawl toward me.

I didn't try to pick it up, but pulled myself a bit nearer and stuck out my own hand in imitation of its shape. I mustn't have been quite able to make the mental switch from my game of soldiers, because I remember thinking that the two sets of fingers, opposite each other in a sort of confrontation, were like armies on a battlefield. Then I noticed how delicate the hand was. Pretty, almost, even with the dirt on the skin and the soil that was wedged underneath the long fingernails. I inched my own hand a little closer, and I think I would have touched it, but I suddenly saw that not all of the nails were the same length. The one on the little finger was bitten off short. The instant I saw that, a picture came into my mind of my sister Vera at Christmas, the cheerful, bright sitting room and her with a sketch pad in front of the fire, drawing, and Dad leaning over her, picking up the hand with the pencil in it. "If you go on chewing your nails, you'll grow up to look like George Formby."

She giggled. "Then I'll only bite the little ones, so I'll only look a *tiny* bit like him."

They told me afterward that I ran into the house covered in mud and earth, shouting Vera's name.

HALDANE M(arjorie) M(aud) (1904–1967), creator of Tom Tyler, Boy Detective, was born in Suffolk, where she spent most of her life. Daughter of a bookseller, she wrote of her early childhood that she and her younger sister, Matilda, had "an enchanted existence, living a perpetual delight from day to day." Their happiness was shattered in 1916, when their father returned, shell-shocked, from serving in the First World War. His subsequent mental breakdown, which Haldane was later to describe as "an evil shadow," took its toll on both her parents' marriage and the family finances. Both girls became actresses, although Haldane only worked briefly in the professional theater before marrying stockbroker Arthur Haxton in 1922.

When Haldane became depressed by the couple's failure to conceive a child, Haxton suggested writing as a distraction, and in 1924 her first book, a retelling of Shakespeare for children, was published. Folk tales and fairy stories followed, and her first original work of fiction, **Kitty's Unicorn,** was published in 1929. This was followed by **Kitty's Birthday Wish** and **Kitty's Christmas Wish** (both 1930). The "Kitty" books were followed by a series of "Amy" books, beginning with **Amy's Secret** (1931), but it was not until the publication of **Big Bad Bessie** in 1934, with its eponymous heroine, the naughty schoolgirl Bessie Brown, that Haldane became one of the best-selling children's authors of her day.

By 1937 there were eight "Bessie" books, and Haldane created the boy who was to become her best-known character, the "boy detective" Tom Tyler. For the next thirteen years she produced, on average, three "Tom Tyler" books a year, culminating in **Tom in Trouble Again** in 1950. Tom's adventures with his cousins Peter and Jill and their dog, Scruff, invariably include unmasking spies, bringing thieves to justice, and finding lost treasure. They have been adapted for the stage, televised, and serialized as a comic strip that ran for over thirty years in **Buster** magazine.

Haldane and her husband adopted a daughter, Vera, in 1928, and in 1930 a son, Gerald, was born. However, the couple's relationship, difficult from the beginning, did not survive the tragic death of Vera in 1944. After the war, Haldane wrote little except to continue the "Tom Tyler" series.

Although her work has generally received a favorable critical reception, Haldane's last book, **Friends in Spirit** (1959), thought to have been influenced by her interest in Spiritualism, was universally reviled as morbid and sentimental. It was, as one critic put it, "such a far cry from the robust common sense displayed by Tom Tyler and his fellow thief-takers that it is hard to understand how they could have been created by the person who wrote this book." Haldane, whose health was deteriorating, was said to be very upset by such attacks. She spent the last five years of her life in a nursing home and died in 1967.

DICTIONARY OF CHILDREN'S LITERATURE

"Get in there, you kids," said the man with the eye patch, "and remember, if I hear a sound from either of you, there'll be trouble!" The tall man slammed the door shut, and Jill and Peter heard the sound of a key turning in the lock. The room was pitch black.

"At least there doesn't seem to be any furniture to bump into," said Peter, "but I can't find a light either."

"There's something nailed across the window," said Jill. "Boards, I think." She sat down on the floor and rubbed her ankle. "Oh, Peter, whatever shall we do?" Peter wanted to comfort his sister, but he could not think of anything to say. With all his might, he wished that Tom were with them. If only Tom could find them, he'd get them out of this fix all right!

"I wonder where Tom is," said Jill, as if she could read her brother's thoughts.

"So do I," said Peter. "And I'm starving. I wish we had some of that delicious picnic with us."

"We ate it all up," said Jill. "Every scrap. I'm rather hungry too. Supposing they leave us locked in here all night?"

"Don't worry, Jill. I'm sure that Scruff will stay by our bikes until Tom comes back, and then they're bound to come and sniff us out."

"Poor old Scruff," said Jill. "I hope those beastly men didn't—hullo, what's that noise?"

Tap-tap-tap! Tap-tap-tap! "It's coming from the window," said Peter. There it was again! Tap-tap-tap-TAP! Then they heard a voice, whispering, "Peter! Jill! Are you in there?"

"It's Tom!" shouted Peter. "Good old Tom! Good old Scruff! I knew they'd find us!"

"Keep your voice down or they'll hear us!" said Jill. "Come on, let's see if we can get the boards away from the window." They pulled as hard as they could, and after a moment, a crack of light appeared, with Tom's face behind it. "How on earth did you get up here, Tom?"

"Climbed up the back porch, of course. Scruff's in the yard. What happened?"

"Those horrible men came back to the clearing while we were tidying up the picnic things," said Jill. "We tried to hide, but they caught us and pushed us into their van. Scruff tried to follow, but they threw stones at him. He is all right, isn't he?"

"He's fine. He showed me the way here. It would take more than a few stones to put him off!"

"Jill's sprained her ankle," said Peter. "She's being awfully brave about it, but I know it's hurting her dreadfully."

"There's something much more important than my silly old ankle," said Jill. "You'll never guess what we saw in the van, Tom! Aunt Sarah's picture!"

"And half a dozen others as well," said Peter.

"So they're the art thieves," said Tom. "No wonder your mother thought they were suspicious characters. Well, we'll soon put a stop to their tricks, shan't we?"

**Tom in Trouble,** 1939

## Jo

*Well, I didn't know* whose son he was. I still think he's creepy. It's not anything he *does,* so much, it's just the way he sits there by himself, really quiet. He's just like this big white *blob* sitting opposite me, and . . . I don't know, he's just really *odd.* Like when he has his lunch, it's the same thing every single day: tuna fish sandwiches. He brings them from home and they smell disgusting. Then he has an orange and he makes this big thing about peeling it with a special knife that he keeps in his drawer. He's a total slaphead as well. There's this bloke, John, who works in our loading bay, and he's quite funny, some of the things he says. Well, I was down there last week and I was talking to him when Gerald comes in and starts going on about something. You could tell John was getting pissed off with him because it was really straightforward, but Gerald just wouldn't leave it alone. When he'd gone, John goes, "I've got more hair on my bollocks than he's got on his head." I was trying really hard not to laugh, because Gerald was only in the corridor and I thought he might have heard, but he never came back. Then I said something about how I suppose his mother loves him or whatever, and John said, "Do you know who his mother was?" I said, "What do you mean, who she was?" and he told me that Gerald's mother was M. M. Haldane, the children's writer. I said, "I don't believe it," because she'd have left him all her money, wouldn't she? But John says it's true.

I mean, I didn't even know M. M. Haldane was a woman. I used to love those stories. I had all the books and I read them loads of times and I kept them and everything. Mel's got them now. Mel's my daughter. She's twelve. Gerald's always asking me about her. I think he thinks he's being friendly, you know, like he always asks me if I've had a nice weekend, but it just never sounds quite right, you know? I told my mum about him and she said, "Oh, you're being mean," but she doesn't have him sitting there looking at her all day, because he does. He watches me. I'm, like, checking a list or something, and then I look up for a second and he's staring straight at me. My mum goes, "Oh, he probably fancies you." I said, "Thanks a lot, Mum, that's like saying Mr. Blobby fancies you." Actually, he did do something quite sweet the other day. Our boss at work, Neville, he's got this really annoying habit where he always calls everyone by their initials. It's stupid, because I never know who he's talking about. He comes into our office and says to me, "Oh, J.F., can you tell P.G. to have a word with C.S. about an order?" and I go, "Who?" Anyway, he came in last week and he said, "Have you seen J.P.?" and Gerald goes, "Try the W.C." I thought that was quite funny, really.

Apart from that, I'm sorry, but he is *really* strange. I was telling Mum about his shirts and how the collars and cuffs are always all frayed and dirty, and I said I don't understand why he doesn't buy new ones because . . . well, I mean, even if he didn't inherit any money from his mother, I earn less than he does and I don't go round with my clothes falling to bits. *And* I've got Mel to look after. He's only got himself. Actually, she's being a real *pain* at the moment, you know, buy me this, buy me that, when she knows I can't afford it.

I was only seventeen when I had Mel. When I found out I was pregnant I was really scared to tell my mum because I thought she'd go nuts, because she'd had me when she was really young as well and she was always saying to me, you know, you want to wait. . . . So I was really nervous, but I kept thinking, I've got to tell her, I've got to tell her. I was getting really stressed about it and one night I just blurted out, "Oh, Mum, I'm going to have a baby." She would have shouted at me, but Colin—that's her boyfriend, but they've been together for so long he's like my stepfather—was really nice to me. But my mum though, all credit to her, she never said, "You've got to get rid of it," you know, have an abortion. To tell you the truth, I did think about it, but then I saw this doctor, and he was all, "Are you sure you want to do this," and then he started telling me about the baby and how it was growing inside me. . . . He didn't show me a picture or anything, but I could sort of see it in my mind, this little pink thing with tiny little hands and everything, and then it was like, that was that, and I really wanted to have it.

I'd have liked to go to college and travel and all that and then have children. I mean, I think I did the right thing having Mel but it was just at the wrong time in my life. Don't get me wrong, okay? Because I love Mel, she's my baby and I'd do anything for her, but if I had my time again I'd have waited before I had kids. But my mum's been really brilliant, because she knows what it's like when you've got a baby and you're on your own. I was still living at home and everything, and she looked after Mel while I did my computer course. I got the qualification and then when Mel started school I got a job, and that's when I moved into my flat. It's just rented, I don't have a mortgage or anything, but it's better having a place of my own. My mum does loads of baby-sitting—I sometimes think it'd be nice if Mel's dad lived with us, but I know he wouldn't be as much help as my mum is. Sean—that's Mel's dad—he was only eighteen when I found out I was pregnant. At first it was, "Oh, I'll get a job, we can get married," and all this, but when she was born he couldn't handle it and he started being really . . . you know, he never came round to see me or anything, and his mum was horrible to me. She started going on about how Mel wasn't Sean's kid and I was just trying to get money off them. My mum was furious, especially 'cause I never asked him for any money, and she was going, "Oh, that bitch, I'm going to go round there and sort her out," but Colin wouldn't let her.

They moved away in the end. It did upset me, but it wasn't like, *disaster*. I mean, I used to try and imagine the three of us living in this nice little house and—oh, I don't know, going on holiday and all that, but I knew it wasn't going to happen. It's like those books, the ones that Gerald's mum wrote. When you're reading them and you're really into the story and everything, it's like you're part of this whole world and you just want it to go on forever, but at the same time you know it's not, like, *real*.

It *is* funny about his mum writing those books. They're about fifty years old now, so it must have been when he was little. I can't imagine him as a kid. I sort of want to ask him about it, but I haven't got the guts.

## Gerald, 1938

*My name is Gerald Arthur Haxton.* I am 8. I live in a house called Broad Acres, in a village called Finching in a county called Suffolk. I am going to do a dairey but it is only paper because I have not got a book yet. When I get one it will be proper. Now I have to say the peopel that live in our house. It is me and my sister Vera. She is 11. My mother is Miss Haldane but her name is Mrs. Haxton really. My father is Mr. Haxton. His name is Arthur and he goes to work in the train to London where his work is. And there is Mrs. Paddick, she looks after us and cooks the food and Mrs. Everit but she only comes in the morning. Tom is the gardener. Our dog is Sammy. He is black and white. He is super but he is not any specil sort of dog but lots of diffrent ones. Aunt Tilly comes to stay. She is nice. And that is all the peopel in our house.

### Monday, September 19th

Mr. Chamberlin went to Munick. It was his first time of flying in an aeroplane. I wish I could go in one. He had ham sandwiches and wiskey on the way and chicken sandwiches and clarit on the way back. Clarit is a sort of wine. I would have the same but with lemonade. But he did not get pudding. Mother says there wont be a war now. Father says he should of stood up to Hitler. Mother said I would like to see you do better.

*Tuesday, September 20th*

It was noisy in the kitchen. Mrs. Paddick said dont worry there wont be any war but then Tom came in and he said if Hitler wants a war he will have one and then we will have one too wether we like it or not. Mrs. Paddick was cross because mud from his boots came on the floor. She gave me a cheese and onion sandwich and then was more cross because I piked the onions out.

*Wednesday, September 21st*

Tom said a rude word. He said the war was bad and he would kill Hitler and Mussoleny too if he could but I think he is silly. Mrs. Paddick says Mussoleny only kills blacks. Then he said not to tell Mother about the rude word and I said I wont. We had ham and salad for tea and stewed damsins and custud.

*Thursday, September 22nd*

I went downstairs after I went to bed. The wierless woke me up and when I went to the door of the sitting room it was an argument. She was shouting but he did not say anything. She said he was a mouse and not a man. Then he said if there is a war I will go away and then you will get rid of me. She dropped her cig on the blue rug and went to pick it up but it made a hole and she said it will spoyle everything. Then he saw me by the door and said go back to bed theres a good chap. She looked at me. Her eyes went big and I thought she would shout at me but she did not. I don't want Dad to go away.

*Friday, September 23rd*

I want a book to write in because my paper has nearly run out so I asked her. She was writing and she said don't distrub me how many times have I told you. I said about the book because she promised but she said I never said you could have one of my specil books. But she patted her hair at the back when she said it and that means A LIE. Mrs.

Paddick said she had some paper and I can have it. She gave it to me and I sat at the table and Tom came in and they were talking about gas masks. Mrs. Paddick said they are horrid things you can suficate in and she may as well go to the semitrey and dig a hole and get in it now.

*Monday, October 3rd*

I have not done the diary for two days because I forgot.

Scriture 8/10 Spelling 5/10 Arithmatic 6/10

There are two new boys in the class and they are twins. I said I am a twin too and they said wheres your twin then and I said he was dead and they said well it does not count. I said I am because it is true but they said no because there is two of them and only one of me. I did not know what to say but IT IS TRUE.

*Tuesday, October 11th*

Not well all day. Had wierless in bed and ate dijestiv biscuits but it hurt. Missed arith test. Talked to Jack. She says his name is Leslie because it is on the sertificat but I know it is Jack because he told me.

*Wednesday, October 12th*

Dad came to see me. He said is there anything you want old chap and I said a book to write in. He said are you going to be a writer like your mother? But I said no it is just for a diary.

## Gerald

*Stacey was working the box office tonight.* I went to say hello and she told me she'll only be there for another week because she's getting married and then she's going off traveling with her husband. They've got the money saved. I said that's nice, because she told me they're going to Sri Lanka. She asked me if I had a lady friend, which was a bit cheeky, but I don't mind. When I told her no, she said, "What a pity." I asked her why it was a pity, and she said, "Then you'd have someone to come with you to the theater," but I told her I like coming on my own. They had two new ones in the chorus tonight, both boys. I kept a lookout for them, but it went off all right.

I always meet the cast. *Cats* I saw 105 times, and I knew all the people. One of them—Becky, her name was, Becky Stocker—she said to me, "Don't you get sick of it, coming back to see the same show week after week?" Because that's what I do, Tuesday and Thursday nights, I go to the theater. I said, "I never get sick of it, it's always wonderful." She said, "Well, I'm getting sick of it and I've only been in it three months." I told her, "You should stick with it, it's a good show, this one." I've been going to another show as well, *Starlight Express.* I've seen it 215 times so far, which is my personal best. But you've got to have a change sometimes, so last summer I stopped with *Cats* and went to *Oklahoma!* instead. That was a bit of a departure for me, and I don't mind admitting I was a bit worried about it at first, because I thought, being as old as it is, it might be a bit slow for modern tastes, but it's first rate. There's good singing and dancing, wonderful sets, clever story, everything you want. The first few months with a new show are always difficult, but once I've got it all off pat I can really settle down and enjoy myself. Tonight was my thirty-ninth performance.

I always eat after the show. I make myself a sandwich before I leave the house, whole-grain bread with tuna fish and lettuce. I put it in an airtight tupperware container in the fridge for when I come back. I have to share the kitchen with my landlady, you see, and with the best will in the world, it's not unknown for things to go missing. I pour myself a glass of milk too—the proper milk, not this half-water stuff—and that goes in the fridge with a playing card on top. The ace of spades. Face down.

I like to know what I'm doing, get it all organized. Some people find their happiness with money or fast cars, but for me, it's when I've got things planned out. Knowing what the next step is going to be, that's the key to happiness for me. I know some people find me a bit strange. I've even had them calling me mental before now, but I always say, well, at least it keeps me happy. A lot of folk go through their whole lives and never find happiness, so I say I'm better off than most.

I had a good old chin-wag with Jack on the way home. It's always the best time, after a show. I wouldn't call it talking, exactly, it's more like signals, sending them out and getting them back, all in your mind. Just as well, because people really would think I was mad if I sat on the bus talking to myself—well, that's what they'd see, anyway. They wouldn't understand what was really happening. Because it's hard to explain—if I'm honest, I don't understand it myself. I don't want to be big-headed, but I will say I'm special in that regard. Being a twin is special—from the moment you're born it makes you different from other people, because they're only one. If you're a twin, it makes you less and more at the same time, if you see what I mean. You're yourself, but you're something else as well—part of a pair. You're a whole and a half, both at once.

Jack was stillborn. There's no point in saying, "what if," because you can't turn the clock back, but I sometimes think it would have been nice if we could have started a business together. I'm in the hiring game. Not cars or vans, but props for stage and television. That's where I get my interest in the theater. It runs in the family, because my aunt was an actress. But if you've been to the theater or watched TV in the last forty years, you'll have seen some of the things we've supplied. Bath chairs, dressing tables, garden shears, jukeboxes, stethoscopes, we've done the lot. Channing & Mason, one of the best-known firms in the business. We're in White City, near the stadium. I don't own the company, of course, but I've worked there since they started. I'm coming up for retirement next year, but I've often thought I'd like my own little business—with Jack, not by myself, but that wasn't to be. Besides, if Jack were alive, we might have gone our separate ways by now, who knows? This way, he's always there—I'm not saying he actually answers my signals every time, any more than someone who's alive always wants to talk to you. Everybody wants to be private sometimes, and Jack's no different from anybody else in that regard. But just because you can't see something doesn't mean it's not there. No one's ever seen God, but plenty of people believe He exists. I do myself, as a matter of fact. I believe I'll see Jack in heaven. I often wonder if he'll look like me. Some twins are identical and some aren't, so who knows? I've always assumed we look the same, but I can't be sure. Perhaps I ought to hope we don't—for his sake! When I was a child, I used to look into the mirror and talk to him and that sort of thing. Make-believe. My mother used to get angry if she caught me doing that. Funny, really, when you think how she was always using her imagination to make up stories. You'd have thought she'd be pleased that I was doing the same. But we never saw eye-to-eye about Jack. She called him Leslie, but that wasn't his true name. It was Jack.

So that's how I get along. I'm not resentful, but I did miss out on a fair bit. In the education department, for one. I suppose I'm not what you would call clever, but it was the war that did that for me, the disruption. Not to mention disruption at home. Never fulfilled my potential, you might say.

My sister, Vera, was much cleverer than me. I always thought that was funny because she was the adopted one and my parents were both intelligent people. When I was a boy, I used to think Jack might have been very clever too, and then he could have helped me with my schoolwork, but now I'm of the opinion that he's the same as I am. Being brainy isn't everything, but I do wonder if there isn't something in me that's been missed. Fallen by the wayside, you might say. If I'd been like those children my mother wrote about, I'd probably have been running the country by now, but there it is. My surname being Haxton—my father's name—people don't make the connection, and I don't push it forward. I don't want to be an object of curiosity, I don't want people raking up the past, and I don't want them coming after me thinking I've got money either. After the death taxes, all that went to the Haldane Children's Foundation, not to me, but as long as I've got enough for a good seat at the theater, I don't mind. I've got Jack, and he's better than money.

## My Diary by Gerald Haxton Age 8

*The paper is thick.* I am scared to write on it in case I make a mistake as I do that a lot at school. I did not put the date it is October the 18th. Now I am ill. It is my tonsells and they have to COME OUT. I am going to hospital.

### Tuesday, October 25th

I did not put about the hospital because I was ill but there were 11 other children as well as me. They put a mask on my face with stuff on it and it was suffickating like Mrs. Paddick said about the gas mask. When I went home I had jelly and ice cream then Mother came in with some bread and driping but it hurt to eat because it was to hard and I did not have it. Vera just came in she said that is not how you spell driping and I said don't look its private. She showed me her picture of Dad and Sammy in the garden and it was good.

### Thursday, October 27th

Talked to Jack a lot. I got the hair brush. The back is shiny and I can see my face so it is like a conversaison even if he does not talk. Mother came in but I did not put the hair brush down in time and she saw it. She said it was a silly game. I said Jack is not silly. She said his name is Leslie so why are you doing this? But he is my twin and I have got more rigte than she has. Leslie is a girls name. Jack is touf so he would not have a stupid girls name.

### Tuesday, November 1st

I went into the kitchen. It was steamy from the boiler and Mrs. Paddick doing washing. We had rabbit stew. Tom came in with a marrow we will have to eat it. It will be very horrid and Vera said she will not eat it she will put it in her nickers.

### Thursday, November 3rd

My birthday. Now I am 9 years old. I got good presents of soldiers and a puzzle. Mother stayed in her room all day. I said should I go and say thank you for the puzzle but Dad said don't upset your mother. We had rost beef and potatos v good and more marrow v bad. And Mrs. Paddick made a cake and we had two pieces each but she still stayed in her room. Aunt Tilly came for tea. She says all the plays are rot but the lines are easy to remember. That is good because she says there is a different one every week. Quite a lot of peopel forget the words but there is a lady with a book to tell you.

### Tuesday, November 8th

I wanted to play with the twins today but they said I couldn't because if I had a twin I would have a picture and then it would be real. But I have not got one. If there was it would just be a little baby and not Jack at all. But I don't care. I talked to him all the way home for dinner. It was tappioka with cripsy bits. My favorite

### Friday, November 11th

There is an artist in the village. He moved into the big house at the end. Dad said the best of British luck to him that house is a reck. But I think it is good it has got a pond and we have not and a super garden.

He has got 6 children Mrs. Paddick said but I have not seen them yet. It will be better than Mrs. Bancroft because she chased us away. He came to see Mother and she said he can draw Vera. But when Dad came home he said why did you say that and she said he was jealous. So then he said to me and Vera to go away. I said to Vera do you mind about the drawing and she said she wanted to.

*Tuesday, November 15th*

After lunch I played ball. I was bouncing it against the wall but it smashed a window in the kitchen and Mrs. Paddick came running out. Mother was cross that it distrubed her writing. When Mrs. Paddick went to get the brush she said Leslie would not have done that. But I know he would because it was not on perpuse.

*Wednesday, November 16th*

We are going to a seons it is where you talk to dead people. I went with Mother and Vera. Mother said Mrs. Paddick we are going to the seons and she said Well that is not very cheery is it? Then she said ask the medium if there will be a war. That is the lady who talks to the dead people but if you don't think it is true then it will not work. Now we have come back from the seons it was a room with an old woman with a red light and lots of people. It was very horrid and smelt funny. The woman made a noise like a pig and then she shouted Marjy and got a smack on my leg. Then the woman said to Mother oh it is your father he is passed to sprit. Mother said no then she ran down the stairs and we could not find her so we went back and they shouted at us because the old woman fell off her chair but it was not fair as we did not do it. Then Dad came in the car and we went home. Dad said we must not go again because it is old woman's nonsense and there was a big row. I said to Vera were you frigtened and she said no but I think she was. I was too but I did not tell her.

## *Tilly*

*The new doctor was here this morning,* going on at me as usual. "You really ought to give up smoking, Miss Haldane." I said, "Why?" I'm eighty-seven years old, for God's sake, and you've got to die of *something*, haven't you? I said, "Well, Doctor, I have butter on my bread, cream in my coffee, a glass of sherry before dinner, and a scotch before I go to bed, and I'm not going to give those up either." He can't be more than thirty, and he's telling me I ought to give up smoking. I thought, who's the old woman here, Doctor, you or me? I damn near said it too, but that would never do. I can't understand some of these young people—frightened to do anything, in case it's taking a risk. No sense of humor either, half of them. Puts me in mind of that Tommy Cooper joke: "Doctor, how long have I got?"

"Well, Mr. Smith, if I were you, I wouldn't buy any long-playing records."

You come into this world, you're going to go out of it, and that's a fact. I'll wait till Nicky goes to heaven, and then I'll go too. Nicky's fifteen, which is old for a dog. He's a French poodle. Black. I'm the only one here allowed to have a dog. They were all set to tell me I couldn't, then in walks the manager and it turns out we were in the same company in 1952. Newquay. Dreadful. I said, "Oh, you were *marvelous*." Which was a downright lie, but it did the trick. But I remembered him, all right. Pardon my saying it, but he used to break wind on stage. He was only young, and it was his nerves, you see. Affected the stomach.

There aren't many here I can talk to, really, not what you'd call a decent conversation. Gerald comes up to see me though, and we have a little chat. He's a good boy, but I worry about what'll happen to him when I go, because he doesn't have a lot of friends. Even when they were children, Vera would always say, "Oh, I had tea with this one," or "I did such-and-such with that one," but when Gerald used to tell me about his school and all the rest of it, he never mentioned any pals. He's always been too much in his head for my liking. I blame his mother for that. I don't like to speak ill of the dead, but my sister was a dreadful woman in a lot of ways. If I'm going to be charitable about it—there's no earthly reason why I *should* be charitable, but I will—I'd say that what happened to my father had a lot to do with her turning out the way she did. We didn't have so much money after Dad got ill, and I think she felt as if everything had been taken away from her . . . personally, I mean, almost as if he'd done it on purpose. And you can see it with some of her books, it's as if she's trying to get back this wonderful childhood she felt she'd lost. She was twelve when it happened, I was only eight, so she'd had more of it than I did, if you see what I mean. But the funny thing is, to hear Marjorie talk, you'd think it was all like fairyland. What I remember is that it was perfectly *nice,* but not idyllic, not by any means. I remember arguments between my mother and father right from when I was a tot, but to Marjorie it was all sweetness and light. I think that the more she left it behind—in years, I mean—the more . . . golden the memories became, so of course the loss seemed even greater. And I think she really did blame Dad for that.

She had this . . . *determination,* if you like, that she wasn't going to be disappointed in life. It was as if she had to get things and keep hold of them so that no one would be able to take them away. Very secretive. And always wanting to be special, to be the best. I think she thought it would protect her, somehow, standing out from other people, being the exception. My mother was always the strong force in our house—she certainly felt her life had been a disappointment. My father was very mild, and I think Marjorie felt he'd just allowed himself to be herded into the army, really.

If she thought something was hers—her territory, if you like—she wouldn't let anyone else get near. Even the grief she felt for Gerald's twin, the baby who died. Marjorie was convinced that if he'd lived he would have been the perfect son, like those kids she used to write about. Well, you can imagine what that did to Gerald, always being second best. Every time he had a birthday, she'd be upstairs all day in her room, crying. I used to say to her, "What about Arthur? Don't you think he's upset as well?" But oh, no, she was the one with the broken heart, nobody else could have any idea of how she felt. Of course it ruined the day for poor little Gerald.

There's no doubt about it, he's grown up odd. He got into a bit of trouble with the police a few years back. . . . He was very upset about it, kept saying they'd bullied him, but when I asked him why they'd questioned him, he wouldn't tell me, got himself in such a state over it I gave up asking. I told him, I'm broad-minded enough, he needn't be ashamed, whatever it was. There was a time, you see, when I thought he might have gone the other way. I've been over sixty years in the theater, so I've known plenty of homos, but I haven't a drop of prejudice in me so far as that goes. Mind you, if it was that, I don't see what the police wanted with him, because it's all legal nowadays. But Gerald never had a man-friend that I know of, and he never had a woman either. I don't know what it was, really. I used to say to him, "Why don't you find yourself a nice girl and marry her?" and he'd say, "I don't know, they're always after something, aren't they?" I think he meant after money, not that he's got any, because Marjorie left all hers to her blessed foundation, and Arthur left his to me. I offered to give Gerald something to put toward a nice little flat, but he wouldn't take a penny even though he's only got the one room.

It's my afternoon to have my hair done. There's not as much as there used to be, but I always have the color and the wave. We both had blond hair, Marjorie and I. I don't know what Marjorie used to do to hers, but I always think you should give nature a bit of a leg up where you can— so I've still got my blond hair, even today. Fair hair and brown eyes, both of us. Unusual. Marjorie must have been first in the queue for the eyes though, because hers were *beautiful,* and she had this look—not that poor old Arthur ever saw it much, or Gerald, for that matter—but you'll see it in all the pictures, head slightly to one side, and even in black-and-white her eyes are lovely, deep, and soft. She looks exactly the sort of person who ought to be writing stories for children. If you'd only seen the pictures, you'd never have guessed what she was really like. I could see through it, of course, but then, I'd known her all my life, hadn't I? I always knew when she wasn't telling the truth, because she had this way of fiddling with her hair, at the back. We all knew she did that, even Gerald. She was taller than me too, which I always envied, because I'm quite little—mind you, being smaller meant I went on playing the younger parts far longer than if I'd been big, so that was a benefit, really. Marjorie never bothered to disguise what she thought about my work—second-rate, because it was always touring, not the West End or the cinema. But that didn't bother me—I mean, I knew I wasn't Gertrude Lawrence. I've played in some terrible old tat, it's true, but it was my job, and I liked it. I've supported myself all my life doing it too, and I bet there's not many can say that nowadays. Mind you, it's different now; a lot of the theaters where I worked have gone—you'd have to be off your head to go into the business today.

They're going to paint my nails for me, because I can't do it any- more. I like to look nice. It's habit as much as anything else. *Must dress well, on stage and off,* that's what the ads used to say, because you had to bring your own clothes, you see, for the modern plays. It was all quite different in those days. We didn't sit round discussing the motivation or prance about pretending to be farm animals or whatever it is they do now. No directors either, not when I started. The stage manager told you where to stand and when to move, and you went on, said your piece, and came off, simple as that.

That's what I told the doctor: I've said my piece, now I want to get off. He said, "Let's hope you've got a good few years yet, Miss Haldane." I said, "I don't *want* a good few years!" In a lot of ways I've had a good life, seen a lot, done a lot, had a lot of pleasure. I'd like to think I've given pleasure, too, along the way, and you can't ask for more than that, can you? But death's a dirty word to him, same as all doctors nowadays. They think the best thing they can do is to keep someone alive, but it isn't. I couldn't explain to him, it's not death that frightens me, it's going on too long.

Marjorie had a heart attack, and that was how my mother went too, quickly, not at all nasty. I've always said that'll do for me when the time comes. One big gasp and that's the end of it. I don't want to be a cripple, and I don't want to lose my marbles. But it's not just that—it's sitting here day after day with nothing to do but remember. Doesn't matter how much you want to, you can never undo what you've done. Listen to me, going on like Marley's ghost: *I wear the chains I forged in life* . . .

We wanted to protect Gerald, Arthur and I. We thought we were doing the right thing, but I don't know so much now. Whenever I've seen Gerald these last few years, I find myself wondering if what we did made any difference, knowing how his life turned out. We can't ever know those things, can we? But I keep coming back to it, and it bothers me.

I'll never forget the state Arthur was in that night. I won't deny we'd been close for several years before that—well, I'm no angel, never pretended I was, and Marjorie didn't want him, so why not? We were never in love. I don't know how Arthur went on, but I had other men around me, and if I took a fancy to one of them I'd go with him. It was more of a friendship, really, with a bit of the other thrown in from time to time. You'd think you'd be able to put the two together and that would be love, wouldn't you? But it isn't. I think it's a damn sight better, if you want the truth—being in love won't make you happy in the long run, even if he's got all the money you could want!

But what I'm saying is, that Yank they hanged didn't kill Vera. He'd been with her, mind you, and so had quite a few of his chums, from what I heard. Of course, Arthur never wanted to believe that, he was protective of her like any father would be, but all I can say is, it takes one to know one, and I knew all right. Eddie Mayo, his name was. Came from Chicago. He was only twenty-three and not too much upstairs either, by all accounts. I thought about writing to his mother, many times, but of course I couldn't. I'd made a promise to Arthur, and even after he died I felt I couldn't break it.

## Gerald

*My thermos flask got broken on Wednesday.* It was in the morning. I'd just arrived at work, and I was about to go into the office when someone in the loading bay called me to look at an order. They were having trouble finding something, you see. All the sections are labeled—*Kitchen Equipment, Shop Interiors,* and so forth—but people don't always put things back in their right places, unfortunately. This time they'd managed to lose a hostess cart. I said I'd go and have a look, and I put my flask down by the door because I didn't want it damaged—famous last words. It was one of the young chaps who called me, and I wasn't surprised he couldn't find the cart because it was right at the back, behind the cash registers—old money, new money, electronic, whatever you want, we've got one—and someone had plonked a dirty great tin bath down on top of it so that all you could see were the wheels.

Just as I was bending over to check it, I heard an enormous crash from the front. Some idiot with a heavy box he'd no business carrying by himself had knocked over a glass case full of songbirds. We keep the taxidermy at that end because some of the bigger pieces, the tigers and bears, can be very tricky to maneuver, and you can't get replacements for love or money. Well, when I saw what was happening, I shouted, "Put that down!" I got over there as fast as I could, but not before the whole thing had come smashing to the ground and the chap had jumped backward and caught my flask with his foot. I didn't notice it at first because I was too upset over the birds, and it was only when we'd got all the glass cleared up that I looked round for my flask. It had rolled right into the yard and there was a tinkling sound inside when I picked it up, so I knew right away that it was shattered.

I suppose you could say it was my own fault for putting it there in the first place, but it's Friday now, and I still haven't got a new one. Jo— that's the girl who works in the office with me—said, "Well, there's always the machine." Because we've got this contraption that makes tea and coffee, or an approximation of tea and coffee, for 30p. I said, "No, thank you, I'll stick with my flask." But when I went after work on Wednesday to see if I could get another one, I found they'd discontinued the line. Well, I've had trouble like this before, over a hot-water bottle, so I said to the girl behind the counter, "Are you sure you don't have any in the stockroom?"

"Oh, no," she said, "we wouldn't have anything like this."

I said, "Well, this is the shop where I bought it, so perhaps you wouldn't mind going to check." Then she asked me when I'd bought it. I had to think about that one for a moment, I don't mind telling you. It was in 1978. That brought some raised eyebrows, but she called the manager and he took one look and told me the manufacturer had gone out of business! So that was that. No new flask. They showed me some others, but I couldn't make the decision there and then.

Well, on Thursdays I have to go straight home—it takes half an hour, walking—and then I've just got time to make my sandwich and pour my glass of milk and put them in the fridge before I have to turn back around and take the tube into the West End. I like to leave plenty of time for that, especially on Thursdays, because I have to get to the Apollo at Victoria, and that means taking the Hammersmith & City line from Shepherd's Bush and changing onto the District line at Hammersmith, and then it's seven stops. I like to arrive at the theater at least a quarter of an hour early so I can talk to everyone and get properly settled before the show starts. Obviously, with doing all that, there was no time to go back to the shop, and I still hadn't decided what I was going to do about the new flask. It bothered me all day, and I made a silly mistake with an order, which is most unusual.

This morning, it so happened that I had to pay a visit to our military department, which is just round the corner from the shop where I bought the flask. I wouldn't normally have much to do with army stuff, but we've had a big run on the Second World War with the VE Day fiftieth anniversary coming up, and I've had to go down there several times in the past few months. I was debating with myself whether to drop into the shop on the way back and take another look at the flasks they had on display. I wouldn't normally take advantage of the firm's time like that, but I thought, I can't allow this state of affairs to go on, I've got to do something.

When I got to the military department, the place was in such a state that the flask went clean out of my mind. I don't like to be a bearer of tales, but it looked—I don't say this to be funny, but it looked like a battlefield. They have these dummies, you see, mannequins, in the front office, and Paul—Paul Cosworth, the chap who runs it—he dresses them up in uniforms. It's like an ad, really, so that the customers can see the sort of thing we've got, and usually it's quite a good display. But this morning it was chaos. I came through the door and the first thing I saw was this torso. No arms, no legs, no bottom, and the head wrapped up in bandages. There were three other mannequins in bits on the floor, arms and legs all over the shop, with what looked like red paint spilled over them. Then I looked up and there was one sitting behind Paul's desk, stark naked, with sticking plaster all over its face. I almost jumped out of my skin when I saw that, I can tell you. When Paul came in I said, "Is this someone's idea of a joke? Because it's not very funny." He'd left the door wide open, and it might have given someone a nasty turn if they'd walked in off the street. He said, "It's my daughter. She's been off school for a few days, so I let her play hospital with them. She wants to be a nurse when she grows up."

I said, "You shouldn't let her do that." I mean, she'd taken all the clothes off; it wasn't nice. "She's got them covered in paint," I said. "You'll have a job to get that off."

He said, "That's all right, it's only ketchup." And then—I couldn't believe my eyes—he picked up one of the legs and licked it, right down the shin. "I'll have that with my chips."

I said, "You shouldn't do that, you don't know where it's been."

Paul said, "Yes I do. This is Charlie, and I'd never let him out of my sight, he's far too pretty." Well, I was so disgusted, I didn't know what to say. I thought it would be best to get on with the job at hand, so I told him I'd come to collect some Home Guard bandoliers. He said, "You must be joking, mate. We haven't got any of those. Rare as hen's teeth, they are. Why didn't you phone me first?" Which I suppose I should have, but with worrying about the flask I didn't think of it.

Then this other chap came in—I recognized his face, but I couldn't immediately place him. I put him at about forty or so, ordinary looking, with brown hair. No distinguishing marks, as they say, but I knew I'd seen him somewhere before. Paul turned to him and said, "Gerald here only wants some Home Guard bandoliers." The man laughed, quite unkindly, I thought. "You'll be lucky." Then he said, "What do you want those for, then?"

"It's for a television program. *The Real Dad's Army,* it's called."

"Is that who you work for, the television? Because you lot should get your facts sorted out. It wasn't always the Home Guard, you know, it was the L.D.V. until July 1940. Local Defense Volunteers; or Look, Duck, and Vanish, depending who you talk to. There weren't any uniforms or weapons in those days; you had people going on patrol with shotguns, crowbars, even golf clubs, some of them. They didn't have all that fancy clobber until very late on in the war, you know. We've just done a display at Dover Castle; you should have come to that if you want to know about the Home Guard."

That made me a bit cross, so I said, "I was alive during the war, and I remember quite enough about the Home Guard, if it's all the same to you. In any case, I don't work for the TV. I work in the other department here, and I just came by to collect some equipment."

Well, I thought, that's stopped him in his tracks, but he said, "I'm from the local precinct; don't I know you?" Of course, as soon as he said it, I placed him, all right. He was the one who said they'd be watching me. "We'll be keeping an eye on you in the future," that was the last thing he said to me. Same nasty tone in his voice. Because unfortunately I've had some dealings with the police in the past, and I didn't like it one bit. They're a lot of bullies, the police, in uniform or out of it. And this one—Steven Palfrey, he said his name was—evidently got straight out of one uniform and into another, though it's beyond me why anyone should want to reenact the war. They wouldn't want to if they'd been there, I can tell you. All muck and bullets—I forget who said that, but it's true.

It really rattled me, him saying that, and I left as soon as I could. All I could think of was what he was telling Paul about me, and whether Paul would tell Neville and then I'd lose my job. It wasn't until I got back to the office that I remembered about the flask. I'd almost made up my mind to go to the shop after work, but I got a headache from worrying about it all, so Jo said why didn't I go home and she'd lock up, which was kind of her.

My landlady, Mrs. Clarke, was waiting for me in the kitchen. She called out to me but I could tell by her voice that she was going to nag at me about something, so I pretended I didn't hear and went upstairs to my room and sat on the bed. She came up about five minutes later and knocked on the door. "Didn't you hear me calling?" I told her I hadn't, but she said, "Oh, I don't believe that for a moment," and then started talking about how I'd left the kitchen in a right old state and put all her things back in the wrong drawers. Then she said that when I'd put the butter away in the fridge I left it too near the edge and she'd knocked it on the floor and the lid of the container was cracked. I said, "I don't think it's fair to blame me for that. It wasn't my fault."

"Yes, it was; you put it in the wrong place. I wasn't expecting it there and now I've had to throw the whole lot away."

I said, "But you said it was only the lid that got broken."

"Yes, but there's still germs! It fell right out onto the floor, and it's no good keeping the bottom part without the lid, is it?" My head was very sore by this time, so I put my hands up to my temples, and she said, "Oh, you can pretend, all right, but there's others have to live in this house as well as you." Which isn't true, because there's only the two of us. She left eventually, but I hate things like that; they make me feel ill.

I lay down on my bed and tried to talk to Jack, but it was no good because he never answers when I'm like this. I must have fallen asleep after that, because when I looked at my watch it was eight o'clock. I'd missed my suppertime, so I thought I'd go for a walk and buy some chocolate to cheer myself up a bit. I walked around for a while, hoping it would do the trick, but I just kept on worrying. It was everything, really, getting me down: the flask, having words with Mrs. Clarke, and, worst of all, meeting that policeman. The thing that was really upsetting me was knowing I'd have to go back to the department on Monday to get the rest of the stuff, because I'd gone there with a whole list of bits and pieces to pick up, not just the bandoliers. I thought about sending one of the lads from the loading bay, but they'd only make a mess of it, and then I'd have to get involved all over again. I thought of asking Jo, but then I thought Paul might say something to her. My headache was getting worse, not better. I can't bear the thought of going through all that again.

I know most of the streets near my house, but I must not have been noticing where I was going, because I suddenly found myself in this cul-de-sac I'd never seen before, with no idea how I'd got there. It was dark, I hadn't got any chocolate, and I didn't know what to do. I didn't want to go home, in case Mrs. Clarke was waiting for me. I could see all the houses, the lights behind the curtains, the televisions, and I imagined all the people sitting in their nice warm rooms, eating and talking, with me shut out of all of it.

Well, I still wanted the chocolate, so I thought, I'll see if there's a gas station nearby with a shop, and I was just about to go and look for one when I saw this young girl hop over the fence at the end of the road. It was just a wooden thing, not very high, and she made this neat little sideways jump with her legs in a sort of scissors movement. I couldn't see her very clearly because the street lamp was some way away, and I don't know what it was exactly, perhaps something about the way she jumped, but it suddenly put me in mind of my sister, Vera, and just for a split second, I actually thought it *was* her, running through the garden to fetch me for dinner, just like she used to, and it made me feel . . . well, happy. Contented, suddenly.

The girl started to run along the pavement toward me, but then she stopped and turned left, down a passageway I hadn't noticed before. At first I thought it must be where she lived, but when I went a couple of steps closer I saw it was a footpath, so I decided to follow. Partly because I wanted to see where the path would lead—I thought it might be a shortcut to a main road with shops—and partly, I must admit, because I was interested in the girl. When she came toward me I'd had a chance to see her face in the light, and she really did have a look of Vera. Her hair was the same color—a sort of bright brown, like a conker, pretty and curly. Vera's used to hang round her face, but this girl had hers pulled back in a ponytail. I wasn't close enough to see if she had freckles on her nose. Vera had freckles, so I was particularly interested in that. She was the same shape too—bony chest and skinny legs—that was Vera when she was eleven or twelve, of course, not later. Her clothes weren't anything like what Vera used to wear though—not that I'd expect them to be, fashion's changed so much. She was wearing one of those jackets that bunch up round the waist, a miniskirt, and a pair of white tennis shoes.

As I said, it was getting quite dark, and this particular footpath didn't have any lighting. On one side, there was thick wire netting with conifers behind it, and on the other, a high brick wall. So the gardens would be private, I suppose. It seemed wrong for a young girl like that to be out on her own in the middle of London. It makes you wonder what the parents can be thinking of when you see young girls wandering about the streets late at night. It's just asking for trouble.

I didn't want to frighten the girl, so I didn't go after her straightaway. She wasn't running anymore, just walking fast, so it was easy enough for me to keep up. A couple of times she stopped and looked round, but I managed to press myself back against the netting. I was wearing my dark blue jersey, thank goodness—and she didn't see me. Just to be on the safe side, I tucked my shirt collar into the neck, because it was a pale fawn color and I thought it might show up. That made me feel like somebody in a film, Humphrey Bogart or someone of that sort, a private detective.

The girl kept up a fair old pace down the footpath, and then she turned right into a street. That was more difficult for me, because of the lights, and I had to duck behind a car more than once, but I still managed to keep up with her. Then she took me down a few more streets, turning left and right, and before long, I was able to recognize where we were. Emneth Avenue, not far away from where I live. It isn't a very long street, so I waited round a corner behind a hedge until I'd worked out what she was going to do. It was a good job I did too, because she only walked a few steps before she went up one of the paths. She looked up and down the street, and then she opened the door and in she went. She had her own key—I saw her pull it out of her jacket pocket—so it must be where she lives. It's no distance at all from my road, and the house looks similar too—Victorian terrace with a bay window at the front and a strip of garden with daffodils and whatnot. I waited until she was safely inside before I went and took note of the number—that was easy enough because it was the only house with a red front door—and then I went home.

It was funny, really, because everything seemed to get better after that. The things that had been bothering me so much didn't seem so important anymore. All I could think about was the girl. Walking her home like that, seeing no harm had come to her, I don't mind admitting it gave me a bit of a glow—made me feel like a sort of guardian angel, even if nobody else knew what I'd done. I wondered if she was lonely— it seemed odd for her to be out like that, all alone. Perhaps her parents don't care. Perhaps they're divorced or the mother goes out to work and isn't interested in her. Or perhaps she works nights and the daughter's just left to fend for herself while she's away. You read a lot about things like that nowadays—parents who can't be bothered. Latchkey children, they used to be called. Poor kid. I thought I might try and find out where she goes to school, see if she's got any friends.

Do you remember that feeling of happy tiredness you had as a child, when you'd been out playing all day in the sun and it was time for bed? You've had your game or your adventure, and now it's time for sleep. That's how I feel now, lying in bed. Peaceful. I haven't felt as good as this in a long time. I've even patched it up with Mrs. Clarke. She was in the kitchen when I got back, sitting at the table with one of her catalogs. Hundreds of them, she's got. I said I was sorry about the butter dish, the lid getting broken like that, and she said, "Oh, never mind about that." Then she looked at the clock and said, "You're late—it's not one of your nights for the theater, is it? Been somewhere nice?"

I had to smile at that, but I just said, "Yes, very nice, thank you."

She put her finger on one of the skirts in a catalog and said, "What do you think of that, then?"

I said, "Very nice."

"I'm going to have that. They've got it in mauve, blue, and green. Which do you like best?" Well, it was hard to tell because they only showed a photo of the purple one, which looked a bit garish to my mind, so I said, "I think the green would be best."

"Well," she said, "I'll have one of each." She always does that. Buys clothes, three or four at a time, same pattern but different colors. Handbags and shoes she buys as well. She never sends them back and she never wears them either. That is, I've never seen her wearing them, but I'm beginning to think she must put them on when I'm out at work. The reason I suspect that is the amount of washing she does— heaps of it. She's always got the machine on. More detective work, you see!

Anyway, it's nice that we're getting on again. Because we've always rubbed along all right in the past and it would be a shame to spoil it. She's said to me on a few occasions, "You're a funny one," but she's just as funny in her way. She watches the clothes going round and round in the machine, for one thing. Just sits there looking at it until it's finished. She said to me, "You should try it sometime, calm your nerves." And she teases me about the theater, always going on the same nights, but she's got her telly programs that she has to watch—she has to see it there and then, she won't record them—and that's three or four times a week, at least. To my mind, that's no different from what I do; she's just as much a creature of habit as I am.

Still, perhaps they won't be seeing quite so much of me at the theater from now on. I won't abandon them completely, of course. After all, I've got my record to beat, but let's just say that my time may be taken up with other things. Tilly's always telling me to get out there in the real world—which is a bit rich coming from someone who's spent her whole life in the theater!

I'll go back to that shop and buy a new flask tomorrow. They had some that looked a bit like my old one—blue tartan, and the handle of the cup was almost the same, if I remember right. I'll do that first thing, and then—who knows? I might take the long way home. Via Emneth Avenue. Get a look at the house in daylight. I shan't hang around though—don't want to find myself in trouble with the police again.

Rather a shame I never got close enough to check on those freckles. Perhaps next time . . .

## Gerald, 1939

### Monday, August 28th

*Mrs. Paddick's husband went to the lecture* for the air raid wardens. He came back and said to Dad, Oh we had a treat tonight we went into the gas chamber. I said I dont think it is a very good treat they shoud have given him some chocolate instead and he laughed but then Mr. Paddick said to Dad that lot do not know what they are doing if you ask me it is a mess. Mrs. Paddick said it takes all the heart out of you. Then Mother came in and said why should we fight for Poland and I dont want to hear any more about the war in this house.

### Tuesday, August 29th

I picked blackberrys with Vera after school and then we played with Sammy in the garden but it was too hot and we had to stop. Mrs. Paddick said the government will move to Canada. She said to Dad will there be a war and he said yes. She said I hoped you would not say that and he said no one knows what is going to happen. So then she said to me and Vera you pick a good lot of those blackberrys so there will be lots of jam for when it is the war.

### Wednesday, August 30th

I helped Mrs. Paddick washing Sammy. She put Rekit Blue on him only the white bits. We went to get our gas masks and it was a long queue. We saw Mr. Treece the artist carrying a parcel. We could not see what it was and Mother said is it a puppy under your coat. He said no it is a gas mask and showed us. It is black with a pig nose and Mother said what a horrid thing. Then Vera said what if Sammy is killed because they dont have gas masks for dogs. Mr. Treece said dont worry you are too pretty to be frightened but then Mother said you are a silly little girl. You have to go to the village hall for the gas masks and they pile them up on a big table. They still had the painted cloth from Peter Pan with the desert island at the back we saw it last year. It was a good show especaly the pirates but now there wont be any more because of the war.

### Thursday, August 31st

Mrs. Paddick went to town to buy the ARP paper from Woolworths. Aunt Tilly wrote me a letter. It had a good joke so I told it to Jack.

Tripper: I wish I had come to this hotel last year.

Owner of Hotel: It is very kind of you to say that.

Tripper: Yes, this fish might have been a lot better then.

Vera and her friend Beryl played jacks in the garden. I coud not do it because the grass was bumpy. Then Dad came home and we made Mecano. He said that when the children come from London a boy will come to stay with us. I think it is good but Beryl said Hitler is a selfish old pig who wants to boss everybody and its all his fault because she will have to share her bedroom with them and they will be dirty. Dad said they might be clean but Beryl said her Mum said they wont because they live in the slums.

### Friday, September 1st

The children came from London and Mother and Mrs. Paddick went to the hall to get the boy. His name is Eric and his room is next to mine. He wispers all the time. He is 8 and has got two big brothers but they had to go to a diffrent place. I wanted to ask him about the slums but

Vera said it would be rude. Dad said they will have their school in the morning and we will have ours in the afternoon.

### Sunday, September 3rd

Mrs. Treece came to get blankets. Mother said we have not got any but then Mrs. Paddick got some and gave them to her. A mother and two girls are staying with them but the mother does not like it because we havent got a shelter like they have in London. Vera said if we had a shelter we could put Sammy in it but Dad said they dont let dogs go in the shelters in London which is not fair because it is not the dogs fault. Mrs. Treece said the children put a slice of bread down the lav.

We lissend to the radio saying the war is on and then I ran out with Eric to see if there were bombers but there was nothing. Then it was the air raid signal. It was a man on a bicycle shouting take cover but we thought it was supposed to be a siren with a funny noise and Dad said oh it is a joke but then the man rushed into the garden. It was Mr. Jevons and he said get into the shelter. We said we haven't got a shelter and he said well get under the stairs so we went in but Sammy ran away and got lost and when we found him it was time to come out so we missed it. Eric said now he wont be allowed to go home but I said we will win because Mr. Trent at school said it is in history that England has never lost a battle and when we win he can go home. Then we had a game of football with my gas mask case. It was nice but the case got broken and Mother said we are savages.

### Monday, September 4th

Mr. Paddick has lost his teeth. It was dark and he rode his bicycle into some sandbags in the lane and the teeth fell out and now he cannot find them again so it is the first casalty of the war. Mrs. Paddick said Hitler has got a lot to answer for. Aunt Tilly has come to stay with us.

*Wednesday, September 6th*

Eric wet his bed and made Mrs. Paddick cross. Also because of the blackout taking a long time and Mrs. Everit said its enouf to drive you crackers. I like helping Mrs. Paddick puting up the blinds but we might as well not bother having a war for all the fun it is and now I cant even play with Eric. He ran off to find his brothers and did not come back til after tea time so Mother said he could not have any.

*Friday, September 8th*

I went to the woods with Sammy to find Eric and I met his brothers. They are called John and Charly. He is older than Eric. They said they have got a hut and it is a secret but they will show me and we played spys. It was fun but when we went home Eric said he does not want me to follow him any more so I went to my room and talked to Jack. He is better than Eric because he woud not wet his bed like a baby.

*Sunday, September 10th*

I want to find the hut in the woods but Eric woud not show me even though Charly promised. He said it is private for him and his brothers but I will find it because I have been in the woods lots more times than him. I coud not find it but Vera was in the woods and Mr. Treece. They were doing painting. Vera was sitting under a tree in her vest and nickers because it was hot. Mr. Treece said we coud go back to his house for tea. It was salad with ham and scons and bananas with cream. Mr. Treece said everybody in England is a pigme and all they care about is fining you five bob if you have not got your gas mask. Then he said about how Mr. Jevons the warden said to him he can see the light in the passidge when he looks through the glass and Mr. Treece said if a German comes he is not going to get out of his plane and press his nose up to the front door. I thought it was funny but Vera said the German might do that and she was upset so Mr. Treece said I will save you from him if he comes. Their evacuees have gone back to London. They said it is because the milk is not out of a tin and they cant go to the pictures. I dont want Eric to go so I will ask Mrs. Paddick to get him some milk in a tin.

*Sunday, September 17th*

It is not Eric's hut at all but Mr. Treece for his painting things. It would be a good place for a camp because it has got blankets and cushions for a bed and a lamp. I found a picture he did of Vera in her vest and nickers. It was funny but when I said that to Vera she said shut up laughing

## Tilly

*The first time I had sexual intercourse* with Gerald's father was on September 24, 1939. I'd gone to stay with them, you see. The government had closed all the theaters for the duration—well, that's what they *said*, but most of them were open again within the month, and the cinemas and dance halls too, because people wouldn't put up with it. Anyway, I lost my engagement because of it, so I telephoned Arthur and he said to come and stay with them. I got there on the fourth—the Monday—he wasn't at work that day and he came to meet me at the station. We were in the car, and I was saying how I was all at sixes and sevens and didn't know what to do with myself. Arthur wasn't a great talker, but he was always a good listener, so I wasn't surprised when he didn't say much, but all of a sudden he stopped the car and said, "Whatever you do, it won't make any difference. We're seeing the end of civilization, Tilly, not just the theater."

We were in a little lane and he'd parked the car to the side on a bit of grass, and then he turned round to face me. He'd got the window open and he was resting his elbow on the frame, I remember that. He was wearing a dark suit, beautifully cut—Arthur's suits always were. He was an elegant man, almost a matinee idol sort of look, but it wasn't just how he dressed—he was handsome too, and he held himself well. I always thought he looked rather like Jack Buchanan. I said as much to Marjorie once, and she stared at me as if I had a screw loose. "Jack

Buchanan? *Arthur?*" I don't think she'd looked at him properly since their wedding night.

He said, "We've been so stupid."

I said, "Do you mean the government?" and he said, "No, I mean our generation. We've failed. All those fine ideals about peace in Europe—you can't just make a resolution not to have war, you've got to make it mean something. And we didn't. All we did was talk. We allowed this to happen."

I said, "Well, it's too late for all that now. It's started, so we'd better get it over with."

He said, "The way we're going, it won't be over until Herr Hitler dies of old age." I'd never seen him so depressed, and I wanted to cheer him up, so I said, "We'll just have to make the best of it."

He said, "You know, I don't think it's even occurred to Gerald that we could lose this war."

I said, "Well, he doesn't know what the last one was like," because I remembered my poor father, what a wreck it made of him. "What about Marjorie? What does she think?"

"To hear her talk, you'd think the only reason Hitler invaded Poland was to stop her writing those wretched books. She's been playing merry hell about this boy we're putting up." That was the first time I'd ever heard him speak bitterly about Marjorie, and I was a bit taken aback. I thought it best to change the subject, so I said, "Oh, have you got an evacuee?"

"Yes, a boy. Quiet little chap. Seems a bit nervous, but that's to be expected with Marjorie behaving the way she is." He stared through the windshield for a moment, then he said, "Tilly, I don't know what to do; I can't see any way out of this."

I said, "Well, I'm here now. There must be something I can do to help."

"I don't mean the house—Mrs. Paddick takes care of that." He thumped his hands down on the steering wheel. "It's unbearable! Here we all are, going to lectures on poison gas and waiting for the world to come to an end." He stared straight ahead for a moment and then turned back to me. "I'm sorry. You're probably right to concentrate on practical things." Then he started the car again and drove me back to Broad Acres.

It was as if something had opened up between us. Up until that point, we'd always got along well enough, but I'd say that was the beginning of our friendship, really—and what came next, of course.

Marjorie was at the door, waiting for us. She didn't come out to greet me, just stood there with her arms folded while Arthur got the bags out of the car. I said, "I hope my arriving hasn't disturbed your work," but she just looked irritated and said, "I don't know how I'm supposed to get anything done. We've had an evacuee foisted onto us, did Arthur tell you?"

"Yes, he did mention it."

"It's fine for him; he's not the one who'll have to put up with it."

"But, Marjorie, one little boy—"

"One little boy who sounds like a herd of elephants," she said sarcastically. "It may have escaped your notice, Tilly, but I have a responsibility to all the children who read my books, not just *one little boy*."

She clattered off to her study, leaving us standing in the hall. Arthur rolled his eyes at me. "Oh, dear."

"I see what you mean."

"Go on into the kitchen. I'll take these up. I expect she'll have calmed down by dinnertime."

At least Mrs. Paddick looked pleased to see me. Marjorie was the one making all the fuss about taking in an evacuee, but poor Mrs. Paddick was in the middle of it all, trying to muddle through as best she could. Little Eric had two brothers but Marjorie refused to play host to more than one child. The long and the short of it was, the brothers got carted off to someone else, no one knew where they were for three days because everything was so badly organized, and Eric got into a terrible state and started wetting the bed. Mrs. Paddick tried raising up the end of it with blocks so the feet were higher than the head, but it didn't make any difference.

One lunchtime Marjorie was sitting there complaining, as usual, and I lost my temper and told her that if she had a pair of sheets to wash every day—this was by hand, of course—as well as running a house the size of Broad Acres, then she'd have the right to feel hard-done-by. The minute she heard that, she threw down her napkin and went storming across the garden after poor Eric. "You disgusting, filthy little boy!" She grabbed him by the scruff of the neck and shook him so hard that his eyes nearly popped out. Mrs. Paddick said to me afterward, "You shouldn't have said that." She was quite right. I should have known better. I thought I'd make Marjorie see how selfish she was being, but all I'd managed to do was get Eric into trouble.

It was obvious that Marjorie and Arthur weren't getting on at all, and she didn't seem to want much to do with me either, so I ended up spending quite a lot of time in the kitchen with Mrs. Paddick. It's funny what sticks in your mind. I don't recall much about how the kitchen looked; it's the smell I remember more than anything. Arthur was always coming down with coughs and colds, and Mrs. Paddick always had saucepans full of handkerchiefs boiling away on the stove. Aluminum pans full of bubbling soapsuds, with the white cotton puffed up like a big mushroom on the top, and a thick line of scummy foam around the rim. They had a sort of wet smell. Warm and damp. If Mrs. Paddick was sitting at the kitchen table with one of her Player's, the cigarette smoke would mingle with the steam from the pans and the two smells would mix together.

The evenings were the worst. If Arthur wasn't staying at his club, he'd come back dog-tired, and after we'd had dinner and the children had gone to bed, the three of us would go into the sitting room and listen to the wireless. Broad Acres was in the mock Tudor style, very big and grand, with lots of dark, heavy beams. The sitting room had a thick,

royal blue carpet with a big pattern of gold leaves, and it was all clut-
tered up with great hulking bits of furniture with lion-paw feet.
Marjorie had a particular armchair that she used to sit in—I never saw
anyone else sit in it—and she'd play patience for hours, sitting there
hunched over rows of cards on a little table. Or she'd want us to play—
childish games like beggar-my-neighbor, I don't think she knew any
others. She never spoke to Arthur unless it was to snap at him. Most of
the time she just ignored him. And if either of us so much as mentioned
the war, she'd say, "Haven't you got *anything* else to talk about?" Or else
she'd jump up and leave the room, and then Arthur would have to go
after her and calm her down. He and I took to having little walks round
the garden before dinner. I always tried to cheer him up, though God
knows I wasn't feeling exactly on top of the world myself. I had nothing
to do, for one thing. Gerald was always moping about the place, and as
for Vera, I hardly saw her. She was always off sketching in the woods—
not that I blamed her, because with Marjorie the way she was, everyone
in the house was walking on eggshells.


Sunday the 24th was the day we went to the séance. I didn't really like
the idea, to tell you the truth, although it used to be very popular in
those days, much more than now. I was a bit surprised when Marjorie
suggested it, because we'd never been to church much as children and
she'd never shown any signs of being interested in religion or anything
like that. But it was a funny business altogether, the way she went about
it. Something a bit cloak-and-dagger about the whole thing, I thought.
She didn't say it in so many words, but I knew she didn't want me to tell
Arthur where we were going. She just said he wouldn't understand and
she had to have her own life. The thing was, I didn't really understand,
either, why she wanted to go. When I asked her who she wanted the medium to contact, she got very cagey and said, "Oh, I just want to see if
there's anything in it, that's all." I said, "Are you sure you've never been

before? Because you seem to know an awful lot about it." She said she hadn't, but I had a feeling she wasn't telling me the truth, so I thought I'd ask Mrs. Paddick.

I found her sitting on a chair outside the back door, peeling spuds, with Eric and his brothers sitting in a line on the top step, munching away at their biscuits. Marjorie insisted that they weren't to be let into the house, so they had to have their tea in the yard. God knows what she thought they were going to do in the winter. Gerald wasn't there, so I suppose it must have been in the afternoon, because the village kids and the evacuees had a split-session arrangement at the local school.

I plonked myself down on the step next to the boys and asked Mrs. Paddick about the séance. "Oh," she said, "I'll be surprised if she goes back to the same one."

"She's been before?"

"Oh, yes. It can't have been any good because I told her to ask if there was going to be a war, and this woman says oh, no, no war, and now look what we've got. I don't think much of that, do you?"

"Do you know what else she said?"

"That was all Mrs. Haxton told me. Except that this woman got on her nerves." Then Charlie—that was Eric's older brother—interrupted to ask for another biscuit, and Mrs. Paddick went into the kitchen. While she was away, he leaned over to me—all of ten years old—and said, "She's a very 'andsome lidy." They were all cockneys, of course. Terrible accents. "When I grow up, I'd like ter marry 'er." I did my best not to laugh, because Mrs. Paddick was a big, strapping woman, and Charlie was a scrawny ten-year-old with bandy legs, who barely came up to her waist. Charlie the charmer. I'll bet my bottom dollar that he grew up to be a real lady-killer.

Mrs. Paddick came back with more biscuits and said, "Is she going again, then?"

"Yes, and she's asked me to go with her."

Mrs. Paddick sighed. "Well, if I were you, I shouldn't say anything to Mr. Haxton. He doesn't think much of it, I can tell you."

I went back inside to Marjorie. "Why didn't you tell me you'd been before?" She didn't attempt to deny it, just looked shifty and said something about how she didn't want to say too much because the spirits won't come if you don't believe in them. I said, "Well, that's a good excuse if ever I heard one." She didn't answer, so I said, "Come on, I want to know who you're trying to contact," but she wouldn't tell me. She said, "This is a different medium. I knew the other one was a fake as soon as she started. If the spirits are present, the air in the room goes cold."

The séance was in Harbury—that was the nearest town. We went into this very ordinary-looking little house with a notice outside that said SPIRITUALIST SERVICES and gave the times as if it were a church. It cost 3d to go in, I remember that. It was crowded with chairs of the sort you get in churches, with a shelf for the hymn book at the back and a few tables covered with vases of artificial flowers. There was a great big Union Jack pinned up over the fireplace, with a sentimental painting of Jesus in the middle. I didn't know what to make of any of it.

The medium—I can't remember her name—was a dumpy little thing in a faded print frock. Not remotely ethereal—I remember thinking she sounded like George Formby, but perhaps that was just the accent. She stood in front of the mantelpiece with her hands clasped and her eyes closed, telling us a lot of soppy stuff about "our angel friends" and swaying from side to side. She kept calling Jesus "the great Nazarene," which made him sound like a magician—not a good one either.

We wobbled our way through a hymn, and then the medium moved forward like a sleepwalker and stood in front of the woman at the far end of the row and said, " 'Ave you got something for me, friend?" The woman held out a cigarette case to her. The medium took it and started stroking it. When I looked along the line, I could see that almost everyone had some object or other in their laps—keys, a pair of gloves, a scarf, a piece of jewelry, and one woman had a silver hairbrush. I had a look to see what Marjorie had brought, but all I could see was something white, material of some sort, all bundled up.

Well, it must have been half an hour before she got to us. " 'Ave you something, friend?" When Marjorie held up her white material, I saw what it was—an embroidered christening robe. For a moment, I couldn't think why she'd brought it, and then I realized: It must have been made for the dead baby.

"There's a beautiful light around this." The medium lifted the robe up to her face and scrubbed her cheek with it as if it were a towel. Then she said, "Is there something you want to ask, friend?"

I didn't look at Marjorie, but when she spoke, I could tell she was near tears. "Is the baby—my baby—" She couldn't get any further. Cue the medium. "Don't distress yourself, friend. The spirit friends 'ave shown me a beautiful little baby, a plump little baby with rosy cheeks. I see 'er beside you, friend; she wants you to be of good cheer, she is up-lifted. . . . God bless you, my dear." I glanced at Marjorie and saw that her eyes were wet. A woman in the row behind us began to sob.

The medium gave Marjorie back the robe and started to move away from us, back to the mantelpiece, but then she paused, as if something had just occurred to her, and turned round. "I 'ave something else for you, friend. Can you place Jack in spirit?"

Jack was our father's name. John Haldane, but everyone called him Jack. Marjorie was staring at the floor as if she hadn't heard, so I said, "I can." I felt as if I were a child again, owning up to something in front of the rest of the school. The medium's manner changed from sleepy to shrewd in an instant and she gave me the once over.

"Are you together?"

"Yes, sisters."

"I see. Well, Jack 'as a message—I don't think it's for you, friend, but your sister—'e says, I am Jack from the spirit world, 'e says 'e is healed, 'e says there is forgiveness in 'eaven, you will 'ave forgiveness. . . . 'Ave you a young lady in your 'ome?"

I barely heard Marjorie's answer. "Yes."

" 'E says you must have no quarrel. Does it connect up?"

Marjorie didn't answer.

"Well, friend, I don't speak to please myself, it's the spirit friends, when they get 'old of you. . . . Tell me, friend, are you troubled in yourself? Do you want to make a change?"

Before Marjorie could answer, the medium said, " 'E says, be patient, there will be a change. It will come upon you. But you must 'ave patience. A great change . . . but 'e cannot say more. 'Is lips are sealed."

Then she stepped back and bowed her head for a moment—to pray, I suppose, although you could hear the clasps snapping all round the room as people stuffed their belongings back into their handbags and got ready to leave. "Thank you to our angel friends and I 'ope they 'ave a lovely journey back to their spiritual 'ome." Then she said, "Good afternoon," and that was it.

Walking back—Broad Acres was only a couple of miles away—I said to Marjorie, "So, what did you think, then? Was she a fake?" I was interested to see what she'd say, because she'd obviously been moved by the message from the baby, but if she thought that was real, she'd have to admit the other thing too, about our father, which seemed uncanny at the time although afterward I thought it was probably just a lucky guess. I said, "Wasn't the room supposed to be cold? I thought it was rather warm in there, myself. Stuffy, almost."

"I felt a draft on my neck."

"For heaven's sake, someone got up and opened a window. I saw them. And she said, 'she.' About the baby. I always thought Gerald's twin was a boy."

"That's what the doctor said, a boy." Marjorie was silent for a moment, and then she said, "They wouldn't let me see him."

I said, "Of course not, Marjorie, they didn't want to upset you. Besides, you had Gerald to look after, didn't you?"

"But I wanted to see him. They wouldn't let me."

"Marjorie . . . that's morbid. After all, it—he—was hardly *there*."

"I could have had something . . . a piece of hair."

"Babies don't have hair."

"Gerald did."

"No, he didn't . . . did he? I don't remember."

"You didn't see him until he was six months old."

"Oh, no, I didn't, did I? I was somewhere . . . Scotland. That was it. Touring, all winter. Last time I do that. It was freezing."

I've often wished I could have that conversation over again. At the time, I just thought Marjorie was being fanciful. I'd never had a conversation like that and I didn't know what to say. And it was such an inappropriate place as well. We were walking through the woods, in single file, down a very narrow path—there were enormous clumps of nettles on either side and I was trying not to get stung through my stockings, so I wasn't giving my full attention to what she was saying. I suppose it was a missed opportunity, that's why I regret it. We'd never been very close as sisters—Marjorie'd never been close to anyone as far as I knew, except for our mother—but she was trying to tell me something that day, and I wasn't listening. It wasn't only the nettles, it was . . . well, I suppose I was embarrassed, really. Perhaps that was *because* it was Marjorie. If it had been one of my friends, I might have been more sympathetic. Oh, I don't know. It's all so different now. People know more about the psychological effects of things. In those days, if something unpleasant happened, you just closed the book and tried to forget about it. Besides, we'd just gone to war. Courage was . . . well, I suppose you might say it was *fashionable*, for want of a better word. You had to put your emotions to one side, and anything else was self-indulgent. That was how we all thought, it wasn't just me. So when Marjorie started to cry, I'm afraid I told her to pull herself together. She said,

"That was all I wanted. Just to know he was there. You don't under-stand."

I said, "No, I don't suppose I do. Now can we *please* just get home?"

"Nobody understands."

I said, "I'm an actress, dear. I understand when someone is giving a performance, all right. I'm surprised you were taken in by it."

Marjorie was ahead of me on the path, and she turned round and stood in front of me. "You're not being *fair.*"

"What are you going to do, run to Mother?" I said jeeringly, my hands on my hips. I was almost tempted to stick my tongue out at her. It was ridiculous, two grown-up women with handbags and hats, carry-ing on like children in the middle of the woods. But the thing was, run-ning to Mother was exactly what *I* wanted to do at that moment—that was why I'd said it. Well, not to run to Mother, because I was always Daddy's girl, not hers, but I suddenly felt as if the whole world were being swept away—what with the theaters closing, and the war, and Marjorie and Arthur. . . . It all seemed so precarious, and there we were having an absurd argument about a charlatan who pretended to talk to dead people. I suppose I was frightened, and that made me unkind.

"Well, I'll say one thing for the old girl, she was spot-on about Dad, wasn't she?" I said.

"Someone put her up to it."

"What do you mean, *put her up to it*? And how could they have known?"

"Known what?"

That astonished me. I wouldn't say I was often at a loss for words, but that . . . "You know very well *what.*" I meant what Marjorie and Mother did to Dad, and she knew it.

"Why do you always have to bring that up?"

I said, "I don't always bring it up. We've never talked about it."

"You do, all the time. As if it was my fault. You don't even remem-ber what it was like, you weren't old enough—you just do it to get at me because I've got a husband and a family and you haven't, *and* . . . you've always been jealous of my success."

"*Marjorie!* That isn't true at all, and you know it. You're the one who isn't being fair."

She gave me a cold, superior stare. "Tilly, when we get back, I think you'd better leave, don't you?"

Arthur and I—it was that night. I didn't do it to spite Marjorie, although you could say it came about as a result of our conversation. She hadn't said any more about my going, but I knew that she'd meant it. I couldn't leave then and there because I didn't have anywhere to go—I'd given up my digs when the play was canceled, and the friend I usually stayed with in London was away. Marjorie decided to ignore me, and as she was already ignoring Arthur, we had dinner in complete silence. After that, she said she was going to bed. It was still light, so Arthur and I took our coffee down to the summerhouse at the far end of the garden. The minute we were alone, he said, "What's going on?"

"I think I should go."

"Why? What's happened? You seemed to be getting along so well."

"Arthur, we haven't got along since we were children! But we had an argument. This afternoon. It's not something you can . . . well, it's going to be rather hard to smooth over. It's best if I go."

I knew Arthur wasn't going to be very happy about it, but what he did next really surprised me. He grabbed hold of my hand and said, "I don't want you to go."

I said, "Oh, now you're at it too."

"At what?"

"You sound like a little boy in his first gray shorts. I don't know what's got into us today; it must be all this waiting for bombs to drop on us that's getting on our nerves."

"What do you mean?"

"Oh, just this argument . . ." I didn't want to tell him about the séance, because that would have been tattling, so I said—it was the connection of ideas, I suppose—"Did you ever meet our father?"

Arthur looked a bit puzzled and said, "How could I? I didn't know Marjorie then."

"I don't understand . . . know her when?"

"When your father was alive."

"Yes, you did."

He looked at me as if I were mad, and said patiently, "I didn't meet her till after the war."

"Yes, I know."

"So how could I have met him?" He suddenly exploded. "Oh, God, Tilly, not you as well!"

That completely threw me. "Not me as well what? What are you talking about?"

"That spiritualist rubbish. I can see she's got you at it as well. Or does it run in the family?"

"I don't believe in all that. But I don't see—"

"Your father died in the war, didn't he?"

"No! He died a few years ago—1934. Don't you remember?" Arthur said nothing. I said, "Who told you that?" but I knew the answer before the question was out of my mouth.

"Well . . . Marjorie, I think. I mean, I suppose it could have been your mother, but—"

"It wasn't, was it?"

"No."

I felt as if someone had thrown a bucket of cold water over me. "Marjorie came to the funeral. She was *there*."

"I didn't know."

"He was shell-shocked. Blown up in the air. He never recovered. He used to cry. . . . They ignored him. Mother and Marjorie. I always wanted to talk to him, because it wasn't fair, but I could never think of what to say, so I used to stand next to his chair and he'd take my hand and hold it and . . . His hand shook, so he'd spill things, and then they'd wipe him down as if he were a tabletop. At first she used to shout at him. Mother. We'd hear her after we'd gone to bed. She'd say things about the business, how was she supposed to keep it going and manage the house, she'd tell him he had to pull himself together. He never said a word, he—he—" I started to cry then. "He was such a *nice* man. I used to go down the road to his shop at midday and he'd lock up and then we'd go back for lunch together, and I always wanted to skip and he never cared what people thought. We'd skip down the road together, and sometimes we pretended to be horse buses—how many men would do that? Marjorie must have been *so* ashamed of him. But it came from our mother. We heard her say to him one night, 'My life's been full of disappointments, and you're the greatest one of all.' She was always angry, always disappointed, but it wasn't his fault. I'm sorry, Arthur, I know you're married to Marjorie, but I've never told this to a soul and she just betrayed him. I can't bear it. Arthur, he used to sit there and *shake* and they just walked round him and . . . How could she tell you he was *dead*? He just stayed in the back room and never went out, and I suppose because you never came to the house . . . I thought you knew, that's why I asked. I didn't realize." I had my head in my hands by that point, and when I looked up, Arthur was staring at me.

"I'm sorry, Tilly. I wish I *had* known him."

"He was a good father. I was always his favorite; Marjorie was Mother's. It was like a pair of scales—two on each side, for balance. But when he got ill, nothing worked anymore."

Arthur didn't say anything, and it suddenly occurred to me that what I'd described my mother doing to my father was exactly the same as the way Marjorie treated him. I suppose it must have struck a chord with Arthur too, because he said, "What you said earlier, about us being like children—that was one of the things I liked about Marjorie. She always seemed . . . well, so fresh. She wasn't part of all *that*."

"Part of what?"

"The war. I'd had a good one, but all the same, I wanted to get away from it. Forget it. I suppose, with Marjorie being a few years younger, I thought she wasn't touched by it, complicated by it . . . but she was, wasn't she?"

"Yes. But she's good at ignoring things. Pretending they aren't there."

"You can say that again." We were sitting facing each other across the little garden table, and Arthur put his hand up to my face and wiped a tear off my cheek with his thumb. "Where will you go, darling?" Looking back on it, I'd say that that was the point of no return. When he touched my face and called me darling. There's always a moment like that, when something that was merely possible suddenly becomes inevitable.

I told him I'd have to find somewhere, and he took a key out of his pocket and gave it to me. "What's that?"

"I have a flat. In London."

"I didn't know . . . I thought you stayed at your club."

"I do, sometimes. Look, Tilly . . . I've kept it pretty quiet."

"Doesn't Marjorie know?"

"No."

"Do you take ladies there?"

"Yes."

"Then I'm not surprised Marjorie doesn't know."

"I doubt she'd care. She's got no use for me."

"Are you entertaining anyone at present?"

"No."

"Then are you asking me to be your mistress?"

"Nothing so Edwardian. Is that what you'd like? Ostrich feathers and Madeira?"

"Hardly. I haven't the bosom for it."

"I think you're beautiful."

"What happens if I leave London?"

"You can keep the key. I've got another."

"Where is it?"

"Sloane Street. Second floor. Stop asking questions."

Well, you don't need me to tell you what happened after that. It was comforting—not only for me, I think it was for Arthur too. As I said, I was fond of him, and believe you me, I'd been to bed with plenty of men I didn't like by that time, so it made a pleasant change. The sofa in the summerhouse wasn't really up to it though. Call me old-fashioned, but I'll take the double bed over the chaise longue any day, especially when half the stuffing's been eaten by mice. My bottom was nearly touching the floor by the time we'd finished. We were picking bits of old bird's nest off each other when Arthur asked, "How are you set for money?"

"I thought you said I wasn't going to be your mistress."

"Yes, but all the same, if you're not working . . ."

"I won't take your money, Arthur. It's bad enough that you're providing the roof over my head."

"Very independent."

"I'd rather be, if it's all the same to you."

"But you will tell me, won't you? If you need anything."

"Will you do the same? Not money, necessarily, because I haven't got much, but . . . if there's anything I can do." I held out my hand. "Shake?"

"Shake. Shaken." He looked out into the dark garden. "We'd better say good night, hadn't we?"

"We should go in separately. You first."

"Fair enough. Mind the flower beds."

I went into London with Arthur the next morning, on the train. He went to work, and I went to his flat. Marjorie hadn't asked where I was going. I stayed there for a few weeks, and when they reopened the theaters I got a job in repertory down in Eastbourne. *Dear Brutus,*

*Dangerous Corner,* and I played the Gladys Cooper part in *The Last of Mrs. Cheyney*—that was fun. I shared digs with my friend Phyllis Tiverton, who'd got me into the company, and didn't see Arthur again for seven or eight months. He'd taken me out for dinner a few times in London—this was before everything was rationed—and then I didn't see him after that until I came back, just in time for the Blitz.

I've thought about the war a lot recently. You can't get away from it with the fiftieth anniversary coming up. People seem to think that if you're over sixty-five you must have had the time of your life and you'd never talk about anything else, given the choice. That isn't true. But this year, we've been up to here with it—they've even had Tommy Handley on the radio again. I didn't think he was funny at the time, never mind now.

We had the local television down here last week, filming us. They made us all sit round the piano, and we were supposed to be singing "The Siegfried Line," except that no one knew the words. There was this young woman prancing about in front of us with a clipboard—all of twenty-five, I should think, and as bossy as they come—and she said, "Oh, don't you remember it?" I said, "It was fifty years ago, what do you expect?" She turned round to one of the staff who was there and said, "You'd think they'd cooperate a bit more, wouldn't you?" Then Ken Porter—he's a bit more with it than most of them in here—said he thought he remembered the words, only he's got Parkinson's so someone else had to write them down, and in the middle of all this, Bertie Gilchrist, who plays the piano, had a funny turn and fell off his stool. They're all heart, these television people—Madam Clipboard took one look at him and said, "What about 'The Siegfried Line'?"

I said, "Bugger 'The Siegfried Line,' he's having a coronary!"

Well, that was how I met Tiny. My new friend. They took Bertie off to hospital, and Madam Clipboard said she'd come back the next day with her minions and we'd do it all again, only they'd have to find somebody else to play the piano. The manager—that's my chum from the Newquay rep—said he'd see what he could do, and the next day, in trots this little chap. Very dapper, with a lilac silk scarf and the most unlikely black hair given that the rest of him looked to be over seventy. He sat down at the piano, took his rings off very carefully, lined them all up along the top, and started vamping for all he was worth. Well, within about five minutes everyone was singing away like billy-o, even me. Not just "The Siegfried Line," but "Knees Up Mother Brown," "The Lambeth Walk," "Run, Rabbit, Run"—the lot. The Clipboard was in seventh heaven.

I caught the little chap's eye a couple of times while we were singing, and he nodded at me—huge grin on his face the whole time, as if he'd never had so much fun in all his life. Afterward, he went off to the manager's office and I tottered into the conservatory for a bit of peace and quiet. I didn't think anything more about it until he suddenly appeared from nowhere, skipped across the room like a pixie, and plonked himself down in the chair next to mine. "*Love* the hair, darling."

I told you I'd just had it done, didn't I? I said, "Thank you. I like yours."

He said, "I do my best." He was perched on the edge of the chair, hands tucked under his thighs, palms down, arms braced, and swinging his legs like a schoolgirl. "I'm Tiny."

"Tilly."

"You're an actress, aren't you?"

That made me feel like Greta Garbo—not *you used to be,* but *you are.* "Well . . . yes."

"Lovely. I can tell we're going to be friends. I used to be a dancer—donkey's years ago, of course. I'm going to be coming here twice a week to play. Norman's asked me." Norman's the manager. "I wasn't sure about it at first—I thought, oh, God, look at this lot, half dead—but then I saw you. Did you do much in the musical theater? I know some lovely songs from the shows."

I said, "You didn't seem very sure about 'Roll Out the Barrel.' "

"I was in the navy, dear, not the RAF. On a destroyer. D'you fancy a drink?" He had a carrier bag with him, and he pulled out two little bottles of made-up gin and tonic and a couple of plastic glasses. "Go on, have one."

"I don't mind if I do. Got any cocktail snacks in that bag?" I only said it as a joke, but he said, "Oh, just call me Mary Poppins," and pulled out a packet of peanuts. "Mind your dentures."

I said, "Do you mind, these are my own!"

"Lucky you. The trouble I've had with my top set, you wouldn't believe. . . . That woman from the TV, she was a silly cow, wasn't she?" We laughed, and I knew I'd found a kindred spirit. We talked until suppertime, and he said he'd come back and see me tomorrow. He said, "I'm going to go off now. I'm dying for a cigarette. Do you smoke?"

I said, "Yes, but they don't let you in here. I have to go into the garden."

"Oh, never mind," he said. "I'll take you down to the front."

I said, "Well, you'll have to push me. I can't get that far on my own."

"Oh," he said, "I don't mind. Does wonders for the calf muscles. Night-night."

A friend, at long last. I went to bed feeling so pleased. I haven't had anyone to talk to—not *really* talk to—since I came in here four years ago. Not someone you could have a bit of fun with, anyway. When I look in the mirror I'm surprised to see an old face—never mind what's below the neck, it doesn't bear thinking about, especially if you've just had your dinner—but inside I'm still a young woman, and I want to enjoy myself like one. I know what you're thinking, but it's got nothing to do with all that—I've got Tiny's number, all right. What do you think I was, born yesterday? No, what I mean is, I could tell that he's the same as me. He's grown old, but in his mind he's still the same beautiful young boy he always was, turning all the heads.

That was one of the reasons I never married, really. Every time someone asked me—which they did, fairly regularly, I'll have you know—I'd think, it'd be like turning my back on life, and I'm too young to do that. Don't misunderstand me, they were lovely men, all of them. I know I make these funny remarks about being in love and all the rest of it, but I knew in my heart that none of them were special enough.

There was only ever one man I'd have married, but I didn't deserve him.

## Jo

*I had such a laugh yesterday.* I was walking past Mel's school at lunchtime. I don't normally go round there or anything, it's just it's my mum's birthday, and I got her this video of *All Creatures Great and Small* because she really likes it, and then Mel said she didn't have enough money left to buy a present so I said she could give Grandma the video and I'd get something else. So then of course I couldn't think what to get, so I thought I'd better go round the shops, and that's why I was there. I could hear them all, the younger ones, they were running round shouting out something I hadn't heard before. At first I thought it must be a football team, but it didn't sound right— this was more *ner-ner-ner,* like that, and then one of them came right up near the fence, and he was pointing at this other kid and going, "Spe-cial ne-*eeds!* Spe-cial ne-*eeds!*"

That really cracked me up. I mean, I know it's awful, but it's quite funny as well, because you know how kids used to go in the playground, "Oh, you *spastic*"? Well, they're not allowed to say that anymore, so they go "special needs" instead. I told Mel in the evening, and she said, "Oh, yeah, they all say that," and I was going, "Well, you shouldn't really," but I was laughing: I couldn't help it.

Ron thought it was funny too. You don't know about Ron, do you? Well, I didn't want to go round telling everyone because I only met him two days ago. In The Greyhound. A whole gang of us meet up there sometimes after work, people I've known for ages, and there was this bloke there. I knew who he was, sort of, because he'd gone out with someone at my school years ago, but I'd never spoken to him or anything. Anyway, we got talking, and he was really nice. Nothing's happened, not yet, but we're going out tonight, just the two of us, and Mel's staying at Mum's, so if you see me with a big smile on my face tomorrow morning, you'll know what it's about, won't you?

Don't laugh, but he's got a fish van. With his dad. Ron and Son. His dad's name's Ron as well. It's not fish and chips, it's all the uncooked stuff—plaice and cod and whelks and crab cakes and all the rest of it, like a fishmonger. They even do jellied eels. He said, "I bet you've never eaten jellied eels."

I said, "No, I bloody well haven't."

He said, "I bet you'd like them."

I said, "No, I wouldn't," because I always imagine them *wriggling* inside your mouth.

He was going, "I'm going to make you eat some," and I'm going, "Oh, yeah, you and whose army?" It was a great evening, a real laugh. He said when they go to Billingsgate in the morning, four o'clock or something, they can smell the fish right across the car park, quarter of a mile away. I said, "Well, you don't smell too bad," and I was sniffing him because I've got this trick I can do where I make my nose go like a rabbit's—don't ask me how, it just does. So he's going, "Do that again, it's really sweet," and then he kept trying to do it. In the end I said, "Pack it in or everyone in here'll think I smell," so he grabbed my wrist and started sniffing that and I'm going "Get off " but actually it was really nice. It made me feel, you know, all sort of special.

It was brilliant—all my friends were there but I hardly talked to them at all except when I was buying drinks. Ron went to the cigarette machine—he smokes Marlboro Lights—and my friend Karen comes over and she goes, "You two seem to be getting on well."

I said, "Oh, we were just having a chat," because she can be a real gossip when she gets going, although I've known her since school and she was ever so nice to me when Sean left.

"Well," she said, "it looks like more than that to me. They're all talking about it up at the bar."

I thought, oh, God, that's all I need, so I said, "Then they need to get a life," but Karen goes, "You got plans for later?"

I said, "Yes, I'm going to pick up Mel from my mum's."

"And then?"

"Then I'm going home."

"On your own?"

"No, with Mel."

"I didn't mean that."

"Didn't you?"

Karen said, "Well, if you don't want him I'll have him. I think he's gorgeous."

I said, "I'm not saying any more," but of course I was wondering what was going to happen because he *is* gorgeous. I usually go for dark men, but he's got this lovely floppy fair hair, and blue eyes, really sort of *boyish*. I think he might be a bit younger than me actually, but I didn't ask or anything. Still, who cares, eh? Nothing wrong with having a toy-boy, is there?

Well, when it was closing time, he waited while the others went out, but I didn't think he was going to say anything because he didn't look like he was going to. He was just putting his coat on, not looking at me or anything, but then he suddenly said, "Will you come back with me?"

I said, "I can't tonight," because of Mel being round at my mum's and having to pick her up. I knew I couldn't just ring up and say, "Can she stay the night?" because I tried that once before and got the third degree on the phone: Where are you going? Who with? What's he like? The bloke was standing right next to me and I was really embarrassed. I told Ron—not about ringing up my mum, just about Mel, I mean about collecting her. I always tell people about her straight off. I don't make a big deal about it, just sort of slip it into the conversation, because some men can get a bit funny about it. It's like they think I'm going to go, "Oh, marry me, marry me," all the time because I want my little girl to have a dad. One bloke actually said that to me once. I said, "In your dreams." But there'd be no point in trying to hide it, because all my friends know and one of them would only tell him—not on purpose, I don't mean that they think I'm a slut or anything, because I didn't do any more than they did. It's just I was . . . well, whatever.

It didn't seem to bother Ron though. Come to think of it, he probably knew already, because we know a lot of the same people. I said to him, "You need your beauty sleep if you've got to be up early."

He said, "All right then," and then he took hold of the top of my arm and pulled me toward him and kissed me. That makes it sound a bit rough, but it wasn't, it was really nice. Then his mates started calling him from outside; they were going, "Are you coming? No it's just the way he's standing," and all this, like, *ho, ho*. They're such a bunch of losers, that lot—well, not all of them. I mean, I've been out with a couple of them—Tony, and Billy . . . Steve . . . oh, and Keith. Well, that's more than a couple, but the rest are losers. Actually, Keith's a bit of a loser as well, to tell you the truth. Anyway, Ron said, "Will you come back next time?" and of course I said yes, and then he asked me if I wanted to come out this evening for a meal, so I was really pleased.

When we got outside, everyone had gone—Karen probably told them I was going home with him, I wouldn't put it past her. Ron offered to give me a lift home, but I said I'd get a cab. He kept saying, "Are you sure?" but I didn't want him to. It sounds really stupid, but it was such a nice evening, meeting him and everything, it was really perfect, and I wanted that to be the end of it. I didn't want anything to spoil it, you know? I just wanted to be by myself so I could think about it. I know it's odd, because you'd think it would be like you never wanted it to stop, wouldn't you? I tried to explain it to Karen once, and she said, "It's because you're getting old." I said, "Piss off!" and she said, "All right, then, I didn't want to tell you this but it's because you're mental."

Ron waited with me till the cab came, and it was a bit cold so he put his jacket round my shoulders and gave me a cuddle, which was really nice. When the car came, he was going to the driver, "Do you know where it is? Are you sure?" and asking him how much he was going to charge and all that. It was so sweet. The taxi stank, as usual, but I told the driver to wait while I went in to get Mel. I thought it'd be a treat for her because I usually get a lift to Mum's from one of my mates and then we walk back, and she's always half asleep. But she was chatting away, and even when we got in and I went in the kitchen to make myself a cup of tea, she didn't go to bed, she came in after me. I was just nodding yeah, yeah, not really listening because I was still thinking about Ron, but then I suddenly heard her say something about how she thought this man was following her.

I said, "Are you sure?" because it's an odd thing for a twelve-year-old to say, but there are some real weirdos about. Anyway, I asked her if she meant actually *following* following or just that she'd seen him about, and she said she hadn't seen him by the school, just in the evening, when she'd been coming back from her friend's or something. I said, "Well, perhaps he lives round there," because nine times out of ten it's the same friend she goes to, Sonali—they're like *that* those two, in each other's pockets all the time—but Mel said, "Then he's just moved in because I never saw him till two weeks ago. There was a house for sale on Sonali's road, but this family bought it. We saw them and everything. The man—the dad—wasn't him. But he's not, you know, *running after me* or anything, it's just, like, I'm going along and—then there's someone behind me, footsteps, or even if I can't hear footsteps, you know you get that thing when you just *know* there's someone there? I don't want to turn right round in case it's this bloke, but if I go round a corner or cross the road or something where I can just turn my head a little bit, it is *always* him."

"Always? What, every single time?"

"Well, not every single time, but a lot."

"It could just be a coincidence."

"Yeah, I s'pose. But it's just . . . really *creepy*."

I said, "Do you want me to phone the police? I mean, they probably won't do anything, but—"

"No, because if it's just some old man out for a walk, I'll feel really stupid."

"When you say old, do you mean *old* old, or just old*er*?" When I was her age, I thought everyone over twenty was, like, a hundred.

"About the same as Gran."

I said, "Does he look, you know, normal?" which was a stupid question, really, because that's the whole problem, isn't it? How do you tell if someone's a nutcase? I'll tell you how: They'll come and sit next to me on the tube, that's how. No, seriously, you can't, can you? One minute they're in the supermarket, next minute they're shooting everyone in sight, and then afterward everyone goes, Oh, he was really quiet, kept to himself, didn't bother anyone. I mean, give me a break.

Mel said, "Yeah, he's just ordinary."

"Have you told anyone else?"

"Only Sonali. I didn't want to tell Gran; she'd go mad."

I said, "You catch on fast." My mum flies off the handle at anything; she's always falling out with the neighbors because she's had a go at somebody. I don't know how Colin puts up with her, to be honest. I mean, she's my mum and I love her to bits, but she drives me round the twist.

Mel said, "Yeah, Hurricane Grandma," because that's our joke, and then she said, "You do understand, don't you? About the bloke. I mean, I don't want to make a fuss, I just told you because . . . well, because . . . I don't know, I just wanted to tell you, okay? It's probably nothing, it's just that it's a bit strange, and . . . whatever. I can't explain."

"All the same, perhaps I should call the police—"

"No!" For a second, I thought Mel was going to cry, which is really unusual. "If you do that it's bound to get out, and then it'll be like when that girl was attacked, remember? That girl from my school? Tanya Perrin? You know, last year."

"Yes, but I don't see what—"

"They said really horrible things about her."

"Who did?"

"The boys. And some of the girls. In her year. And some of the others as well. They kept saying what a slut she was, and somebody wrote it on her bag and everything."

"But she was *raped*."

"Yeah, but they went round saying she wanted to and then said she didn't afterward. And some of the boys said they'd, you know, *done it* with her."

"Had they?"

"No! They were just saying it, and they said she really, like, *fancied herself*, and . . . it was just horrible." Mel wouldn't look at me. "I don't want to talk about it, all right? I wish I'd never said anything about it now."

I said, "All right. But you will let me know if you see him again, won't you?"

"Yeah, don't worry."

I said, "No, you've got to promise me. Really promise. Get your head out of the fridge." She'd been sitting up on the counter—I keep telling her not to, because she's making the sink unit go saggy—and she jumped down and started rummaging in the fridge for something to eat.

"There's nothing in here."

"That's because I haven't been shopping. I'll do it tomorrow. There's a packet of crisps in the cupboard; you can take them to bed with you. Go on, or you won't get up in the morning."

I know, crisps in bed. The World's Best Mum. Not.

But I thought, who cares whether she cleans her teeth or not, she's alive and she hasn't been raped or anything, and that's the most important thing. Because I remember that girl Tanya Perrin, what it was like at the time. I felt so sorry for her and her family, but—I know this is really horrible—I just thought, thank God it wasn't Mel, because I'd die if anything happened to her. Well, I wouldn't, because I'd want to be there for her, but you know what I mean. Tanya was a bit older than Mel; I think she was about fourteen. Mel was really upset about it. They never caught the rapist either, so he must still be out there somewhere. As long as he's not the one that's been following Mel. *If* someone has been. I mean, she didn't seem *really* sure about it, but she's not the type who makes things up to get attention, she'd obviously really thought about it before she told me. I'm glad she did tell me though.

Not that there's anything I can do. I mean, I can't lock her up, can I? She's been going out on her own since she was seven or eight—only down to the local shops, not crossing the big roads or anything—and now that she's older she goes up to Hammersmith with her friends. You hear about these parents who drive their kids everywhere, but I couldn't do that even if I wanted to. I haven't got a car, for one thing, never mind passing my test. But I think it's really stupid. I mean, they've got to do things on their own, don't they? Otherwise, what's going to happen when they grow up? I don't let Mel stay out late, but she's got a right to her own life, with her mates, and I'm not going to wrap her up in cotton wool. My mum tried that with me, being overprotective, and look where it got me. But it is hard. I mean, I remember when Mel was born and I saw her for the first time, I just wanted to hold her forever.

I've often thought about having another baby. I wouldn't do it on my own again, but I've never met anyone really special. I suppose I don't trust men, not totally. . . . I mean, it'd be nice to get married and all the rest of it, but then what if I got pregnant and he ran off? Being married isn't going to stop him, is it? But I really like Ron. I mean, I fancy him, but I *like* him as well. He's more, I don't know . . . *grown up*. All our gang, we're, like, late twenties, but half the time, 'specially with the blokes, the way they behave, even if they've got kids and all the rest of it, they're like big babies themselves. But with Ron, he's all, sort of, taking charge and, you know, protective. Like with the cab, I thought, oh, he really cares about whether this man is going to rip me off and everything. And the way he was asking questions—was I going to be all right on my own and all that—I just thought it was really sweet, that's all. I'm not going to tell Karen though. Actually, she phoned me up this morning, trying to find out what was going on, nosy cow. She said that Ron was married, but his wife walked out on him. That sort of made me like him more, actually. Like I said to Karen, it's something we've got in common, because I know what that feels like, being dumped.

I'm really looking forward to tonight. I thought I might ask Gerald if I can leave work half an hour early so I can get ready. He can be a bit of a stickler, but I did it for him a few days ago, so I'm sure he's not going to mind. Oooh, I can't wait, I'm really excited!

## Gerald

*She's got freckles!* And there's another surprise as well. Melanie—
that's her name—is Jo's daughter, from work. Talk about coincidence!
I was tickled pink when I found out. Jo calls her Mel, but I'm going to
call her Melanie. It suits her much better. I must say, I'd never have
guessed the two of them were related. But all the sleuthing has really
paid off—you'll be calling me Sherlock Holmes before I'm finished, I
can tell you. In actual fact, there's no great secret, it's just a matter of
being methodical, and of course you've got to have a bit of patience.

Mind you, I realize now what a stroke of luck it was that first night,
finding out where she lived. Discovering she was Jo's daughter was another piece of luck, really. I'm always careful when I go near the school,
because that's what got me into trouble before. Until last year, I used to
go and watch the girls play volleyball—they used to have a practice on
Saturday afternoons, and sometimes I'd take a walk by the courts and
watch them. I wouldn't say that I follow sport as such, but it was a
pleasant way of passing the time. I used to take my flask with me, and
I'd buy a KitKat on the way there and sit on the bench and eat it. I
always took my litter home with me, and I wasn't doing anything
wrong—although that's not what the police thought. There was an in-
cident when a man exposed his privates to some of the girls, and some
busybody must have seen me near the volleyball court and told them,
because they thought it was me.

That's what I mean when I say that policemen are a nasty lot. That man I saw at the military department, Palfrey, he was one of them. I told him, I'm not like that, but he said some very unpleasant things. Mocking me, telling me I wasn't normal, that sort of thing. Quite un-called for, in my opinion. It was him and another policeman—they wouldn't leave me alone. It was so much like the time before, when they questioned me about Vera, I just seemed to go right back to how I was then. They wouldn't believe me and I couldn't stand up to them.

Three hours they made me wait, and I wasn't offered so much as a cup of tea. Then they kept on and on at me that I must have exposed myself to these girls; they said I'd been seen at the court and there were people who could identify me. I told them I wouldn't do that sort of thing, but they wouldn't listen. It was the same questions, over and over, taking turns one after the other, and I got confused and my mind sort of slipped. They asked me something and I said, "I didn't touch her," and they said, "Who?" and then I realized I'd meant Vera and not these other girls they were talking about. The policeman found the body disturbed, you see. They kept asking me, did I touch it, and I couldn't remember, except the hand, I knew I'd touched her hand, and then the policeman—Palfrey—said, "Did you touch yourself?" and I didn't understand him, I was panicking and shouting, and then he said, "Who's Vera?" and it was almost as if the two things were happening at once, the past and the present. Palfrey said I was shouting her name. He thought it was one of the girls at the school, and I'd . . . I told him, I think that sort of thing is disgusting, but they never listen to you.

They let me go in the end, but I was upset for weeks afterward. I had to go to the doctor and get something to help me sleep. I kept getting headaches and I couldn't talk to Jack at all. I felt ashamed, you see. I knew he knew about it, but it was as if I was the one who had the op-portunity of life, and there I was making a mess of it, getting myself ac-cused of something I didn't do.

I haven't been near the volleyball courts since then, but a few days ago I decided to take the long way home from work. It wasn't one of my theater nights, and to be honest, I wasn't particularly keen on going home. I'm not getting on so well with Mrs. Clarke at the minute. This past week she's been at me about something or other every day. I saw Melanie sitting on the bench by the court with another girl. I was thinking about something else and I nearly walked right in front of them before I realized who it was, but they were chattering away nineteen to the dozen and I don't think they noticed anyone else was there. I sat down on another bench, about fifty yards behind them, and I had the *Daily Mail* with me so I opened that. That's the thing about undercover work—you can't look as if you're hanging around; you've got to be doing something.

I couldn't hear what they were saying, but after a few minutes Melanie took a magazine out of her bag to show the other girl, and something else—it looked like an exercise book of some sort—came out with it and fell on the ground under the bench. Neither of them noticed it. They were too busy laughing over some article in the magazine.

After a few minutes the other girl suddenly looked at her watch. They were obviously late for something, because they rushed off without noticing the dropped book. I stayed put for a couple of minutes before going over to see what it was. I must confess I was a bit worried in case it was a schoolbook with homework in it, because I thought she might get into trouble for losing it. My first thought when I picked it up was that it must be a diary, but there wasn't much in it, just a few poems. A lot of the lines were repeated, so I wondered if they might be words from pop songs. But it said *Mel Farrell* on the front, with the address on Emneth Avenue. That's when I realized who she was. I wanted to be absolutely certain, so the next day I had a look in the folder where they keep the employees' home details in case they need to be contacted, and—sure enough—Jo Farrell, 41B Emneth Avenue. I took note of the zip code and telephone number, just to be on the safe side.

I'm happy to report that I needn't have worried about Melanie not having friends, because she's got plenty. In fact, she could do with being a bit less popular, in my opinion. There's one she goes to see a lot, an Indian girl—I haven't found out her name yet—and she seems all right, a tad quiet. But there's a whole crowd of others that I'm not so keen on. Quite foul-mouthed, a couple of them. Jo mentioned that Melanie goes shopping with them on weekends—I don't go along, someone might notice, but it wouldn't surprise me to learn that they steal things. Not Melanie, of course, but some of the others. I can't understand why Jo lets her go off with them. I've had it in mind to tell her more than once—I could say I was passing by and saw them—but I don't suppose she'd take any notice. Jo's nice enough, but she's like a lot of women nowadays, thinks she can do without men.

I don't mind admitting it's been a fair old upheaval, all this. I decided quite early on that I needed to make some changes to my routine—I'm all for keeping busy, but you can't do everything, so I've stopped going to *Oklahoma!* It was a bit of a wrench because I was enjoying it, but it had to be one or the other and I wouldn't miss my Tuesday nights at *Starlight Express* for the world. Besides, I've got my record to think of— 219 performances, and I haven't missed a single week! I felt a bit lost the first time, when Thursday came around and I wasn't getting on the tube to go to the theater, but then I discovered that Melanie always goes to the Indian girl's house for a couple of hours after school, and I'm easier in my mind if I'm there to see her safely home. Mind you, she gave me a bit of a turn the other week—something must have frightened her, because she kept looking round, and I had quite a time trying to keep out of sight. It's a good thing there are so many parked cars, or I don't think I'd have managed it. But she really shouldn't run. The state of the pavement round here is a disgrace, and she could easily trip and hurt herself. In actual fact, I'm thinking of writing a letter to the council about it. The other troublesome thing is keeping up with her. I wouldn't call myself fat exactly, but at my age I'm certainly not as thin as I used to be, and she goes at a fair old lick. But I always go home and tell Jack about her before I go to sleep. I don't know if it's the excitement, but these days I'm out like a light the moment my head hits the pillow.

One of the best things about this new arrangement is that I can still make my sandwich and put it in the old tupperware box to eat when I get back after seeing Melanie home to her door. I have a glass of milk too, just the same, with the card on the top. In a lot of ways it's like the theater, except it's better because it's real, so there's more satisfaction in it somehow. I've worked out a better route home for her from the Indian girl's house, safer, and now I know the name of the magazine she reads. I've been wondering if I might be able to go to the newsstand first thing on the day it comes out and buy it, then leave it for her on her doorstep. That's the plan, although I do have some reservations—I don't want it to distract her from her schoolwork, for one, and I'm worried about getting into trouble if someone sees me. But what I mean is, generally there's more *involvement,* which I enjoy, although I have to admit, now that I find myself thinking about Melanie, my sister, Vera, comes into my mind more often, and I can't say that's always a good thing. It's set me thinking about Vera and Jack again—and to be frank, there's more than a touch of jealousy there. Because although there's no denying Jack and I are best friends, you could say that Vera got to Jack before I did, and I still have feelings of being left out, even now. I miss Vera in a way that I've never missed Jack, because he's always been there. But when Vera died, the connection was gone and that was it. And she was great fun, none of that "big sister" stuff. Mind you, that did have its . . . shall we say, *unfortunate* side, in the end. It wasn't right, behaving like she did. If women and girls are beautiful, they think they can do whatever they like, and that is bad, but partly it was my mother going after that man Treece and causing the bad influence. That's something I really don't like to think about, because it isn't very nice at all.

On the subject of upsets, I had a nasty one yesterday when Jo suddenly asked me, right out of the blue, if she could leave early. Yesterday being Thursday, I wasn't very happy about it, because I always need to get away right on time to get ready for Melanie, but as I can't fault Jo's timekeeping I said yes, just this once. So she went off at half-past three. She told me she'd got all her work up to date, but—wouldn't you know it—someone rang at quarter to four with a query about one of her orders, and that took me over an hour to sort out, so I ended up tearing home and rushing through all my preparations for the evening. I was rather rattled by the time I made it to the road where the Indian girl lives. I always wait round the corner, because there's some shrubbery and a couple of big trees, so it's nice and hidden. But people take their dogs there, and of course I went and trod in some of the mess. I had to clean it off my shoe with my handkerchief, and then of course that had to be thrown away, so as you can imagine, I wasn't in the best of moods. And then, when Melanie came out, she turned left instead of right, and I nearly missed her!

I suddenly remembered my idea for a different route home, and for a second I thought we must have started communicating with each other through our minds, as I do with Jack. I felt almost dizzy with excitement, but then she turned down another road and I realized she wasn't going home after all. My mind was in a whirl and it was all I could do to stop myself from catching up to her and asking her what she was doing. I must say, it did cross my mind that she might be meeting a boyfriend. At first I thought, no, she's far too young, but then I remembered that Vera wasn't much older and they say children grow up much faster nowadays, wearing makeup and all the rest. I wanted to stop her but I didn't know what to say.

Maybe I speeded up without knowing it, or she slowed down, but I suddenly found myself about five paces behind her, and she must have heard footsteps because she turned round and looked at me. It was quite a dark street, so I couldn't see her face very clearly, but I thought she might have smiled. It happened so suddenly it caught me by surprise, and I think I must have looked a bit gormless, because she didn't say anything, just walked a few yards down the pavement and knocked on one of the doors. I had no choice but to carry on walking, because the house where she'd stopped was dead in the middle of the street. I got to the end and turned the corner, and then I didn't know whether to wait or not. In the end I took my little notebook out of my bag and jotted down the details—*Painswick Road, halfway down, blue door, two garbage cans*—then I whipped out the old A-to-Z and shot round to Emneth Avenue as fast as I could to see what was happening there.

Well, 41B was in total darkness, which made me think that Jo must have gone out for the evening and told Melanie to stay with these other people. So it wasn't the doctor at all, but some man! Jo shouldn't be chasing after men, she should be looking after her daughter. And don't tell me it's all feminism, because I know what I'm talking about. It was exactly the same with my mother and that artist. She should have spent less time making eyes at him and more time thinking about Vera, but all she ever cared about was throwing herself at him and leading him on. I used to think Jo was a good mother, but it just goes to show, what people say and what they do are not the same thing at all.

It was like my mother when the photographer came. She'd want us to be in the pictures. We'd get the attention then, all right—she'd put her arms round us and pose with the book as if she were reading us a story—but it was all for show. It meant no pocket money if you didn't do what she said, so we always cooperated because she was the one who doled it out. Of course, that didn't work with the dog. He was always meant to lie down by her feet for the photographer; he kept getting up and walking away and that would make her angry, but she couldn't show it because she didn't want anything to make her look bad in front of "The Public." Me and Vera always tried not to look at each other, because then we would laugh and Vera was terrible if she started. Her shoulders would shake and shake and she'd have to pretend it was a sneeze coming. But if she told Sammy he must lie down he'd always do it, because he loved her the best of anyone.

Well, I got a bit rattled thinking about all that, but I thought I ought to nip back to Painswick Road and make sure everything was all right. I walked past the house a couple of times but it was too dark to see the number, let alone anything else. Then a man opened the curtains of the front window and gave me a nasty look, so I thought I'd better call it a day, though I can't say I was very happy about it. When I got home I went upstairs to take off my coat and fold up my plastic bag like I always do, and then I went down to the kitchen to get my supper out of the fridge. My mind was still running on Vera and my mother, so I was a bit distracted and it wasn't until I was about to drink some of the milk that I noticed the ace of spades on top of the glass was face *up*. I was so agitated I must have dropped the glass, because the next thing I knew there was a great crash and milk everywhere and Mrs. Clarke came flying into the kitchen. I asked her if she'd touched my supper, and she started shouting at me. "Move it? What are you accusing me of? I wouldn't touch your things with a ten-foot barge pole!" and a lot more in the same vein. I said, "I suppose I might have made a mistake," because it's not impossible, coming home in such a rush.

I felt so frustrated—not only about the milk, but about Melanie, not being able to do the job properly, not knowing who she was with or what was going on. The upside-down playing card and the broken glass seemed to be bad omens. I don't know what got into me. I turned round to Mrs. Clarke and said, "You just bugger off!"

She said, "Don't you talk to me like that. You don't know when you're well off."

I said, "I don't think I'm well off," and she said, "That's what I mean, you're well off here and you've got no appreciation. You wouldn't find another room so easily, you know." I told her I might start looking if she kept on at me in that fashion, and she got quiet after that, just cleared up the spilled milk and went back to her television. But I'd lost my appetite. I ended up putting the sandwich in the bin and going to my room. I felt too depressed even to get undressed, so I just lay down on the bed with all my clothes on. I looked at all my things in their places and thought, fifteen years I've been here, I don't want to start looking for another home. I don't want to live on my own—that's why I refused when Tilly offered me the money. You know, I'm not so stupid that I can't stand back and look at myself and see what other people see. All these things I do, I know it's really a way to keep the loneliness at bay. Being organized, having a routine, it's like a sort of barrier. I've always been a lonely person, always accepted that it was part of me, of my life. I think that's partly because of Jack and partly my own fault. When I was a child I used to wonder if Jack was lonely too, but he's got Vera, hasn't he? And perhaps he's better at making friends than I am. I've often wondered if, when I die, he'll introduce me to his friends and then they'll be my friends too. I'd like that.

## Gerald, 1944

*Friday, September 1st*

*Last night I had a dream about Jack.* He was in a room with some rats, hitting them with a big stick. I wanted to talk to him but he said it is for the ARP and then he told me to go away because it was secret. I shouted to make him hear me but he did not seem to, but went on killing the rats. Then he ran through the door and rode away on a bicycle.

I went for a walk in the woods and saw Eric and Charlie. They were playing spies and they said I was a German spy. I said, "I'm not." Charlie said, "Yes you are." I said, "Go on then prove it," and he said, "We don't need to prove it, we just shoot you." It is quite a stupid game anyway, specially for Charlie because he is older than us.

*Saturday, September 2nd*

Vera and her friend Beryl were in her room getting ready to go out. I was bored so I said can I come and watch and they said yes. They were saying about what they want to do when they are grown up. Beryl said she will be an office girl and marry a rich man and have a motor boat. I don't think a rich man would want to marry her! (But I did not say that.) Vera said she doesn't want to work in an office but be an artist like Mr. Treece. Then Beryl said to me, "What do you want to do?" I said be an engineer because that is what the twins at school want to do. Their

father is an engineer and he has traveled to lots of different countrys
so it sounds like a good job to me. Then Mother came in and was
angry with Vera because she had lipstick. Vera said Beryl gave it to her
but I know that is not true because she said to me that her boyfriend
Eddie gave it to her as a present. I think that is true because Eddie is a GI
and they have got money. He is nice and quite brave too exept he does
not fly.

*Friday, September 8th*

Mother was furios because Vera left her door open and Sammy got
in and jumped on the bed. He chewed one of her Shalley Girl books
that was on the bed. When Dad came back he said, "It is only the cover
so she can still read it." Then he said to Vera, "Anyway, that is baby
stuff." Vera said, "I don't care because I like them."

*Saturday, September 9th*

Dinner was nice and funny because Dad said the chops must be
mouse chops because they are so small. Then Mother said Mrs. Paddick
told her that she can't make the meat stretch far enough and Dad said,
"You'd have a job stretching this, it's as tough as old army boots." She
said, "Well, make the most of it, if this keeps up we'll be eating whale-
meat." Dad said at least you could have a lot but you couldn't fit a whole
whale on the table, the tail would hang off the end and we laughed a lot.
But when I told Eric afterwards he said it was stupid because nobody
could get enough coupons for a whole whale.

I took my cocoa to bed and wrote this diary but then I heard them
arguing so I had to go on the landing and lissen and tell Vera when she
comes home because we promised we would. I did not hear the beginning but they were rowing about Vera's present because her birthday is
quite soon. I heard Mother say, "I think it costs £50," so they must be
getting her a jolly good present. But then Dad said, "Well, you don't

seem to care what she does," so I think Mother is trying to make it up to Vera for being horrid to her. Then it went quiet and he said, "Are you sure?" Mother said something about a negro doctor in London but I couldn't hear what it was. Perhaps it is part of the surprise, so I won't tell Vera because that will spoil it. I wanted to wait and see if they said any more but then I heard Dad open the door and come up the stairs, and I had to run for it. I spilt some of the cocoa on the carpet but it was on the brown part of the pattern so I don't think anyone will notice. I just jumped into bed when Dad came in. He said, "I came to tuck you in, old chap, I hope you don't mind." It was nice of him to do that but queer because he doesn't do it usually. He's going to stay until next weekend. HURRAY! It is better when he is at home even if there are rows.

Eric is stupid and what he said was stupid rubbish. Mrs. Paddick told me whales are not rationed.

## Monday, September 18th

I went to Vera's room and took her sketchbook and pencils. I did it because they were her best things. And Sammy. He is sad because he liked her best of anyone. I wish he had been in the woods with me on that day because then he would know. But saying the words is no good because if it is a dog they don't understand.

## Thursday, September 21st

The police went into Vera's room and took some of her things away. Then they went into my room and messed everything up. I wanted to put it all back in the right place but they said no and made me wait outside til they were finished. They found Vera's sketchbook and pencils in my desk and came out and showed me. "Why did you take this?" I hate them. Then Mother came up and she said you stole the things. But I did not. I just wanted to put them away for Vera but when I tried to say that

I couldn't. They don't lissen when you say something. All they do is ask more questions and it all goes back and forward again. They want me to say bad things about Vera but I won't. I wanted to go away with Sammy into the garden but she said, "Don't you run away from me." I did not want them to see me and when I came back to my room it was all horrible. I hate them and I HATE HER.

### Friday, September 22nd

The police found Vera's dress in the woods. It was burnt but enough left so they could tell. We had to go in the woods with them afterward. They were asking where we play and Eric said they don't go near the hut but they do. Charlie said afterward if you tell things to the police you will get in trouble.

But they said I could have the sketchbook back. I wish I had told her she was going to get a big present.

### Saturday, September 23rd

Eric said Charlie said Vera was going to have a baby.

### Wednesday, September 27th

Eric says he heard Mrs. Paddick say it was from an American soldier. I said Vera would not have a baby with an American soldier but he kept saying it is true. I did not want to talk to him so I stayed in my room. When I went to wash my hands for tea Mother was in the bathroom. She was holding her comb under the tap putting water on for her hair and I said, "Is it true Vera was having a baby?" She did not answer but just put the comb on her hair. She kept fussing with the pins so I went right next to her to ask her again IS IT TRUE? She turned round. There were pins in her mouth she spat them into the basin NO IT IS NOT TRUE and I don't want to hear you say that ever again. She was holding her hair on the back with one hand but she got my arm with the other and said, "Do you hear me don't you ever say that again." She didn't turn the water off and it splashed on her watch, and when she saw it she said, "Get out of here, get out."

She was doing her hair putting the pins in so I don't know if it was a lie.

### Thursday, September 28th

One thing I keep thinking. I miss Vera but I don't think it is fair if she can be with Jack and not me. I don't like that because he is not her twin and it should be me.

## Tilly

*Tiny's taken me out a few times now,* down to the seashore. Doesn't seem to bother him, pushing the chair, and he brings my little Nicky as well, on the lead. Good for the lallies, he says. He's still got all the "polari"—you know, the slang the old queens used to talk. He says it's a habit, but I think he lays it on a bit thick for me because I like it. Yesterday he came round after lunch, and we were getting ready to go when I said something about how I'd had my hair done but there wasn't enough time for my nails, and he said, "Tell you what, give me the polish and I'll take you down to the sea and paint them for you there." It was one of those lovely April days, so I sat on the beach in my chair and he perched on the end of one of the benches with a face towel spread across his knees and he rested my hands on it and did the manicure. Lovely, it looked, much better than the girl does. Then we had the cigarette and he said, "I went to the shop for those little bottles of gin and tonic, but they'd run out. I had to do it myself, put it in a jam jar and shake it all about." And he reached into his carrier and brought out a little jar with a screw-on lid. I said, "Well, I hope you rinsed it out first, or we'll be having gin and marmalade." Because it still had the label on—Golden Shred. "Oh, no," he said, "it'll be delicious. And I've brought some glasses; none of your polystyrene rubbish here."

He poured it out and we clinked our glasses and had a sip. "Do they let you cook, then? In the—" He jerked his head in the direction of the home.

"You must be joking. It's the insurance. They're terrified in case some old dear leaves a pan on and the place burns down. But I've never much been one for cooking. If someone else was volunteering I'd be happy to eat it, but left to myself . . ."

Talking about that reminded me of once when I was in Arthur's flat, making dinner for him. It was the end of 1940 and I'd just got back to London. It was pretty grim, but I thought, bugger the Blitz, I'm going to make Arthur a good meal to come home to. I thought it would be nice to play house, at least for a short time—because you never knew what was going to happen, if the bomb had your name on it.

I was peeling the potatoes when I heard the warning, but I carried on because I wanted to get it all ready. I was standing under the window at the sink, scraping all the peel into a metal bucket. I'd heard a few bangs, but they seemed quite far away, but after a while I thought, this is getting a bit too close for comfort. Well, by the time I'd worked out that they were definitely heading in my direction, there wasn't time to get into the shelter, so I did the only thing I could think of, which was to stick the bucket over my head and huddle down on the floor. I remember a tremendous crash and a whooshing over my head as the window blew in, but nothing else until Arthur came and found me under the table, covered in glass and dust, still with this thing on my head. I could hear him saying, "Tilly, oh, my God, Tilly . . ." He pulled the bucket off me and of course all the lights had gone out because of the bomb, so it was quite dingy, being under the table and everything. Arthur was peering at me. "Are you still in one piece?" Well, I was, but I was pretty stunned, so I didn't move to get up straightaway, and I think he must have been a bit worried, because he touched the side of my face to check if I was, you know, *still there*, and then he suddenly jerked his hand away. I heard him give a little gasp, and then he started saying, "Don't worry, you'll be all right, I'll go and find an ambulance crew, you'll be all right, Tilly." He was staring at me, gabbling all this, and by that time I'd managed to pull myself together a bit so I said, "I don't need an ambulance, just let me get up." But he said, "No, keep still, it's the shock, I must find a doctor."

I said, "Arthur, for heaven's sake, it's a few cuts, that's all."

He said, "No, your head, your face . . ." He took my hand and he was shaking like a leaf; I could feel it. I said, "What's wrong with my face?" and I put my hand up and felt this slimy sort of mush all round my eyes, but it wasn't painful or anything, so I pulled a piece off and had a look, and it was a potato peeling. I said to Arthur, "Whatever did you think it was?"

He looked a bit sheepish. "Well, I couldn't see. . . . I thought it was your brain."

I said, "Thanks, chum. I may not be the greatest genius who ever lived, but I think my brain is a bit better than a few potato peelings." I don't think I ever heard Arthur laugh so much. But someone was looking after me that day, because the house next to us was flattened and everyone inside was killed.

I couldn't stay on at the flat after that because it wasn't safe, so Arthur suggested I go down to Broad Acres for a while. I wasn't very keen on that because of Marjorie, but Arthur had a word with her and came back saying she was perfectly happy about it. I suppose she'd either managed to forget we'd ever quarreled or she'd decided to pretend that it hadn't happened, which was Marjorie all over.

Their little evacuee boy, Eric, was still there—actually, quite a few of them had stayed, which surprised me, given the reception most of them got. Eric's mother, Mrs. Watkins, used to visit every month to see how he and his brothers were getting on. She'd sit in the kitchen for a couple of hours, complain nonstop, eat everything in sight, and then go back home. I don't know why she bothered coming, really; she hardly paid any attention to her sons. Marjorie wanted nothing to do with her, so Mrs. Paddick had to play hostess, and Mrs. Watkins made it clear that she expected to be waited on hand and foot. "The government's paying you to do it."

Mrs. Paddick used to say, "Not at eight-and-six a week it isn't," under her breath, but she put up with it because she was fond of Eric. He was an angel compared to some other kids.

The atmosphere between Marjorie and Arthur was worse than ever. Marjorie was so tightly wound up that she'd rush out of her room in a fury if anyone made the slightest noise. I remember hearing the cleaning woman complain to Mrs. Paddick that Marjorie had shouted at her for banging her broom in the corridor. "Madam's been like a coiled tiger all morning." I saved that one up to tell Arthur, it was such a wonderful description.

I'm not sure if Johnny Treece was the root of the problem between them or just a symptom, but he certainly had a lot to do with it. Arthur wasn't at home much, which was probably just as well for him. He'd volunteered for the ARP early on. Being such a good organizer, he was soon in charge of a lot of people, and that took up a great deal of his spare time. I didn't like Treece any more than Arthur did, but Marjorie thought he was the bee's knees. We—she and I—weren't from what you'd call an *intellectual* background. Actually, that's not entirely true, because my father was a very intelligent man who knew a lot about politics and history, but he wasn't an artsy type of intellectual, if you know what I mean. I've never been very interested in that sort of thing. Anyway, I thought Treece was a phony right from the start, always talking about how England was full of *little* men with *little* minds and *little* ambitions. I used to think to myself, at least all those *little* men are big enough to stand up to Hitler, but I never said it to his face. Marjorie would have gone mad if I had, because she'd fallen for him hook, line, and sinker. She was forever going on about what a marvelous artist he was, but I couldn't see it myself. He did these huge canvases, smothered in oil paint, with great big full-length figures in heavy colors. They were supposed to represent good and evil and life and death and all the rest of it. I'm no expert on art, but the proportions of these things never seemed quite right to me—their legs were too short in relation to their bodies, and it made them look . . . well, a bit ridiculous, if you want the honest truth. Treece was full of how important they were. Talk about pompous—he told me that art was a sacred calling. "People are like sleepwalkers, and it is the artist's duty to open their eyes."

I said, "Open their eyes to what?"

He looked at me as if I were an idiot and said, "To truth, of course. Truth and reality."

It was all I could do not to laugh, but I said, "Oh, of *course*."

To hear him talk, the critics were jealous of his great talent, that's why they'd all rubbished him. "Sniveling pygmies," he called them. Well, as my friend Tiny would say, *get over yourself,* you know? The first time I met Treece, I'd gone to his house with Marjorie and he had all his children digging a massive hole in the garden. I thought it was for air-raid protection—some sort of trench—but it turned out it was for his pictures! He wanted to protect them from bomb damage. I ask you. . . . Never mind that his wife and kids might get blown to smithereens, just so long as the bloody paintings were safe. The man was an egomaniac. Marjorie didn't help, telling him that truly great artists are never recognized until after their death. The two of them hatched a plan to bury a time capsule with some of his pictures in it, to be opened in the next century. Marjorie told me—*in all seriousness*—that by the year 2041 people would be morally advanced enough to appreciate Treece's stature, because true art was timeless. I said, "I hope it keeps fine for them."

God knows what his wife thought about it all. From what I saw of the poor woman, she didn't have much time to think about anything—too busy running after that ragtag mob of kids. She was quite a bit younger than he was, and someone in the village told Mrs. Paddick that she'd been one of his students. Not at a proper art college, just some posh girls' school. It was quite a scandal, apparently, because Cynthia—that was her name—was all set to be a debutante, and her parents tried everything to get her away from Treece, but it didn't work. Sinty, he called her. Always singing out, "Sinty, baby wants feeding! Sinty, baby's got a dirty diaper!" Never occurred to him to lift a finger, of course, and there was never any help, because he only sold a picture once in a blue moon. Marjorie bought a couple, much to Arthur's disgust, but he couldn't afford one child on what he earned, never mind six, and it was obvious that Cynthia's family didn't want to know. You could see she must have been lovely once, but by the time I met her she looked washed out, no spark left.

Treece had plenty of charm when he chose to use it, and there was no doubt in my mind that he was going out of his way to use it on Marjorie. When he asked to use Vera as a model, I'm sure the first thing in his mind was to get in with her—admiring the daughter as a way of flattering the mother. Arthur told me that Marjorie was all in favor of Vera modeling at first. It was when Treece started giving Vera drawing lessons and spending more time with her that she began to resent it.

Vera had no idea about any of it, not at first. She was only twelve or thirteen. But Treece knew what he was about—well, he'd done it before, hadn't he, with his wife? Vera just liked him because he used to help her with her drawing. She'd been keen ever since she was a tot. You'd be sitting there reading a magazine and you'd suddenly catch a glimpse of this little thing on the floor in front of you, scribbling away with her crayons, grinning like anything. I'd say she had real talent. I've got three of her pictures in my room—sketches of their dog, Sammy. She drew them the summer before she was killed.

I always used to think that if I had a daughter I'd want her to be like Vera, because she was nice-looking, clever, kind, popular—got along with everyone except Marjorie, and that wasn't her fault. If she hadn't been adopted, I'd have said she took after me, because she liked the men, all right, same way I do. That's why I didn't put all the blame at Treece's door. I've never felt guilty about the way I've behaved, and I don't suppose Vera did either. It was in her nature, same as it's in mine.

I never liked John Treece, but the more I look back and see what I did wrong in my life, the less I'm inclined to go around blaming others, that's all.

Marjorie made her feelings about Treece so obvious that even the dog must have realized something was up. I remember one awful scene—1944, it was, in the winter, so Vera must have been sixteen—Treece had come over specially, to give Marjorie one of the sketches he'd made. You'd have thought it was a royal visit from the way she carried on, but there was a fair old dingdong about it afterward. Marjorie'd stuck the drawing up on the middle of the mantelpiece, but it came straight down the minute Arthur came home and saw it. He was standing on one side of the rug and she on the other, with me sitting in the farthest armchair, trying to pretend I wasn't there at all.

Arthur said, "Look at it! It's nothing like Vera! Look at that great big nose he's stuck on her; he's made her look like a Jewess!" Maybe that wasn't a very nice thing to say, but it was how people talked in those days. Then he grabbed it and held it out to me and asked me what I thought of it. Well, I'd seen the way Treece looked at the girl, and I was wondering if he'd made it deliberately unflattering in case anyone was getting suspicious, but I wasn't going to tell either of them that, so I said, "Don't bring me into this, it's got nothing to do with me."

Marjorie said, "Why ever should you think that? Please, don't hesitate to get involved—after all, you seemed to have moved here permanently."

Arthur leapt in before I could reply. "Don't speak to Tilly like that!"

"Oh, yes, your precious Tilly. We mustn't hurt her feelings, must we?"

She leaned over to get a cigarette from a box on the mantelpiece, and Arthur and I looked at each other. I widened my eyes slightly. *Does she know?* He made an almost imperceptible shaking movement with his head. It took only the space of a second, but when I looked toward Marjorie I saw she was staring straight at me, and I realized

she'd witnessed the whole thing. I knew she hadn't known before—
what she'd said was just . . . well, *Marjorie being Marjorie*—but she'd
recognized what was behind our exchange of glances. I saw it flash
across her face and waited for her to say something, but she didn't. I
looked down at the carpet, then back at her, and realized she knew
I knew she knew.

I said, "Look, Marjorie, if you don't want me here, I'll leave tomorrow." Which was a mistake, because of course Arthur jumped in with
six-guns blazing: "No! You can stay here as long as you like." He turned
back to Marjorie. "At least there's one woman in this house who doesn't
behave like an absolute bitch."

Marjorie dropped her head. If you hadn't known her, you might have
thought she was about to cry, or apologize, or something like that.
Attack was the best form of defense in Marjorie's book, and she was always sarcastic when she knew she was in the wrong, but this was something else. I couldn't understand why Arthur hadn't read the danger
signal, but I'd noticed he was a bit slow about cottoning on to that sort
of thing. Like most men, I suppose—you have to walk up and down
with a placard before they get the message.

I stood up. "Don't, Arthur. I think I'd better go."

Marjorie said, "Yes, why don't you?" Then she turned back to Arthur.
"You really don't understand anything, do you?"

He looked baffled for a moment, then he said, "I know a piece of
rubbish when I see one!" He still had the sketch in his hand, and he
crumpled it up and threw it onto the fire. Marjorie dived after it and
just managed to grab the edge before it turned into a ball of flames. She
let out a shriek. "You destroy everything you touch! I don't know why I
ever married you."

Arthur just looked at her as she cradled her burnt fingers and said,
"Neither do I."

I looked at the pair of them and thought, that's it, I've had enough. I was so sickened by the whole thing that all I wanted was to get away. Arthur begged me to stay, but I knew I couldn't. He'd told Marjorie that he didn't want her to have anything more to do with Treece. I think he had some idea that she might behave herself if I was around, but he must have realized he was clutching at straws. In any case, I wasn't in any position to act as a policeman—even if I'd wanted to, which I didn't. I may be a lot of things, but I've never been a hypocrite. Besides, it wouldn't have made one iota of difference whether I stayed or not—Marjorie was going to do exactly as she liked, and that was that.

Marjorie never said anything to me about that little scene, then or afterward. That surprised me, until I realized that in her mind, Arthur and I had become an added justification for her behavior over John Treece.

It's easy to condemn other people's mistakes but a darn sight harder when they're your own. I should have told Arthur what Treece was up to, you see. Or warned Vera, watch out, you're playing with fire, but it wasn't my way. It wasn't much fun for her or Gerald growing up with the war on, and I thought, she's got her little secret, where's the harm in that? She reminded me so much of myself at her age, that was all I could see. Nobody was looking out for her, that was the problem. There was me walking around with rose-tinted spectacles, and Marjorie giving her the cold shoulder because she wanted Treece for herself. The only person who really saw the poor girl as a *child* was Arthur, and most of the time Arthur wasn't there. Treece wasn't my type, too scruffy, but he wasn't a bad-looking man, and Vera had to find a bit of affection somewhere.

I came across the two of them by accident. It was the summer after the row about the picture. I'd been working, but the tour was cut short because one of the theaters was bombed, so I went to Broad Acres for a couple of weeks. I was by myself in the woods, taking a walk. There was a little hut where the boys used to play sometimes, and as I got nearer to it I heard voices, whispering. I couldn't tell who was in there—I thought it must be some of the evacuees—so I crept up to the window, and I was just about to tap on it and give them a scare when I saw Vera sitting on a rug on the floor, taking off her shoes. You could only see part of the inside of the hut from where I was standing, and I thought she must be alone until I heard her say, "Shall I take all my clothes off, or just my knickers?"

I thought aye, aye, what's this, a boyfriend? I stepped behind a tree pretty smartly because I didn't want her to think I was spying, and then I saw a man come up to one of the windows and nail up a piece of material to make a curtain. I couldn't see his face and I didn't want to crane my head round in case he saw me, but when I heard his laugh I knew who it was immediately: John Treece.

I didn't know what to do. I thought of trying to tiptoe away, but I was afraid they'd hear, because the tree was right next to the hut and *I* could hear *them* quite clearly. Treece said something like, "That's a very neat pile you've made." He must have meant Vera's clothes. Then he said, "Stop picking at that. It'll bleed."

"No, it won't. It's ready. Look."

"For God's sake . . . leave it alone." Treece sounded exasperated, and I remember thinking, some seduction this is going to be. Then I heard a whacking sound, as if he'd slapped her leg, and her voice: "Mean!"

I poked my head out from behind the tree and saw his shadow against the curtain. He pulled off his shirt, then he disappeared. I suppose he must have joined Vera on the rug, because the next thing I heard was, "My little mistress . . ." and then, "It's never very much fun the first time." I didn't want to listen to any more but I was still worried they'd hear me, so I did the next best thing—slithered down so that I was sitting at the base of the tree trunk and put my hands over my ears. There were some muffled bumping noises, and then I heard Vera say, "Ow!" It sounded so childish, as if some naughty boy in the classroom had tugged her pigtail, that for a moment I wanted to rush into the hut and tell Treece to leave her alone, but by the time I got to my feet I thought, there's no point, it's happened.

I don't know how long it was afterward, but I heard the door of the shed open, and there was Vera, fully clothed, standing on the step, holding her satchel. She said, "I have to go home now." Quite matter-of-fact—if you hadn't heard what had gone before, you'd have thought Treece had been giving the girl a drawing lesson, not deflowering her. He said, "I'll meet you here tomorrow, same time."

"No, I can't. But I can come on Friday." There was a pause, and then she added, "If you'd like."

Treece said, "I'll be here," and I thought, I bet you will, you dirty old sod. Vera put her face up to his for a kiss like a child at bedtime, then she bent down to pull up her socks and ran off with her satchel bumping against her hip. It was like a pang in my heart, seeing her school bag banging up and down like that, with her pencil box shaking around inside, and again, when I saw Treece standing in the clearing watching her go, I wanted to jump up and tell him what I thought of him . . . but I didn't. I had such a clear picture in my mind of myself at Vera's age, because that's when I met my first lover too. I'd just left school and got my first job in the theater, and I was so excited about being a real woman, that I'd *done it* and nobody knew except the two of us. It all came flooding back to me, the thrill of it, and I thought, I'm not going to spoil this for her.

That was how I felt at the time. But sitting there on the beach thinking about it again, so many years after, I felt as if my heart was breaking. One minute I was chatting away to Tiny, happy as a clam, and then all this business about Vera went through my head and the next minute I was in floods of tears. I said to Tiny, "Take no notice, I'll be fine in a minute," but of course the arms came round me, and that only made it worse. I said, "If I told you what I'd done, you'd hate me."

He said, "No, I wouldn't, I couldn't hate you, how could I hate my friend?"

"Oh, Tiny, you don't know—"

"It can't be as bad as all that."

"It's *worse*."

"Oh, darling . . ." When I looked at his face I saw two big tears welling in his eyes, ready to drop. I said, "Don't you start, or we'll never stop."

"Sorry." Tiny stared at me for a moment, and then he said, "You should have got married, girl."

"Why do you say that?"

"Companionship. It's all very well, the other thing . . . but you've got to have someone. To talk to. You've kept a lot to yourself, haven't you?"

"I suppose you're right. . . . I've never thought of it like that." I hadn't, really. But I didn't know what to say to that. What you don't have, you don't miss, do you? I'd always pushed things to the back of my mind. But when Tiny said that, I suddenly remembered my father. He used to say to me—before he got ill, this was—"Life isn't a game, Tilly. You've got to take it seriously." I always thought, why should I? You only get one shot at it, so you might as well enjoy yourself.

Tiny said, "I'll show you something," and he pulled a plastic wallet out of his pocket. There was a photograph inside, a man. "Dennis. My friend. He died last June. We were together nearly thirty years."

"He's got lovely eyes."

"You'd have liked him. He was a bit older than me, but not much. I thought he'd always be there." He bent down to stroke the dog so I couldn't see his face. "We had our little adventures, but . . . I miss him."

"Oh, Tiny, I'm sorry."

"No, don't be sorry, because he was *there*, you see. Thirty years, a happy home . . . we loved each other. You can't ask for more than that. And now he's gone. Here, let's put him away, shall we?" He put the little wallet back inside his jacket. "Ooh, look at the time. Here, give us your handbag." He pulled out my compact and handed it to me. Slipping back into his polari slang, Tiny said, "Better have a vada at your eek before we go back, put a bit of powder on. Don't want a blotchy old eek, do you?"

"Less of the old, if you don't mind."

Tiny told me a lovely joke on the way back. During the war, a bishop goes into a public urinal. While he relieves himself, he looks round at all the graffiti chalked up on the walls—Hitler this and Hitler that—and he turns to his neighbor and says, "What on earth does all this mean, my good man?"

The chap says, "I'll tell you what it means, mate, it means 'Itler wants fucking, that's what it means!"

"Dear me," says the bishop faintly, "what will the man be wanting next?"


It's a bit sad when somebody tells you a good joke and there's no one to pass it on to. I'd probably finish up being arrested for murder if I told it to anyone in here—so I sat down in front of the dressing-table mirror and told it to myself. And before I went to sleep, I said a little prayer to thank God for bringing me such a wonderful friend.

"*Your rabbit pie is absolutely first-class, Mrs. Peak,*" *said Tom, making the housekeeper blush with pleasure. The two boys stared at the delicious tea laid out on the table in front of them: ham sandwiches with plenty of mustard on them, boiled eggs, salad, bananas, homemade lemonade, and a splendid chocolate cake.* "*Where's Jill?*" *asked Peter.* "*She'll miss the first meal of the holidays if she doesn't hurry up.*"

*Just then, Jill and Peter's mother came into the dining room, looking worried.* "*Hullo, Aunt Fenella,*" *said Tom.* "*Is something the matter?*"

"*I was just wondering where Jill has got to,*" *said Mrs. Johnson anxiously.* "*She went out for a walk with Scruff while you were helping Mr. Brown with the bonfire. It's not like her to be late for tea.*"

"*I wish she'd come,*" *said Peter.* "*We want to tell her our plans for tomorrow.*"

"*We thought we'd take our bikes and do some exploring in the woods,*" *explained Tom.*

"*And have a bathe in the old pool,*" *said Peter.* "*Don't forget that!*"

"*Oh, dear,*" *said Mrs. Johnson.* "*Didn't I tell you?*"

"*What's wrong, Mother?*" *asked Peter.*

"*No one's supposed to go into the woods anymore,*" *replied Mrs. Johnson.* "*Dr. Andrews, the famous scientist, has moved into Pendene House. He's doing some top-secret work for the government, carrying out experiments in the woods, and no one's to disturb him.*"

"*Pendene House—that's the big one at the top of the hill, isn't it?*" *asked Tom.*

"*Yes, Master Tom,*" *agreed the housekeeper with a shiver.* "*Big and gloomy. I shouldn't like to live there.*"

"What sort of experiments, Mother?" asked Peter. "Do you know?"

"No," said Mrs. Johnson, "but they must be very important, because the Ministry of Science sent some men to help with the work, and they put a lot of notices up saying Keep Out."

"It sounds fascinating," said Tom. "I'd like to be a scientist when I grow up. Wouldn't you, Peter?"

Before Peter had a chance to reply, there was a pattering of feet in the kitchen passage, followed by a loud bark, and a bright-eyed fox terrier bounded into the room. "Scruff!" exclaimed Peter. "Where have you been? And where's Jill?"

"Now, really—" began Mrs. Johnson, because the dog was not allowed to come into the dining room. Then she stopped in amazement because Scruff, instead of lying down quietly beside Peter's chair, began nosing around his legs, whining, and putting his front paw on Peter's knee. "What is it, old fellow?" said Peter. Scruff backed away from him, shook himself furiously, and began to bark. "Goodness, what a noise! Whatever is the matter with him?" said Mrs. Johnson, as the dog rushed forward, grabbed hold of Peter's shoelace, and tugged with all his might!

"He's trying to tell us something!" exclaimed Tom. "Scruff, old boy, I do wish you could talk."

"Perhaps he's hungry," said Mrs. Peak. "I don't know why—Miss Jill bought him a great big bone from the butcher only this afternoon."

"Jill!" shouted Peter. "That's it! He's trying to tell us something about Jill!"

"I think Scruff wants us to follow him," said Tom. "May we go, Aunt Fenella?"

"Yes, I think you'd better," replied Mrs. Johnson, turning pale.

Scruff ran in circles around the boys, trying to shepherd them toward the door. "Woof!" he barked. "Woof, woof, WOOF!" His mistress was in trouble! Why wouldn't they hurry?

**Three Cheers for Tom!** 1945

## Jo

*All right, then, what's it worth to you?* No, only kidding . . . I was *so* nervous, getting ready. I mean, it's not like I haven't been out with a man before or anything, but it's been a while. I haven't met anyone I really liked for ages, and Mel used to get a bit funny about it if I was seeing someone. I s'pose it was because it was always, like, her and me, and she didn't want anyone else coming in upsetting the applecart, if you know what I mean. Mind you, she's been okay the last couple of years. I didn't tell her though, just said I was going to the pub. But she's not stupid; she kept coming out with why was I doing my hair, why was I wearing my best top, and all this. I mean, I didn't want it to be, like, this *big deal,* but all the same, I was in a right state about my cellulite. Mel came in while I was in the bathroom, and I'm going, "Look at my bum, can you see any marks?" She's like, "Mum, *puh*-lease . . ." and I'm standing on the loo seat, trying to see it in the mirror.

Ron took me to this really nice Chinese place. I've walked past it loads of times and always wondered what it was like because it looked great. They've got a little pool in the middle of the restaurant, with a fountain and fish and everything, and you have to walk over this sweet little bridge to get to the tables. I didn't know if I should offer to pay half—some men can be a bit funny about that and I didn't want him to think I just *expected* him to pay or anything. But when the bill came he held it really close to him so I couldn't see how much it was. I was fumbling round in my bag, but then I thought he might think I was rude if I *did* offer, because he'd booked it and ordered the food and everything. I didn't say anything in the end, just went off to the ladies' room and let him do it, but I think that was all right because he never mentioned it or anything.

He was all very . . . you know, being a gentleman, pulling out my chair so I could sit down and all that. I just felt like everyone was looking. . . . I think we were both a bit self-conscious, to tell you the truth, and the tables were really close together, so it was like everyone could *hear*, you know? Then he started telling me this really complicated story about when his dad got their van resprayed, and he asked the man who was painting the names on the side to put *Wet Fish, Shell Fish, Smoked Fish* underneath. His dad wrote it down and everything, but the bloke forgot to put *Smoked,* and then he said he wouldn't do it again even though Ron's dad went mad and threatened to punch his lights out. So now it says *Ron & Son, Wet Fish, Shell Fish, Fish.* He was telling me all this, and I thought it was quite funny, partly because he was saying it really sort of deadpan, but I didn't know if I was supposed to be laughing, so I looked down at my knife and fork so he wouldn't see I was smiling. Then he goes, "Wet Fish, Shell Fish, Fish," in this big, dopey voice, like the Honey Monster or something, so I knew it was all right. Then the food came, and he said, "Go on, do that thing with your nose again," so that made *him* laugh, and we got on really well after that.

It was fun, but all through the meal he never asked me if I wanted to go back with him or anything. So by the time we got the bill I'm thinking, perhaps he was just having a laugh, perhaps he doesn't fancy me. But when we got outside and I'm saying thank you for the meal, he said, "Don't you want to come back with me, then?"

I'm thinking, try and stop me, because he looked so great with his floppy hair and this *beautiful* leather jacket, and I'm, like, *Easy, girl!*

But then he said, "Only problem is, I do have to get up early."

Nothing ventured, I thought, and I go, "Well, what about if we go back to mine?" It was okay because I'd changed the sheets and the flat was actually tidy for once.

Ron said, "I don't mind at all, but can we get a taxi? First thing this morning, someone dropped a box of haddock on my foot, and it's bloody painful." I just started laughing, I couldn't help it. Ron looked a bit hurt, so I said, "Look, I'm really sorry, but it's like everything in your life comes down to fish."

"Yeah, it does." He stepped off the curb and looked down the road for a cab and I thought it was going to be, like, with some blokes, if you make a joke about their car or their football team they get really huffy. So I went after him, but before I could say anything, he goes, "Well, not quite everything. Some things come down to chips." Then a cab came, so he held out his arm, and when it stopped he flexed his arm like he was showing his biceps, except I couldn't see because of the jacket. "And mussels." We were both giggling by then, so we got in and I go, "And cockles."

"And winkles."

"Winkles?"

"No, more like eels—conger eels!" And he grabbed me and we were mucking around, tickling each other, and the driver's going, "Where to, mate?" All the way back, I'm saying things like "sprat" and "shrimp" and all the little fish I could think of, and he's coming back with big ones like "shark" and "swordfish," right up the stairs to my flat and into the bedroom.

It was great—not just, you know . . . the *sex,* but all of it. I'd been really worried about my cellulite and keeping the light on and all that, but I was laughing so much I never gave it a thought. We're lying there afterward and he's coming out with all these names of fish I'd never heard of and I'm going, "You're making them up!" and he's going, "No, I'm not."

I said, "All right, then, what kind of fish am I?"

"You're an . . . orange roughy!"

"I don't want to be that one, it sounds horrible."

"Because of your hair."

"It's not *orange*, it's more, sort of . . . red. Anyway, roughy sounds like a bit of rough or something."

"Okay, you can be a . . . parrot fish. They're beautiful."

"That's better. Just as long as I'm not a dogfish."

"Course you're not. Anyway, they're not that ugly. Not like a John Dory or something. They've got spots." Then he dived under the duvet. "Oh, no, it's Spot the magic dogfish, and he's coming to get you!"


I only had about two hours' sleep in the end. Ron had to get up at half-past three. He was really trying not to wake me but it was a bit difficult because we were all wrapped up together. I pretended I was still asleep 'cause it was nice watching him get dressed when he didn't know, but then I got up and made him a cup of tea and we had a little chat before he went. I didn't want to go back to bed, so I made myself this huge bubble bath and just lay there, thinking about him.

I knew I'd have to phone Karen and tell her, but I was putting it off all day at work because I wanted to keep it to myself for a while, just to have that special sort of feeling when you've met someone, and anyway, I couldn't because Gerald was in a really funny mood. He kept picking on me for no reason, taking all the orders I'd done off my desk to check them so that I couldn't find anything. By about four o'clock I was up to here with it all, and I was just about to sneak outside for a cigarette when my phone rang. It was only Karen, going, "I know what you did last night!"

"You *what*? How?"

"You were seen. Getting into a taxi. With Ron Russell."

"Who saw me?"

"Donna. She's just phoned me. She said she saw you with him, and you were all over each other."

"Yes, well . . ." Then I didn't know what to say, because she's going, "What happened? What's he like?" and Gerald's come in and he's standing right in front of me. I'm going, "Could you repeat that?" and "When do you want it for?" trying to pretend it's work, and Karen's going, "Have you gone mental?" She said it so loud I was sure he could hear. I'm flapping my hand at him and mouthing, "Be with you in a minute," but it was like he was rooted to the spot, just staring at me, and I knew he wasn't going to budge until I'd hung up. Karen keeps saying, "What's the matter? Is somebody there?" because she can be a bit thick sometimes, so in the end I go, "Well, I'll see what I can do and I'll get back to you tomorrow," and put the phone down.

He's still standing there. "Who was that?"

"Just an order."

He said, "Oh?" like he didn't believe me, but I wasn't going to tell him. It's not as if I'm on the phone to my friends all day, and it was Karen who rang me, so I wasn't exactly running up the phone bill. Anyway, it was none of his business, so I said, "Excuse me, I have to go to the toilet." I knew that would shut him up.

Come five o'clock I was out of the office like a greyhound, because I was really excited to see if Ron had rung, plus I wanted to get home before Mel because she'd told me her judo might be canceled. I missed the bus by about three seconds though, and she was in the kitchen when I got back. She had this big parcel in her arms, wrapped in brown paper. I said, "What's that?"

"I don't know, but it's got your name on it. I found it on the step."

It looked like a chimpanzee had done it up, sticky tape all over the place. I got my nail scissors and cut it open, and inside was this cuddly toy, a big stripy fish, blue and yellow. It had a piece of string round its neck with a label saying *Dear Parrot Fish, Thank you for last night, R,* with a row of kisses underneath. Mel went, "Oh, yu-uck. I *knew* you weren't going to the pub. And you've got a message. Are you going to listen to it?"

I said, "Yes, all right, in a minute." I was trying not to look too pleased, but she wasn't fooled. "I suppose you've already listened to it, have you?"

"Well, it might have been for me, mightn't it? Except I don't know anyone called Ron who barks on the phone." I thought, Spot the magic dogfish, I can't believe he did that. "Mum, you've gone red."

"Oh, cut it out. Why don't you make us a cup of tea?" I dashed into the sitting room—I thought Mel might follow, so I made a big thing of shutting the door behind me. Ron's message was really sweet. I was worried after what Mel had said that it might be something rude, but he was just asking if I wanted to go out again on Saturday. I thought, all right, I'm going to ring him back before I get all nervous about it, so I did. We arranged to meet in The Greyhound. Then I thought, okay, can't put it off any longer, so I went back into the kitchen and of course the first thing Mel said was, "Have you met someone, by any chance?"

She sounded a bit sarcastic, so I said, "Would you mind if I had?"

"No! You might have told me though. Is he good-looking?"

"Course he is."

"Are you sure? I mean, he's not, like, really *bald* or anything?"

"He's got quite a lot of hair, actually."

"He's not bald with a ponytail, is he? Because that is *so* sad."

"He's gorgeous."

"Mum?"

"What?"

"Look, I know it's been really hard for you, being on your own with me and everything. When I see Sonali's mum and dad, they're, like, really good friends, and you don't have anyone, so it's more difficult, and . . . you know. Anyway, if he's a nice person, I mean, special, then I'm really glad for you. And I think you're a brilliant mum."

"Oh, *Mel* . . ." I went and gave her a hug. I was so touched.

She gave me a squeeze back and said, "I think you should wear your blue dress on Saturday. I've got to go and finish my project now—it's due in tomorrow. Your tea's gone cold, by the way."

I just stood there thinking, she is turning into a really nice person. It's not as if *I* was thinking, you know, I'm, like, this really great mum or anything, it was more thinking I'm so lucky she's my daughter. I could feel myself filling up and I thought I'd better take myself off and have a shower before I really got into it. I put the fish on my bed. You probably think it's really stupid, but I left the label on as well.

I was so knackered I fell asleep in the middle of *Friends*. Mel had to wake me up when she came in to say good night. I dragged myself off the sofa and I was just about to go to bed when she said, "*Mu*-um?" like she does when she wants something.

So I go, "*Ye*-es?"

"You know I said I thought someone was following me? Well, I saw him. Properly, I mean."

"What, today?"

"Last night. When I was going round to Gran's. I knew who it was because of the footsteps. They were really close but I wasn't scared—well, not much, anyway—because I was on Gran's road right by her house, so I knew it was okay. I turn round and there's this man, staring at me."

"What did he look like?"

"Just this bloke. Quite old, and sort of dopey-looking. Not scary or anything. He had this plastic bag, really faded like he'd washed it or something. He wasn't carrying it by the handles, he had the top all bunched up in his hand."

"Never mind the bag, what about *him*?"

"Well, just . . . you know."

"No, Mel, I *don't* know. Was he tall?"

"No, sort of medium."

"Fat? Thin?"

"A bit fat. Not huge or anything. Pudgy."

"What about his face?"

"Pale. Dopey, like I said. But I don't think he expected me to turn round, so perhaps he doesn't look like that normally. He's got a big . . . well, sort of like a moon face. But it was a bit dark, so I couldn't really see."

"Did he do anything?"

"What, like flashing? No, he just stopped, then I started walking again. I never heard footsteps, but I didn't turn round or anything. Like I said, I was practically outside Gran's house."

"Do you want me to phone the police?"

"No, because it's not like anything happened. But you said to tell you, so . . . I mean, I don't think he's, like, really bad or anything. I just didn't want you to think I was making it up, that's all."

"Oh, Mel . . . I don't think you're making it up. That's why I think we should call the police."

"*No*, Mum!" We were in my bedroom by this time, and she's sitting on the bed in her bathrobe, cuddling Ron's fish and looking really panicky. It was just like last time, when she told me about Tanya Perrin. It was weird, because she never said anything about it at the time, but Mel can be really deep. She'll think about something for ages and then all of a sudden, like *months* later, she'll come out with all this stuff and I'll be going, "What are you talking about?"

"Why not?"

"I just don't want to make a fuss about it, but you said to tell you so I told you, okay? I mean, it's not a big deal, all right?"

"Well, if you say so, but, Mel . . ."

"I know, if I see him again I'll tell you. I'm going to bed now. Don't fuss, okay?"

"Okay."

She got up off the bed and came round to give me a kiss. "Good night, Mum." Then she gave the fish a kiss on its nose. "Good night, *darling* Parrot Fish. Thank you for last night." Then off she goes to her room, giggling her head off.

Of course I'm left there sitting bolt upright in bed, wide awake, thinking what am I supposed to do? I know what Mel means about not making a fuss. It's like when I was pregnant and I didn't tell my mum for ages because I knew she'd go ballistic. But this man could do anything—I mean, it wouldn't take much just to drag her off into the bushes and . . . he might kill her. He might—oh, God, I can't even think about that. It's like, if I even *think* about it, it might happen, you know? I might make it happen. I know it's stupid, but *still* . . . It makes me feel sick even thinking about it.

Actually—you'll think I'm going off my head when you hear this—when Mel was telling me what happened, I kept thinking about Gerald at work. I know it's not very likely. I mean, there's what? Ten million people in London? And I don't even know if Gerald lives round here. Come to think of it, I don't really know anything about Gerald, apart from him being M. M. Haldane's son.

It was just when Mel said the man had a moon face. That and the plastic bag. The one Gerald's got looks like he's had it for about ten years. And she said he stared at her—well, Gerald's always gawking at something. Me, usually. Sometimes, like when Karen rang this afternoon, I feel like telling him to get a life, but he is my supervisor, so . . . I could find out where he lives, I suppose. Bit paranoid though. Like spying on someone. It wouldn't be difficult—all I'd have to do is look through the personnel file. I mean, if he lives in . . . I don't know, Catford or somewhere, he's hardly going to spend his evenings prowling round here, is he? And I could walk Mel round to Mum's tomorrow night before I go out, just in case. I'd better ring her tomorrow, check if it's all right.

I must have gone off to sleep after that, because the next thing I know, Mel's shaking me. "Mum, it's eight-fifteen! You forgot to set the alarm!"

## Tilly

*I didn't find out about Vera* until a week afterward. It was my own fault, because none of them knew where I was, and I didn't telephone.

I had met the most *wonderful* man. It was in '44, at the end of June, about six weeks after I witnessed that little scene I told you about. I'd gone back to touring after that—I was jolly lucky to get it because a lot of the companies had disbanded—and I was on my way back to London on the night train. It was pretty grim: a third-class carriage packed with soldiers, and very slow. I couldn't find a seat, and every time we stopped, more men would come piling in. The carriage was almost pitch-dark because of the blackout, and sweaty bodies kept shoving their way past me and treading on my feet.

"*Do* you mind?"

"Here, watch it, you bastards, there's a lady present."

"Look out, we're stopping again."

"Where are we?"

"How the bleeding hell should I know? Anyone got a smoke?"

One of the soldiers lit a match for him, and I could suddenly see a whole gang of faces crowded round me. Most of them were a bit the worse for wear, judging by their breath, and they were all larking about—except for one man who was standing very quietly. He was in the middle of the group—I'd noticed him when the match was lit—but he didn't seem to be taking any part in the horseplay and I never heard him speak. Every time someone lit a cigarette, I'd catch a brief glimpse of his face: sunburned and very handsome, with black hair and a mustache, and he seemed to be staring straight at me.

It was a long journey, and at the end of it I staggered off the train more dead than alive. One of my big toenails turned black and fell off after a few weeks, but other than that, I didn't think much about it.

I had some clothing coupons saved up, so I went to Galleries Lafayette on Regent Street to see if there was anything worth buying. By some miracle I managed to find something I liked, so there I was, strolling along feeling pleased with myself, when I suddenly became aware that someone was following me. Well, it was broad daylight so I wasn't bothered, and in any case I've never been the nervous sort, even in the blackout, but I took a quick look behind me—nothing too obvious, just a glance—and blow me down if it wasn't the man from the train. So I walked on, nice and slowly, and then I went and looked at the posters in front of a cinema to see if he'd stop as well. After about five minutes I began to think I must have misunderstood—he was quite a bit younger than me, after all. Not that I've ever looked my age, but I was in my middle thirties by this time, and I'd guessed him to be about twenty-four or five. I thought, oh, well, and I was just about to turn round and go home when I spotted him leaning against the wall, scribbling something on a postcard. When he saw me looking, he ran up to me, thrust this little card into my hand, and rushed off without a word. When I turned it over there were big capital letters, scrawled in pencil: I AM IN LOVE WITH YOU. MY NAME IS JOE. MEET ME HERE TOMORROW 18:00.

*Well!* I'd been going to see a friend, but I canceled that, make no mistake, and when I turned up there he was, waiting for me. "I didn't think you'd come."

"I'm here, aren't I?"

"I don't normally do that, hang about and write on postcards."

"Well, I don't normally turn up to meet men who hang about and write on postcards. No, that isn't fair—I can hardly say 'normally' when it's never happened to me before."

"It might be habit-forming."

"Yes, I'm rather worried about that. My mother warned me there were some types of men you had to be careful of, but she didn't mention your sort."

"The postcard sort?"

"Exactly. And the hanging-about sort."

"When I saw you on the train I thought you were beautiful."

"And now?"

"I think you're better than that. What's your name?"

"Tilly."

"Well, Tilly, what about it? Shall I take you to the pictures?"

"That's what we're here for, isn't it?"

It was the Gaumont we went to, but I don't remember the film. We went up to the dress circle—there were always fewer people up there because you had more chance of being hit if there was a raid, and people were frightened at that time because the Germans had started sending over their doodlebugs. But that was the place where men used to take their girls, so quite a bit of hanky-panky would go on and you'd hear all these strange noises in the dark. . . . Well, I must have seen the film before or we didn't like it or something, because we started talking, and everybody round us was up to God-knows-what, so they weren't bothered. We were laughing and smoking cigarettes—they let you do that in those days—and we had a marvelous time.

I think we must have sat through some of the program twice, because it was quite late when we came out. I was interested to see what would happen next, because he hadn't done anything more than put his arm round me. He said, "I've got a week's leave. Can I see you again?"

"Well, I'm not going anywhere."

"All right, then, tomorrow. Same place, same time."

"Like going to the pictures, do you?"

"We don't have to go in, just . . . well, it's easy to remember, that's all."

"You could always write it on a postcard."

"You have my last one."

So I fished about in my handbag for a piece of paper and wrote on it *Joe and Tilly are going on a date,* and then I wrote the time and the day of the week and all the rest of it and gave it to him. He looked at it, and I could tell he was a bit disappointed, so I said, "What's the matter?"

"You didn't put as much as I did."

I said, "I *see.*" So I took the paper back and wrote *It may take me a whole week to fall in love with you.*

Joe read it and said, "Then I'd better see you every day just to make sure, hadn't I?"


The next night we went to a restaurant. The meal wasn't up to much and I was worried because I knew soldiers didn't get a lot of money, but Joe insisted on paying for all of it. It was coming down like bullets when we came out, so we huddled in a doorway, hoping it would let up—some chance, that was one of the wettest summers I can remember. There was a family with a little girl there, and we were chatting to them when she suddenly shouted, "Buzz bomb!" We didn't have time to run for cover, so we all sort of fell down in a heap in this doorway. Doodlebugs didn't have pilots, you see, and at a certain point they'd cut out, then they'd drop to the ground, and—*bang!* They used to make a *put-put-put* sound, a sort of motorboat gone wrong. . . . We could hear this noise coming closer and closer, then right above our heads. And then it stopped. That's the part I remember best, that sudden silence, and you'd be praying, please, God, don't let it fall on me, don't let it fall on me, like that—which was a bit awful, really, because that meant somebody else was going to cop it. Joe was lying on top of me, and this little girl's father was on top of him, all higgledy-piggledy. There was the most enormous crash and a rattling noise like a giant stick in a tin pail, and we felt the vibration of it go right through us. Joe shouted, "Keep down!" and then you couldn't see a thing for smoke and dust. When we picked ourselves up from this heap we looked like coal-men, covered in dust and soot. You couldn't see from one side of the street to the other, and there was glass everywhere, crunching under your feet whenever you took a step. The mother had a great gash down one side of her face where she'd been cut. We told the father we'd stay with her and the child while he went for some help. I'll never forget that woman, she was so brave. We got her to sit down again, propped against a sandbag or something, and after a while I got a bit worried because she hadn't moved or spoken, so I took her hand and asked her if she was all right, which was pretty stupid because she obviously wasn't. There was blood pumping out of her; you could see it down the front of her coat, red against the plaster dust, but she said to me—I'll never forget this—she said, "Well, the street's nice and flat."

The building opposite was just rubble. I don't think there was a window left intact in the whole street, and all that was left of the curtains were little fringes at the top. Doors were blown off their hinges, bricks everywhere, people calling out . . . it was chaos.

The woman's husband came back after a while and took her off to a first-aid post, because all the ambulance crews were occupied with the people being dug out of the rubble. They had men to do that, what they used to call the demolition squad, and of course their job wasn't made any easier because the rain was still coming down in sheets. I was in a bit of a daze and I think Joe was too, because we stood there in this pouring rain for about five minutes trying to wipe the muck off each other. Then he said some silly thing like, "I always like the evening to end with a bang," and it was obvious he was on the point of saying good night, when I thought, this is ridiculous, so I said, "Why don't you come back with me?"

"Oh, no, I couldn't do that."

I said, "Joe, we've just missed being killed and we could both do with a bath."

He said, "Well . . ." Then he winked at me and said, "You've got the bit between your teeth, haven't you?"

"Yes," I said, "and there's nothing you can do about it. Besides, I don't like to be alone with the geyser."

He said, "An old geyser, is it?"

I looked him straight in the eye and said, "Yes, a smelly old geyser. Frightens me to death."

"Well," he said, "we can't have that, can we?"

It wasn't Arthur's flat. I was sharing a place with an actress friend, Millicent Jones. It wasn't quite true about the geyser, although it fairly ponged of gas and you couldn't leave the door open because the bathroom was on the stairs, so that left this tiny little window, which only opened a couple of inches. Millie'd left a bottle of brandy on the table with a note propped up against it saying I could help myself, so we did.

Just in case you're wondering, it wasn't one of us at each end with gallons of bubbles, like something out of a Hollywood film, because this was wartime, remember? For one thing, the bath wasn't big enough, and for another the bathroom wasn't a place you wanted to spend a lot of time in, being freezing cold and full of fumes. Add to that the fact that you were only allowed five inches of water, and you'll understand it was hardly what you'd call a romantic setting. The water looked like black soup by the time we'd finished. And we didn't bolt straight into the bedroom afterward either. Our clothes were in an awful mess, so I borrowed Millie's dressing gown and lent mine to Joe. We had a drop more brandy and he started mucking around, doing soldiers in skirts. With the frill round his neck and his great hairy arms and legs sticking out in all directions, he looked really comical, and soon I was laughing like a fool— although some of it may have been the brandy and being glad to be alive, because it could take you like that sometimes.

After a while we curled up on the sitting-room rug and had a talk, telling all about ourselves the way you do at the beginning. It had needled me at first, the difference in our ages, but I soon forgot about it. I was telling Joe about my father and I suppose I must have got a bit emotional, because he said, "I'll tell you about my father, if you like." Well, I told him I'd like to hear about him, and he said, "Before I say anything, I want to tell you that meeting you was one of the best things that ever happened to me, and nothing's ever going to change that."

I asked him what he meant, and he said, "Well, you might not be so keen when you know."

"Know what?"

"My father was a docker." He said it in a flat voice, as if that was going to be the end of the conversation, because of the . . . well, the social aspect, I suppose you'd call it. I thought, I'm going to knock this on the head straightaway, so I said, "Look, Joe, I couldn't give two hoots if your father was a circus clown; it doesn't matter to me."

He said, "Are you sure, because . . ." and then he started telling me all this stuff about how he'd got a scholarship to the grammar school and the other kids had given him a rotten time about it. It was a great torrent of words, rushing out of him, and I thought, he's never told anyone about this before, ever. You'd never have guessed, because he'd changed his accent to fit in with the others at school, and his father had said, "What you talking like that for? Got a bloody plum in your mouth?" He'd left home as soon as he could, and his dad had been crippled in an accident and died before he'd had a chance to patch it up. My heart went out to him—all the times I've thought I should have stood up for my father against my mother, when he had his mental breakdown, and when he died. Poor Joe, I felt for him so much.

There we were, getting all sentimental, so I said, "Come on, give me a smile and I'll tell you the most embarrassing thing that I've done in my life." So I told him this story, partly as a sort of test, really, although I probably wouldn't have done if it hadn't been for Millie's brandy, because it still makes my toes curl when I think of it. It was when I was seventeen or thereabouts, and it was one of my first engagements. Well, I've never been backward in coming forward, as they say, but I thought these older actors and actresses were the most glamorous people in the world, and I would have given my eyeteeth to be like that. The theater was in Manchester, and the landlady where I was staying was the chatty sort. She'd told me this story about how her friend's eldest was working at the Grand and how they had a new dining room there, all done up in oyster-colored silk with French furniture and all the rest of it. Very la-di-da. Anyway, there was a new member of the company, a boy about my age, very handsome, and I was determined to show him how sophisticated I was. So I was telling him about this dining room as if I'd been there, about the fancy curtains and food and the wine—"Oh, but you simply *must* go there, darling . . ." talking all like that—and this chap was looking very impressed, and then I said, "Oh, yes, it's all Lewis Cunt in there, you know."

Well, as you can imagine, *dead silence.* Suddenly all the heads were turned toward me, and the boy started shuffling his feet and looking very embarrassed. I knew I'd said something terribly wrong, but I didn't know what it was, because I was just repeating what the landlady had said to me, how she'd pronounced it, and I thought it was the name of the man who'd made the chairs. And then one of the older ones said, "Oh, you mean *Louis Quinze . . .*"

Well, when I told Joe, his eyes went as big as saucers. I thought, now I've blown it, I shouldn't have told him that, and I was about to apologize for being vulgar when he started roaring with laughter. Honestly, I thought he'd never stop—he'd rolled over so he was lying on his stomach, and he was beating the floor with his hand like a wrestler, tears coming out of his eyes, everything. He said—well, it was more of a gasp, really—"Oh, dear, I can't believe you said that."

"Well, I didn't know what it meant until one of the others explained, and then I was so embarrassed I thought I'd die on the spot."

"Oh, no, it's wonderful, I haven't laughed so much in years."

After that we had a cuddle, and one thing led to another, so I said, "Would you like to come into the bedroom?"

He said, "Why, did your friend Lewis design the bed?"

"I *knew* I shouldn't have told you that story! I'll never hear the last of it, will I?"

Joe said, "Not if I can help it," and swept me up in his arms like Rhett Butler in *Gone With the Wind*.

He was the best lover I've ever had. We saw each other every day for a week, and then he had to go back to his unit. They were going to Europe, because it was just after the Normandy landings so the troops were needed, but that was all I knew, really. When we said good-bye at the station I had an odd feeling that I might never see him again—not just the usual worry, but a very strong sense of it. I said, "I'll send you a postcard," because that was our joke, and he said, "What, like the one I sent you?"

"I don't need a postcard for that. I love you, Joe." And then I walked away, quickly, because I didn't want him to see me cry.

Well, I got a letter from him soon after, and I thought, perhaps I needn't have worried—after all, there were men going off the whole time and leaving wives and sweethearts, and some of them had to come back. I knew Joe was in Belgium, but his letter didn't really tell me much apart from how pissed off he was hanging about with no smokes. Of course, they weren't allowed to write anything important in case it got into enemy hands. I remember the ending though: *I hope you like the color of your bedroom ceiling, because you'll be seeing a lot of it when I get home. Give my best love to your friend Lewis!* That made me laugh.

He never came home though. I got a letter from one of his mates a few weeks later. Apparently Joe had asked him to write to me if anything happened to him, because otherwise I wouldn't have found out, you see, not being the next of kin. By the time I got the letter, I knew I was pregnant with his child.

## Jo

*I never had a chance* to look up Gerald's address because he hardly left his desk all day. He was huffing and puffing because this huge lorry came back off a film set, full of taxidermy, and when I went down to check it I discovered one of the wallabies was missing. I'd tried to get it sorted before Gerald found out, but of course he was eavesdropping on my end of the phone call and immediately it was, "What's missing? What's got lost?"

He nearly went into orbit when I told him. "Who was it? We'll never deal with them again!"

I said, "It's one of our biggest clients, Gerald. Actually."

I rang Mum when I got home. I didn't say anything about Mel's man, but she said Colin could pick her up at half-past seven, so that was one less thing to worry about, at least. Ron was at the pub when I arrived. We were having a drink at the bar and he was in stitches about the stuffed wallaby, when this man standing next to us suddenly taps me on the shoulder and goes, "Excuse me, but are you Jo Farrell?"

Well, it was weird, because when I'd heard him ordering drinks a few minutes earlier, I'd thought, I know that voice, but I couldn't place him. So I go, "Yes," and he says, "I'm sorry, I couldn't help overhearing what you were saying and I thought, that's got to be Jo. I'm Paul Cosworth. From Militaria."

It was amazing. I mean, I've been on the phone to this bloke every week for the past few months, sorting out orders for Second World War stuff, but I hadn't a clue what he looked like, because I'd never been round there. So I introduce him to Ron and we find a table and we're all talking away when Paul goes, "How's Gerald?"

"Don't ask."

"That bad, is it?"

Ron asks me who Gerald is, and I'm thinking I'd better not say anything too bad about him in case it gets back, but Paul's coming out with all this stuff I didn't know, about how he goes to see the same musicals over and over again, and Ron's going, "What a nutter."

I started feeling a bit guilty—even though I'd been halfway convinced he was this sort of mad stalker—because Paul's making him out to be a real head case. I thought I ought to stick up for him a bit, so I said, "Oh, he's all right really, just a bit of an old woman, that's all."

Ron's going, "Well, so long as he's harmless," when Paul says, "My mate Steve, he's a policeman, and he reckons that old Gerald's a flasher."

"You're joking."

"Straight up, I kid you not. Steve told me they've picked him up quite a few times."

"What, round here?"

"He only lives down the road. He used to sit on the benches up by the school and . . . you know, get his tackle out."

"Did they catch him?"

"Well, not red-handed, so to speak. But they kept getting complaints about a man hanging around, and then this girl got raped."

I thought I was going to be sick. "Tanya Perrin?"

"That's the one. At one stage they thought that might have been him."

"What, that he raped her?"

"I don't know about that, but they thought he had something to do with it."

"Was he charged?"

"No, he's too tricky for that. My mate Steve said they were sure it was him but they couldn't prove it."

"Did anyone identify him?"

"No, it never got that far. Like I said, they didn't have the evidence. But he came in last week when Steve was in the shop, and as soon as Gerald realized who it was he couldn't get away fast enough. And some-thing else Steve told me—Gerald's sister got killed when she was six-teen. It was during the war, but it wasn't a bomb or anything. She was *murdered*." Paul nodded his head knowingly at us. I didn't know what to think. I could hardly take it in.

"Did they find out who did it?" Ron asked him.

"It was a GI. *Apparently.* Of course, they had hanging in those days, so we'll never know, but it makes you wonder, doesn't it?"

"How old is he?"

"Who, Gerald? Early sixties, I should think. Jo?"

"Wha— Oh, yeah, he's just coming up for retirement."

"So he'd have been, what"—Ron counted backward on his fingers—"1995, '85, '75 . . . fourteen? Fifteen at the most. Bit young, isn't it?"

"Except it runs in families, doesn't it, abuse? I mean, if he was mo-lested as a kid, and then when he gets a bit older, he starts doing it . . . well, they think it's normal, don't they? What everybody does . . . they get mixed-up, warped."

Ron goes, "You can say that again."

"Well, they think it's love, don't they?"

Ron got to his feet. "Another drink, anyone?"

"Thanks, I'll have the same again."

"Jo? Jo, are you all right? You've hardly touched your drink."

"Yeah . . . can I have a mineral water, please?"

Ron went off to the bar and I said to Paul, "You know who his mother was, don't you?"

"No, but she can't have been much of one if she produced *him*."

"She was a famous writer. M. M. Haldane. The children's books, re-member?"

"Tom Tyler? I always thought that was a bloke."

"Well, it wasn't, it was Gerald's mum."

"Well, I never!"

"Well, you never what?" Ron put the drinks on the table.

Paul said, "Gerald's mum was only M. M. Haldane."

"As in Tom Tyler?"

"And the rest. Weird, or what?" Paul asked me, "How did you know?"

"Someone at work."

"You sure he wasn't pulling your leg? I mean, you'd think if that's his mum he'd be really clever. And rich as well. Not some pathetic little pervert."

I'm sitting there listening to this and my stomach's really churning, and all the time I'm thinking, am I going to tell them? Ron suddenly looked over at me and said, "Are you sure you're all right?"

"No, not really. I just can't believe I'm hearing this. It's *horrible.*"

"I know, he's just filth. I don't see why you should have to work in the same office."

Paul says, "I know what you mean, but it's kids he's after, isn't it? I've got two myself, a boy and a girl, and if anything was to happen to them, I'd—"

"That's what worries me!" I couldn't help it, I was in a real panic. It all just came pouring out, about Mel and the man following her. "What am I going to do? When she told me what he looked like, it really sounded like Gerald but I thought, it can't be. I didn't even know he lived round here. I've never seen him on the bus or down the shops or anything, and he doesn't come in the pub."

"That sort never do though, do they?" said Paul. "They don't have friends, not in the normal sense. They just get together to leer over photographs and swap information and all that. Well, they're always looking out for kids, aren't they? Preying on them, trying to lure them in an' all that."

Ron said, "He shouldn't be allowed to walk the streets."

"That's what I said to Steve, he ought to be in prison, but Steve says they can't touch him. They can only keep them for twenty-four hours, you see, otherwise they start screaming about their rights and all the rest of it—"

"*Their* rights? What about Mel? Doesn't she have any rights? What am I going to do? I mean, he must know where we live—I'm not in the phone book, but it would only take him ten seconds to look it up at work. I was going to look up *his* address today, only I never got the chance. Christ, I can't believe this is happening—what am I going to do? I can't be with her every minute of the day." I could *not* believe it. I mean, there I was, a few minutes before, sticking up for him!

We never went out for dinner. Ron and Paul were brilliant, really sympathetic. I'd gone to the ladies' room—honestly, it made me feel so sick I thought I was going to throw up, but I was all right in the end—and when I came back, Ron said, "We've made a plan. You find out where he lives, and we'll go round there and warn him off."

I said to Paul, "But he knows you, doesn't he? What if he goes to the police?"

"Doesn't matter. I know Steve, don't I?"

"I suppose so . . . but you said they haven't got anything on him."

"I reckon it's only a matter of time. The police can't do much unless he's actually done something, so it's up to us to stop him before he does. Look, Jo, even if they catch him and he gets convicted and all the rest of it, they're going to lock him up for six months and then he'll be free to do it all over again. Honestly, it makes me sick."

Ron said, "He won't forget us in a hurry. We'll sort him out."

"Yeah, we'll scare the crap out of him, don't worry. He won't be bothering your daughter again, we'll see to that."

"But what if he goes to the police?"

"*Him?* Not likely. He came into the shop the other day when Steve was there, and when he saw who it was he started acting all shifty. He shot out of the door like a rat up a drainpipe. Couldn't get away fast enough."

Ron said, "In any case, he's hardly going to go down the station and say, oh, these two men threatened to work me over if I carry on pestering young girls, is he?"

"I suppose not. . . ."

"Well, then. I know it's a cliché, but with these people, it's the only language they understand."

After that I felt a bit better—well, I stopped feeling sick, anyway. We had another drink, and Paul started telling us about the military displays they had planned for the VE Day anniversary in May. I was thinking how I was going to face Gerald on Monday, because I don't want to be on the same *planet* as someone like that, never mind the same office. I told Ron I'd phone him the minute I got his address, and then he swapped numbers with Paul. He said, "We'll arrange this between us. The less you know about it, the better."

That was fine by me, because I didn't want to ask too many questions, to be honest. Paul's a big bloke, and Ron's not exactly a midget either, but they'd said they were going to warn Gerald, not beat him up or anything. It's all very well to say that people like Gerald need help and counseling and all the rest of it, but if it's your children they're after, well, you'd do anything to protect them, wouldn't you? It's easy to say you shouldn't take the law into your own hands, but it's like Paul said, there's nothing the police can do and when something like this happens, you've got no choice.

## Gerald

*I must confess I got into quite a state* after that fiasco with the milk—disappointment with myself more than anything, I suppose. It got me thinking about the time when I was fourteen and I wanted to join the air training corps but they said I wasn't good enough and I had to go into the Home Guard cadets instead. Mother'd put Tom Tyler in the air corps—the book had been published the year before so of course I'd had my heart set on it and I knew Jack wanted it too, but it wasn't to be. It was all the same year as Vera . . . a few months after, it must have been. The sky was full of American aircraft—I remember Mother said it got on her nerves, having all the noise while she was trying to write, but it became part of our lives, really. Vera and I used to count the planes leaving the base and then coming back in again. There were always a few who didn't make it, and that used to upset Vera very much, because she knew a lot of the airmen. I didn't like that, the way she went on, making up to them all the time. I knew that wasn't right. I liked the Americans though—well, we all did; we had never seen Americans before except in the films. We thought they must all be like that, tall and brave with a lot of money, but they thought they could just come in and do what they wanted. That is what happens when people get above themselves. Good people can be turned bad because of sex—that's what happened with Vera, and the Americans took advantage of it.

Eric's brother Charlie spread a lot of rumors about how she'd been with this one and that one; he even said he'd seen her in the hut with a man. I called him a liar and we had a fight. Not much of one, I admit—he knocked me down with the first punch, because he was a year older than I was and quite a bit stronger. I didn't know how much of what he said was true, but I didn't want it to be true and that's why I fought him. Then of course it all came out about her being pregnant. Mother told me that wasn't true, although she must have known I'd find out sooner or later. I can't say I blame her for trying to cover it up, because people weren't above making nasty remarks—"She was asking for it," that sort of thing, and at school some of the boys would say, "Your sister was a prostitute." Filthy-minded, even at that age. I didn't know what a prostitute was in those days, but I knew it was something disgusting. Of course, when I was a bit older, if you went to certain places there'd be women who'd come up to you, offering themselves, and I would tell them straight off I wanted nothing to do with them, but they'd make a nuisance of themselves. Sex-mad, the lot of them.

I have to stop myself thinking about those things, because it makes a big muddle in my mind and everything goes out of control. It is hard, but I know I have to stop or it begins to look as if the whole world is just chaos and full of sex and when that happens you can't make sense of anything, because if that could happen to Vera, then how can anyone be safe? That's why I started the scrapbook for Melanie—the idea just came to me out of the blue. That was the color I chose, in actual fact. I visited several shops and found a lovely one—it was on sale too! Reduced by 50p, so that was a piece of luck. As soon as I saw it I knew it was the right one for the job, and I must say, things have brightened up considerably since I bought it. It doesn't do to dwell on the past too much. I know Jack would agree with me there, because I've been able to talk to him again these past few days, and I must say he's really bucked me up. There's the responsibility too, of course, that goes with it, I can't deny that, but I feel better in my mind now he knows I'm not going to let him down this time. Positive thinking, that's what it is. You've got to look on the bright side.

I've pasted in some photographs I took—one of the house on Emneth Avenue, and a couple of her with her friends. Well, I say that, but one of them was with those girls she goes shopping with, and I wasn't having them in the scrapbook, so I just cut out the part with Melanie and threw the rest away. There's a nice one of her with the Indian girl too, walking down the road. They're a bit on the blurry side, I have to admit, but it was jolly difficult getting anything at all. I must say, I take my hat off to these undercover types. I never realized how hard it is to take a picture of someone without being spotted. I'm thinking of investing in one of those Polaroid cameras—they cost quite a lot of money, but I think it'll be worth it. I won't have the worry of some idiot losing the film when I take it round to Boots, which is quite a consideration—those people you have to deal with look like they're half asleep. There was a piece in the local paper about how Melanie's school is having a special art exhibition for the VE Day anniversary, so I put that in as well. I thought that was a nice touch. The past and the present coming together, you might say.

There's one picture that's really rather good, if I do say so myself. I managed to get it when she was coming round the corner from Emneth Avenue. There's a place opposite, you see, it's a row of terraced houses but it's broken in the middle by a path where you can cut through from the main road. I don't know why they did that, but it's been most useful these past few weeks. There's a big tree at the end of it so you're not in full view of every busybody who comes along. Funny, really. To think I must have walked past it a thousand times and never taken notice of it before— this sort of thing makes you much more aware of your surroundings— and I got a good snap, a profile. You can see the face, the hair hanging down the back, everything. I put it alongside an old photo of Vera, and I wasn't mistaken because there's really quite a good likeness. Of course, mine's in color and the one of Vera is black-and-white, but still . . .

I'm sure there would have been more about Vera in the papers if it hadn't been for the war. Of course where we lived it was big news, but I mean the national papers. They were too busy reporting about Europe—the invasion and all the rest of it. There was a paper shortage as well, so you only got a few pages. Not like now! I always read a news-paper. I think you ought to know what's going on in the world, but really, some of it . . . I wouldn't mind being on that program with all those politicians, *Any Questions* or whatever it's called. I'd soon put them straight! It's a funny thing, because this time last week I was so down in the dumps I wouldn't even have thought of something like that, but now I'm on top of the world again. Even Jo telling me she's got to be off early again tomorrow didn't spoil things. I've been taking my eye off the ball at work recently, with so much else going on, and what with all the extra orders and people putting things back where they shouldn't, we're long overdue for a spot of stock-taking. So I'll fix up my sandwich and glass of milk so I can work late and have them ready for when I get home.

## Gerald, 1944

*Friday, September 29th*

*The police came again to see Mother.* It isn't fair because I want to know as well but they wouldn't let me stay. I have got a right because she was my sister AND I WAS THE ONE THAT FOUND HER but they don't care about that.

*Monday, October 2nd*

They have got more information but nobody will tell me. It's not fair because I'm not a spy. When I came back for lunch Mrs. Everett was in the kitchen so I took my milk out on the step because I knew they wouldn't say anything if I was there. Mrs. Paddick told Mrs. Everett that Eddie stole Vera's purse and it was found at the base. Mrs. E. said, "I don't know why he had to do that, those Yanks make more in a week than our boys do in a month." Mrs. Paddick said, "She met him at a dance at the base with that Beryl who is a piece of work if you ask me and I don't know what Mrs. Haxton was thinking of letting them go." Then she said, "Oh, that poor lamb, I never would have thought it." Mrs. Everett said, "I'm not surprised, they are always getting drunk, we had another of their blessed jeeps through our hedge last week." Mrs. Paddick said Mother said to her at least it was not a Negro because she could not bear it, but Mrs. Everett said, "That's not so bad, some of those colored boys have lovely manners."

*Tuesday, October 3rd*

I went outside the kitchen again and Mrs. Paddick said, "The one they want to talk to is that man Treece. If you ask me there's something not right about him," and Mrs. Everett said, "He has a seedy look." Mrs. Paddick said, "Drawing lessons!" Then she did a snort and said, "I believe in clean living. Some people have not got any idea of what is decent." But then I sneezed and she came out to see what it was and said, "You run along." It is the only thing anyone ever says to me but it was queer she said that about Mr. Treece because he's not a bad man. He says funny things

*Wednesday, October 4th*

Mrs. Paddick said the police arrested Eddie. Mrs. Everett told her, "Good riddance to bad rubbish." Mrs. Paddick said, "If they have got the right man."

*Thursday, October 5th*

Eric told me I could come and meet him and Charlie and Johnny in the woods after school so I did. Charlie said we had to go to the hut even though the police said we can't, but when we got there it was empty. I asked if he stole the things because there were blankets and cushions but he said the police took them away. There was a mark on the floor and he said it was blood, but that was a lie because it was only paint. I wanted to get out but Charlie said we had to stay. He shut the bolt on the door and I thought he was going to bash me for what I said about stealing but he said, "That night they reckon your sister was killed, there was someone sleeping in here." I asked, "How do you know?" and he said, "Because I saw them." I asked him who it was but he said he didn't know because it was dark and the person was rolled up in the eiderdown. I said it might have been a log because Tom did it in a book once but Charlie said it was too lumpy so I said how could he see if it was dark and we had a row about that till I asked him what was he doing in the woods. He wouldn't tell me so it must be poaching. He said, "She used to come in here with all her boyfriends," so I bashed him and he bashed me back then they ran off. So I sat by myself and Mr. Treece came and told me off for being there. I was pretty pissed off so I said, "Well, the police said no one should be here," meaning HIM and he said he was working but he didn't have any paints so I think he was snooping.

### Friday, October 6th

I tried to get into the house without anyone seeing because my shirt got torn from fighting, but Mrs. Paddick was in the hall and she said, "What have you done to your face?" and made a lot of fuss because there was a bruise. She made me go into the kitchen and put stuff on it and then she asked me if I was fighting about Vera. I said yes, and she said, "You don't want to take any notice of what that Charlie says." I hadn't said who did it because it would be telling tales, so I said, "How do you know?" and she said, "Never you mind." Everybody keeps acting like a Know-It-All pretending to be much better than me because they know some clever secret and I am sick of it so I said, "Eric said you said Vera was going to have a baby from that American soldier and that was a lie."

"Then Eric's been listening where he shouldn't."

"But you told a lie about Vera!"

She started to say something about "I thought your mother—" then she stopped. "It isn't a lie, dear."

I told her, "I wrote down everything you said," and she said, "If it makes you feel better, dear," as if I am a little baby who doesn't know anything. "I could show it to the police, what you said."

Mrs. Paddick said, "But they know, dear. They were the ones who told us."

And that is bad because it means it must be true. But it is worse than that.

*Saturday, October 7th*

Mrs. Paddick is just a stupid old woman pretending to know everything, but she doesn't know what Eric told me. He saw Mother going out with Sammy that night. It was late and she was banging about outside with Sammy at the gate because he didn't want to go. She was pulling him, and Eric's room is at the front so it woke him up. I said, "Why would she go out in the middle of the night?" He said, "I don't know, do I?" He said she went down the lane and didn't come back for a long time but he doesn't know how long because he went back to sleep.

*Monday, October 9th*

There was another row again last night. Dad came home and we didn't know he was coming. Me and Eric had our dinner in the kitchen when I heard him come in. I went into the hall to see and Mother was putting on her coat. She said, "I wasn't expecting you. I'm going round to see Johnny Treece and I will have my dinner on a tray when I get back." He was angry because he looked like Sammy does when he growls and you can see a bit of his teeth. He grabbed both her arms. "You're not going anywhere." She said excuse me and tried to get past but he said, "Take your coat off." He shouted at me to get in the kitchen so I went in and shut the door but it still felt as if the house was going to explode. He put his hand on her back and gave her a push into the sitting room, or that's what it looked like except it was through the glass bit of the kitchen door that makes everything look wavey.

When we finished Eric said he was going to see Charlie. I said can I come but he said no so I went upstairs. Jack was not there. It is always just me by myself especially now Vera is not here. Once I said to Dad how it's not fair if other people have all the secrets and not me and he said it wasn't a secret if someone else knows but only if it is you and you don't tell anyone. I could see what he meant but it's not much fun that way. I just heard a glass smash downstairs so I picked up a cup on the windowsill and threw it at the wall and it made a big smash but no one came. Even if I smashed up the whole room they would just say, Run along.

### Tuesday, October 10th

Mother was not there at breakfast. Dad had to go to a meeting about the ARP and Mrs. Paddick and me went out to wave him off. Then he backed the car down the lane and said good-bye all over again for no reason and gave me 10/-. As soon as he drove off Mother came down with her coat and went out. I don't know why I thought of it except he never gives me my pocket money and 10/- is too much, and I get it on Saturday not Tuesday. Also the car had luggage on the backseat and he said he was only going to a meeting. Or perhaps Jack made me think of it. So I asked Mrs. Paddick if he was coming back and she said, "I don't know dear." Then she got some chocolate out of her apron and said, "I was saving this but you might as well have it now."

## Jo

*I don't know how I've got through* these past three days, I honestly
don't. Seeing bloody Gerald sitting there opposite me the whole time,
all these things kept coming into my head about what he'd done and
inside I'm thinking, "You *bastard!*" and I really wanted to say it to his
face. I'm not a violent person, but I really, really wanted to hit him *so
much* . . . and all the time I'm pretending—yes, Gerald, no, Gerald,
three bags bloody full, Gerald—honestly, I don't know how long I can
keep it up 'cause it's doing my head in.

Ron took me home after the pub, and I'm sitting in the taxicab tick-
ing off on my fingers what Mel does after school. "Monday's judo,
Tuesday she goes to Mum's—I'll give her a ring and ask if Colin can
pick her up from school—Wednesday she's got the dentist, so that's—"

"Jo? Just calm down, yeah?"

"I *can't!*"

"Look, we said we wouldn't tell anyone, right? We can get it sorted—"

"Yeah, but what if I can't get his address? If it's not in the file? This is
*my daughter,* Ron. She's all I've got, and if anything happened to her,
I—" I could feel myself welling up, I couldn't help it, and of course I
started crying right in the back of the cab. Ron put his arm round me
and said, "Calm down, it's all right," and all this, but I just felt like nothing would be all right ever again in my whole life.

On Sunday morning I sat down with Mel and went through what she was doing after school and how she wasn't to go anywhere on her own. She kept rolling her eyes and telling me to chill out—I didn't tell her about Ron and Paul's plan, but I think I got the message across.

I looked through the personnel file on Monday while Gerald was in the warehouse and rang Ron on his cell phone with the address.

"I looked it up in the A-to-Z. It's only about half a mile away from me."

"I'll check it out this evening, then come over to you. Will you be in?"

"Don't worry, I'll be there. You can meet Mel."

"Great. I'll call you first. Be about nine, I should think."

I couldn't get my mind off the whole situation, so when I got home I rushed round the flat cleaning up, doing the ironing, *anything* to try and stop thinking about it, but come half-past eight I was nearly climbing the walls, and Mel was looking at me and going, "What are you *like*?" I knew I couldn't tell her, but I wanted to talk about it so badly. I nearly told Mum when she phoned, but I didn't because I thought, she's going to go nuts and I can't handle it, and anyway, Ron told me not to.

By the time Ron arrived, which was almost a quarter to ten, I was going out of my mind. I'm, like, "Where have you *been*?" and he's saying, "At least let me get in the door." So we go into the kitchen and Mel's in there. I'd told her he was coming and everything, but I could see she was a bit shy.

Ron says to her, "You must be Mel. Nice nails!" Because she had this green varnish on.

"Thanks. Mum thinks it's disgusting."

"Oh, cheers. Gang up on me, why don't you? D'you want a drink, Ron?"

"I'll have a beer if you've got one." Then he turned to Mel. "Show us again," and she put her hands out so he could see. "No, I like it. It's the same color as liquor."

"What's liquor?"

"It's the liquid you get when you cook eels. Like a parsley sauce."

"Oh, gross!"

"No, it's quite nice. Pie and mash and liquor, that's what they used to have."

I said to Ron, "You've got eels on the brain, you have."

Then he gave me this really wicked look. "I brought you some."

"You haven't!" I couldn't tell if he was being serious or not.

"In here." And he held up this plastic bag. "Live ones. They're better when they're fresh."

"What am I going to do with them?"

"Skin them."

"You've got to be joking."

"It's easy. Look, I'll show you. Careful, 'cause they're slippery and they can really move when they want to." He put his hand right into the bag and I swear I could see something moving about in there. I was out into the hall like a flash and Mel was hiding behind the fridge screaming, "No!"

Then he pulled out his hand and he's holding this one little prawn.

I said, "You really had me going there."

"You should have seen your faces!"

"I've never seen you move so fast, Mum."

"No, you're all right, we got these in this morning. Tiger prawns. They'll be fine tomorrow if you put them in the fridge."

Mel started laughing. "Well, she's not going to arrange them in a vase, is she?" What she meant was that men normally bring roses or something, and for a moment I thought Ron might think it was a bit rude if he didn't get it, but he said, "I'll bring flowers next time. For both of you. How's that?" and Mel came straight back with, "What? Sea anemones?"

"I just might, at that. To go with your eel-colored nails."

"That does it, I'm taking it off. Can I use your remover, Mum?"

"Thanks for asking." I said to Ron, "She doesn't usually bother."

"Oh . . ." Mel stuck out her tongue at me, then she turned round to Ron, really grown-up like. "Nice meeting you."

"You too."

The minute she'd gone, I said, "What happened?"

"Well, I went round there in the van."

"Not the fish van? Ron, what if—"

"Not that one, the other one."

"*And?*"

"Well, I saw him go in—there was a woman there. I thought you said he lived on his own."

"I thought he did. He's never mentioned anyone. Well, he wouldn't have a wife, would he? Not if he's a—" I didn't even want to say the word. "Anyway, judging by what Paul said about going to see those musicals over and over—I mean, who'd put up with that?"

"I don't know. . . . From what I could see, she was what my dad would call 'a bit of a walrus.' "

"Could be the cleaning lady."

"Not watching telly at nine o'clock at night it couldn't."

"Well, his lodger, then."

"Could be. Or his landlady. But in any case, we can't go round there and have a word with him if there's someone else there."

"Jesus, I can't stand this. What am I going to do, Ron? It's like the world's closing in on top of me—"

"Wait a minute. Wait a *minute*. What about if we go to your work?"

"*What?*"

"It's just a small office—two, three people, right?"

"Three."

"You, Gerald, and . . . who?"

"Neville. He's the boss, only he's on holiday at the moment. Christ, I'd forgotten about that."

"So it's just you and Gerald?"

"Next week it is, yeah."

"What time do you knock off?"

"Five. Us, that is. The blokes in the warehouse go at half-past four."

"Okay. Well, if you were to say you had to get off early . . . then it would just be lover boy, wouldn't it?"

"Yeah, but—"

"Is there anyone else around? Security?"

"No, they come on later. And it's, like, general security. They go round all the units, not just us. Bit risky though, isn't it?"

Ron shook his head. "Piece of cake. Paul knows where it is, doesn't he?"

"What, the office? I wouldn't know. I'd never seen him before that night when we were in the pub. He must have been in though."

"Right. I'll give him a ring. Which day?"

So I said Thursday, and then he said he was going to try and get Paul on his cell phone, so I went to Mel's room. The door was shut—she was on the phone and I knew she had to be talking to Sonali. So I'm standing there listening in case she says anything about Ron. I know that's bad— she's my daughter, and I'm sort of *spying*—but I really wanted them to get along. I'm practically holding my breath in case she says he's a plonker, but she didn't. She was going, "No, honestly, he's all right . . . I know, I was really surprised. . . ." Then Sonali must have asked her what Ron looks like, because she said, "Oh, not bad. Nice eyes. And he's got hair like Gary Barlow a bit, only it's more blond . . . anyway, he's just . . . really nice . . . what, out of ten? Oh, seven, at least. Maybe seven-and-a-half."

I know it's stupid, but I actually stood there and went, "Yes!"— whispering, of course—and punched the air with my fist. Because if it's an actor or someone in a band, they might give him, like, eight or nine out of ten, but with people they know—boys at their school or what-ever—it's usually, like, *two,* so seven-and-a-half is brilliant. And I was so pleased that Ron wasn't making this big effort with Mel, you know, trying really hard to get her to like him, because it's so embarrassing when blokes do that and she's just, like, *oh, you are SO SAD.* . . .

Then Ron stuck his head out of the kitchen door. It's only a small flat and all the rooms come off this one little hall, you see.

"Did you speak to him?"

"Yeah. Thursday's on."

"What are you—"

"Look, Jo. We agreed it's better if you don't know too much, right?"

"All right, but—"

Ron shook his head at me. "It's not like we're going to kill him, is it? Much as I want to. Now . . ." He put his arms round me. "I can't hang about 'cause I've got a few things to do, but I'll give you a ring tomorrow, okay?" He started going backward to the front door, sort of pulling me with him.

"Yeah . . ."

"Stop looking so worried!" He sounded really cheerful. "It'll all work out, you'll see." Then he gave me a peck on the cheek, shouted out, "Night, Mel! Nice to meet you!" over my head, and let himself out. I heard him whistling on the stairs. A second later, Mel opened her bedroom door and stuck her head out. "Oh, he's gone." She sounded really disappointed.

"He has to get up really early in the morning." To be honest, I felt a bit disappointed too. I mean, he hadn't said he'd stay the night or anything, but . . . I don't know, I suddenly felt like I was making excuses for him. It just left me feeling a bit down, him rushing off like that.

Mel shrugged. "Never mind. He's all right. Hunky, even. Well, sort of. In a, like, *old* way." I suppose it was the thing with Gerald, but I suddenly felt really unsettled.

"Mum? What's wrong?"

"Nothing, really."

"Were you worried in case I didn't like him? 'Cause I think he's great."

"I'm glad you like him. Come on, love, it's well past your bedtime."

It was only half-past ten and I wasn't that tired, but it suddenly seemed like the end of the evening, so I did a quick tidy-up round the kitchen, then I went to bed too. This book I'm reading, I was really into the story, but I just couldn't concentrate on it. I couldn't get to sleep either. It was like something was nagging at me—I don't know what exactly, just this weird sort of feeling, and I couldn't shake it off.

## Tilly

*I still don't understand how it happened.* I'd always used Rendell's, and of course Joe had French letters—all the soldiers did—so you'd think I'd have been all right, wouldn't you? There was this rumor going round that the government had ordered the factories to make a certain percentage of the contraceptives with defects, in order to keep the birthrate up. I didn't believe it, because they wanted more legitimate ones, not the other sort, but you never know, do you? In any case, what were we supposed to do, fill it up with water first? Talk about a passion killer . . .

There was no question of having it. I knew that from the start. I spent a couple of weeks kidding myself that nature would take its course without my help, before I faced up to the situation and got myself blind drunk on gin, hoping that would do the trick. I was all by myself, crying my eyes out over Joe, and when Millicent came in she found me passed out on the sofa, snoring my head off with the empty bottle in my arms. "You were holding it like a baby," she said, and of course that started the waterworks again, so I told her what a mess I'd got myself into.

"Quinine." That was the first thing she said. She knew a woman who'd used it three times and swore by it. She'd bought the tablets at the pharmacy—you didn't need a prescription and you could get fifty for seven and six—and she'd taken them with castor oil and it worked like a charm. So I thought, there you have it, and the next day I took myself off to the pharmacy, but—wouldn't you know it? Not available. The army had commandeered the lot and I was back to square one.

Well, everyone knew that there were nursing homes where they'd get rid of the baby and write it up as some other sort of treatment. I'd even heard of a WAAF who got sent for an abortion by the services—her husband was overseas and she'd had an affair with her CO. Mind you, I don't suppose she was the only one by a long shot. But the cost was about £75, which put the kibosh on it as far as I was concerned.

It was Millicent who came up trumps in the end. She asked around— there was always someone who'd done a favor for a friend, that sort of thing—and she came up with this woman's name. Mrs. Pavey. There's no harm in my saying it, because she'll be long dead and besides, it's all legal now. Anyway, this woman hadn't passed any medical exams but she'd helped quite a few people and Millie said she only charged £2, which was pretty well all I could afford. "Millie, you are an absolute darling. Where does she live?"

"Camden Town. But she wants to come to you."

"What, here? Why can't I go to her?"

"Well, I suppose because someone might see you going in."

"Yes, but they'll see *her* coming *here*, won't they?"

"Yes, but if she has a succession of women . . ." I realized that Millie was starting to look a bit uncomfortable. "Someone could get suspicious and . . . well, the police might—"

"*Police?* Why? For crying out loud, she's not doing one every half hour, is she? And for all they know, she could be shampooing our hair!"

"Oh, you know . . ." Millie suddenly went quiet, and I noticed she wouldn't meet my eye.

"What did she actually *say* to you?"

"Well . . . I suppose I ought to tell you. She said that if anything . . . you know, *went wrong*, well . . ." Millie took a breath before she gabbled out the rest of it. "She said she couldn't risk ending up with a dead body on her hands."

"Oh."

Millie said, "You don't *have* to do it. I mean, you could have it adopted, or . . . well, there's probably some men who wouldn't mind . . ."

"What men? And what sort of lunatic is going to adopt a child in the middle of *this*? Don't be daft, Millie. Joe's never coming back, and I don't have any choice. And even if he *were* . . . Oh, I don't know what I'd do. But he isn't."

"Sorry. But I just thought, if there's a chance—what Mrs. Pavey said—"

"Don't! I don't want to think about it. Let's just . . . let's have a drink, Millie. Honestly, it ought to be you telling me to pull myself together, not the other way round."

Millie went back to Mrs. Pavey and they made an arrangement for her to come and see me at the flat. For some reason, she couldn't come round immediately—there were several days to get through between that conversation and when she arrived, and they were awful. I did my best not to think about it, but of course that was impossible and every time I *did* think about it, it brought Joe right back, which was . . . well, even after all this time, I can hardly bear to remember what that was like. I was frightened, as well, after what Millie'd said, because I wasn't really sure what it involved. Of course, I'd heard of people who'd had it happen—I don't mean just theater people, but women with big families who didn't want another one, but I didn't know any of the details. I just wanted to get it over and done with. I can't say I felt any connection with the baby—well, not in a direct way, although I did have this very particular dream, several times over. It was strange, because I could tell the origin of it—it was something I'd seen a few years before, in the first Blitz, but I'm sure I never dreamt about it then. There was a direct hit on a house, and this poor little thing had obviously been flung right out of the building into the road, and with the impact . . . it was *burst*. And all its little insides, just smashed down like that onto the ground, and the horror of that . . . it all came back to me in this dream but muddled-up so I was in the street, doing a sort of human jigsaw with the pieces of this baby. I knew I had to put it back together, but it wouldn't fit. Some of the parts seemed to be made of flat cardboard, like a puzzle, and others were real limbs, flesh, so they wouldn't join up, and then I'd look at them and notice that they were dirty or the toenails needed cutting and I knew it was because I hadn't looked after this baby and that's why it was like this and I couldn't make it whole again.

Millie was very kind to me—I was always waking her up in the night, because we'd go down to the basement to sleep during the raids and we'd be lying right next to each other, and she'd give me a cuddle. She couldn't have been a better friend, but I could tell she was getting uneasy. She kept asking me, "What if something goes wrong?"

I said, "Look, you mustn't be here when this woman comes." Well, she got very upset; she kept saying, "But I can't leave you on your own."

I said, "You've got to. That way, if anything does go wrong, you'll be in the clear. You can say you didn't know anything about it."

I was determined not to let her see how scared I was. She agreed in the end, so when the time came, she went off for her shift at the W.R.V.S. and I was left waiting for this woman to turn up. I was in such a state of nerves I nearly jumped out of my skin when the bell rang.

She was a stout, elderly woman with a round face surrounded by tight, greasy rolls of gray hair. She looked sort of kind and brisk at the same time, like a nurse. I remember staring at her bag, wondering what was in it.

"Are you going to let me in? I don't want to stand out here all day." She pushed past me into the hall.

"Oh, yes, of course. Mrs. Pavey?"

"That's right. Would you be Mrs. Haldane?"

Without thinking I replied, "No, it's Miss."

As soon as I said it, her expression changed completely. "I *see*." She looked at me as if I were something she'd trodden in. "Your friend didn't tell me that. I don't normally do this for unmarried women. I don't think it's right."

If I hadn't been so worked up I'd have told her a few home truths about the pot and the kettle, but as it was I told a white lie. "He was a soldier. We were engaged." I was wearing a nice ring with a blue stone that Arthur'd bought me, and I held up my hand to show it to her.

"Was he killed?"

I nodded. "He never knew."

She still looked a bit suspicious—I told you I've never looked my age, but I wasn't exactly a girl either, and it crossed my mind that she might think I was some sort of prostitute. "Please help me."

For a moment I thought she was going to refuse, but her face softened a bit and she said, "I don't know. What d'you want to go and do that for if you're not married? It's bad enough afterward." She must have seen my desperation because she said, "I'll help you. But don't you tell anyone what you've had done or who did it, do you understand? Not a one."

I promised her I wouldn't tell a soul and she said, "All right, get a towel and put it on the bed, then take your drawers off and lie down."

She knelt down at the foot of the bed. I was lying down flat but I raised my head and saw her open her bag and take out a black rubber tube with a bulb halfway along and a nozzle at one end.

"This is going to be safe, isn't it?"

"Well, dear, you've already taken the chance, haven't you? But I've never had a bad one yet and I don't see why you should be the first."

I sat up. "What do you mean, a bad one?"

"Well, there's always a risk. If the air gets in, you see, then you're in trouble ... but I know what I'm doing, and I always have a good boil-up beforehand so it's clean."

"But—"

"Look, dear, are we doing this or aren't we? Because if not, I've come all across London and—"

"Yes! Yes, we are. Doing . . . what you've come for. I'm sorry."

"Then you'll have to trust me. If I were you, dear, I'd shut my eyes," she chuckled, "and lie back and think of England."

All I could think of was Joe.

Mrs. Pavey stuck this thing with the soapy water inside me, and although it hurt, it wasn't as bad as I'd expected. To be honest, I was just relieved it wasn't a crochet hook or a piece of bark or any of the other things I'd imagined, something that would wound me inside, because I'd heard all the stories. . . . Afterward, she said, "That should do the trick." She told me not to move for a while, and she tidied everything up. She obviously wanted to get away as quickly as possible before it started. I had my purse ready beside the bed, with the money all counted out, so I just leaned over and tipped it into her hand. I remember she asked me didn't I have any notes, because it was so much change, and then she said, "I can let myself out. Now, just remember, if you do have to go to hospital, you've never seen me and I've never seen you."

I don't know how long I lay there afterward, but I remember I turned over onto my left side and tucked my knees up because it hurt, and I could feel tears sliding across my nose and a wet patch on the pillow under that side of my face. There was nothing at first, just a pain—not sharp, but a deep, cramping feeling. Like the time of the month, really, if you get it badly, but then I felt as if something was yielding inside me—*giving way,* that's the best I can describe it—and then I knew the miscarriage had started because I was flooding all over my skirt where I pulled it down. I knew it must be soaking through the bedspread and I tried to stand up to get to the toilet, but I felt so faint and light-headed that I had to sit down again.

I was sort of crouched over on the edge of the bed and my foot knocked into something, and I saw she'd left a bowl from the kitchen on the floor, a big enamel thing with a blue rim, and I leaned over to try and pull it between my legs. Well, I just managed it before I could feel it passing from me, but I kept my eyes closed and then I lay back down on the bed. That was where Millie found me when she came back. That was the next thing I remember, her face in front of mine, and she was saying my name, over and over. . . . When I opened my eyes and looked round for the bowl, it was gone. She must have emptied it down the toilet.

I think I must have slept after that, but I felt so weak and wobbly the next morning it was all I could do to get out of bed. I went through to the kitchen, holding on to the furniture. I was very thirsty, so I got hold of the kettle to fill it up, and then I started hemorrhaging again. I called out to Millie, and she took one look, pulled the cloth straight off the table, and said, "Stay still." I was holding on to the edge of the sink and she was wadding this material, pushing it up between my legs, trying to stop the blood. She said, "We've got to get a doctor."

I said, "No, you can't," but she rushed out and fetched one of the neighbors, a first-aider, and he said, "You're going to hospital." He went and got one of his pals and they came back with a rough-and-ready stretcher—canvas slung between two wooden poles—and they strapped me onto it and took me down the stairs. I don't remember much about it, just seeing the tiles on the hall floor and thinking, that's good, because they were red, you see, so if there was any blood on them it wouldn't show so much.

I remember, after I'd had the D&C, coming round from the anesthetic and hearing the doctor and nurse talking over me, saying it was an incomplete abortion. I tried to tell them that I hadn't done anything, but I kept drifting away and then coming back again, and I don't know if they heard me. If they did, I wasn't believed, because the nurse came back next morning and said, "You're gambling with your life, you know. You mustn't do anything like that again. I'd steer clear of men, if I were you."

They let me go and when I went down the steps of the hospital, there was Arthur standing at the bottom. I was still feeling pretty groggy, but I remember wanting to laugh—it was just after what she'd said about staying away from men and then finding him there. Waiting for me.

I said, "What are you doing here?" because he looked really grim. He said, "Your friend telephoned. She thought you were dying. She was in quite a state. . . . Lucky she spoke to me and not Marjorie." He marched me off to his car—he could still get petrol because of his ARP work—and said, "What the hell were you thinking of, letting some old woman mess you about? Why didn't you come to me?"

"Well . . . it wasn't yours."

"I know that! But I told you, if you needed anything . . . How could you be so *stupid*?"

"Oh, Arthur . . ." I couldn't even cry. It was as if something inside me had gone out, like a light. It was an empty, flat feeling. Nothing there.

"I've spent the last two days trying to get in touch with you. I didn't know where you were."

"Why?"

"Vera's dead, Tilly. She's been murdered."

I just stared at him. I couldn't take it in.

"I needed you, Tilly."

"I . . . I don't know what to say."

I had the picture in my mind of what I'd seen that day in the woods—Vera and Treece in the hut—and then this terrible, dull feeling of it all being too late, beyond repair.

"Aren't you even going to ask what happened? Don't you care?"

"Yes, of course . . . tell me."

"She was battered to death. With a wooden stake. Gerald found her in the woods."

"Why?"

"They don't know why. Or who. She was—" He hesitated, and I realized why.

"Pregnant?"

"Yes. Marjorie got it out of her. She wouldn't say who. Marjorie thinks it was one of those blasted GIs."

I closed my eyes. "Arthur, I've let you down. I'm sorry."

He took me home after that. He didn't offer to come up with me, and I didn't ask. He just patted me on the knee and said, "I know you've been in a bad way."

I said, "Arthur, I'm so sorry . . ." I knew it wasn't good enough, but it was all I could find to say. I couldn't seem to focus on anything, or feel anything except this big lead weight inside my chest, knowing I'd been so wrong.

When I saw Arthur's face like that, so haggard, and he told me . . . He thought I was saying sorry for not being in touch. But I wasn't. It was worse than that. I'd let him down. And Vera. But if I'd known what was to come, my God . . .


I wouldn't blame you if you thought I was as hard as nails, but it's what people always say in the theater: "The show must go on"—and it does, doesn't it? But it means you have to block things out of your mind. If I didn't do that, I couldn't live with myself . . . with some of the things I've done.

It was after seeing Arthur that day that I knew.

God took Joe away from me as a punishment because I didn't look after Vera.

# Gerald

*I was busy counting the teapots* when I heard them come in. We've
got over a hundred of them, fancy ones and novelty ones shaped like
cars and lions, and I was giving them a quick once-over with the old
feather duster and checking for any damage at the same time. It's
funny, because just before I heard the door open I was thinking, I
ought to do this more often, because it's nice when you can get down
to some real work and there's nobody around to bother you.

The first thing that came into my mind was that it must be a delivery
running late. I thought Jo had forgotten to put it on the board and
they'd come through from the street because the loading bay doors were
shut. Of course I couldn't *see* anyone—what with all the shelving units
and the stuff hanging up and the big pieces like kitchen ranges and twin
tubs you can barely see to the end of a row anyway, let alone right across
the warehouse. Well, I thought it was a bit odd that they hadn't called
out—that's what the couriers normally do. So I put down my duster and
started off toward them. I don't really know why I didn't shout, "Hello"
or "Just coming," but I had a sense that something wasn't quite right. For
one thing, I could hear two sets of footsteps, and that was funny because
even with the van deliveries it's usually just one man.

Well, I got to the end of the row, and I'd just stuck my head round
the corner when I heard a shout: "There he is!" and two men—big, fast
men—came pounding toward me. The one in front had a thing like a

cricket bat in his hand, and they were both wearing masks, balaclavas with eyeholes. I saw them come at me in a blur—and it was obvious they meant to do me no good. I was standing next to a shelf of electrical kitchen equipment, coffeemakers and things of that kind, and without stopping to think I grabbed hold of the nearest object—beige plastic, I think it must have been a Teasmade—chucked it in their direction, and ran down to the end of the warehouse as fast as my legs could carry me. I heard a crash and glass breaking and a swear word, so I think whatever I threw at them must have connected, but they were still behind me, catching me up. . . . A couple of rows down was a big basket of plastic lemons, waist high. It was sticking out into the aisle and I turned that over as I passed, thinking to slow them down. It did, but only for a second—one of them cannoned off a shelving unit and I heard it teetering backward and forward and prayed it wouldn't fall over, because if one goes, the whole lot follows—like dominoes—and that would be all our crockery gone. The thought of that made me see red, and I grabbed hold of the first thing that caught my eye: our big orange fishing net with the pretend lobsters and seaweed stuck on it. It was festooned on a couple of poles, so I gave the whole thing a yank and down it went. I heard a grunt and a thump from behind me, and when I glanced over my shoulder I saw one of them was on the floor—he'd caught his foot in the mesh—and the other one had tripped over him.

Well, I made it to the end of the warehouse in one piece, but I had to go all the way up the other side to get to the door, and I was running out of breath. I knew it was only a matter of seconds before they would be onto me, so when I saw the parking meters, that gave me an idea. We've got about thirty of them, all the different models ever made, and we keep them near the back with the rabbit hutches and telephone booths and other odds and ends. When I saw the space behind them, I didn't think twice, just dropped onto my knees and crawled straight into it. I heard them come round the corner, but they couldn't see me behind all these bits and pieces, and I stayed put on all fours and tried to control my breathing.

I could hear them getting closer. One of them said, "He's got to be here somewhere," then there was silence. I could hear my heart beating and I thought, *any minute, any minute now . . .*

"He's not gone behind that lot, has he?"

"Fat bastard'd never fit."

I thought, that's what you think, and I closed my eyes and prayed they'd go away, but then I heard the footsteps come closer and there was a tremendous clattering noise as if one of them was running the bat up and down the row of parking meters. My head was pounding with it and my knees were in agony from the concrete floor—I thought I was going to collapse, but I kept my arms braced and my eyes tight shut. Then the man with the bat must have taken a swipe at one of the shelves, because I heard a clang as something fell to the floor.

I thought they must be vandals, out of their minds on some drug or other, but when I heard them say my name, my stomach turned over, my mouth flooded with saliva, and I thought I was going to be sick. They were whispering it, "Ger-*ald*, Ger-*ald*, Ger-*ald*," almost like a chant, building up louder and louder, closer and closer, and I could feel the blood pounding in my head as it grew and grew, and then one of them cut across it. "Oi, nonce!"

I heard something heavy being dragged across the floor behind me—one of the rabbit hutches. I couldn't do anything—the space was too small for me to turn around in.

"Gerald, you nonce!"

"If he is in there, he'll have to come out sometime."

"Noncey! Noncey-woncey!"

"A ferret, that's what we need."

"He'd probably fancy it."

"Probably bugger it when it wasn't looking, wouldn't you, Geraldo?"

Then I heard a lot of banging as they picked up the parking meters and threw them on the floor, and then one of them said, "Oh, look, I can see his arse." Bile leapt into my throat—I couldn't even turn my face to look at them, there wasn't enough room. I didn't know what they were going to do, but I thought they might start hitting me, so I went down on my elbows and cradled my head with my hands to protect it.

"Well, well, we were wondering where you'd got to."

"I've always liked hide-and-seek."

"Gerald likes playing children's games, don't you, Gerald?"

"He likes playing games with children, that's for sure."

"Ever since he was a boy."

"Played games with your sister, didn't you?"

"Kept it in the family . . ."

"She's gone though, isn't she, Gerald? Got to find someone else now . . . found Mel Farrell, didn't you?"

"Look at him, shaking like jelly. Not so much fun when it's someone your own size, is it?"

I put my hands over my ears to block them out. I thought I was going to lose control of my insides and mess myself.

"We know all about you, Gerald."

"All your little games."

They stopped talking. My head was hammering, but I could hear them moving about and then the sound of the bat swishing through the air as if someone was practicing strokes. "We're going to give you six of the best." Nasty, jeering laughter. I lifted my head and tried to get my mouth working. I wanted to tell them they were wrong and ask them not to hurt me, but I couldn't make the words come. I must have made some sort of noise, because one of them said, "Oh, look, he's trying to say something."

"Pity we're not listening."

"You've been a naughty boy, Gerald, and we're going to smack your bottom."

When I tried to straighten up I felt as if someone had stuck a knife into the small of my back—it must have been from staying so long in one position. The only other way out was to shuffle backward on my hands and knees toward the two men, but when I tried, there was an agonizing pain as one of them trod on my calf with his full weight. I felt the tears rush to my eyes. "Stop, please, you're hurting me . . ." Then I heard a whoosh of air as the one with the bat raised it above his head—"This'll teach you to stay away from Mel Farrell, you pervert!"—and before I had time to brace myself it smashed against my buttocks and my whole body shot forward. The last thing I remember is a blur of red and a cracking noise as my temple smacked into the side of the phone booth.

I must have blacked out, because the next thing I remember it was pitch-dark and I was aching all over, with no idea where I was. It took me quite a while to work it out. I could feel the hard floor underneath me and something stuck round my eyes. When I put my hand up to my face I could feel the wetness, but it was a few minutes before I realized that it was blood—and then it all came back to me. I couldn't hear any noise in the building, and I thought the men must have gone, but all the same it took a good five minutes before I got myself upright, and then I thought I'd better turn the light on. So I started groping my way along the back wall toward the switch. I couldn't tell how far I'd got until I bashed into something—we've got an old tin sign hanging up there for Spratt's Puppy Biscuits—and I must have hit it quite hard, because one side came away from the wall and the sharp corner fell down on my shoulder and ripped my jersey. It knocked me right off balance. I fell over onto some shelves, and I heard a great slew of stuff slip off the other side and go crashing onto the floor.

I was in quite a state by the time I found the switch. My head was throbbing and I couldn't stop myself shaking. When I turned it on and saw the mess, all the things broken and scattered and . . . *demolished* . . . I felt as if the whole world had gone right out of control, and there was nothing I could do, with everything just exploded and no hope of getting it back again. Because it wasn't just the things they'd broken, it was the humiliation and all the names. I heard what they called me—a nonce. I know what that word means. I am *not* one of those people and

I would never do anything like that, but those men . . . I could hear their voices in my head, *nonce, nonce,* and saying my name in that horrible way as if I'd done something when I haven't. I think one of them was Steven Palfrey, the policeman, because I've heard that voice before and I think it was him. He's a bully, but he can do anything he wants because he's in the police. He thinks he can just come and do that to me when it is not fair, and all the police will back him up. They will not listen to me. They are filthy, their minds and the things they say. They can accuse anyone they like even when it's not true, and all they want is to hurt people and make them feel they are small and do not even matter and . . . Melanie.

He said stay away from Mel Farrell, but I would not hurt her for the world. She is my friend and I love her, and he said about Vera, "Played games with your sister." Well, I did, but it was normal and not what they meant because that is disgusting, and anyway it wasn't my fault about Vera. She should not have gone with those men, because it was wrong and I would never do anything like that. It's like the police when they asked if I touched Vera's body or if I did something when I never did anything. It's not fair because I always get the blame, as if I made it all happen when I did not. IT IS NOT FAIR because it was *her* fault, and now I have the feeling that it has all gone haywire again with all this in my mind like a tornado, destroying everything.

I called out to Jack. He was not there but I knew he'd seen it all, and now he thinks I am no good. Like when I was young, if *she* caught me talking to him she'd say, "He can't hear you, you know," in a nasty way. But he can and he saw it because he can see everything, like when they hit me and my trousers got all filthy and ruined. . . .

Then I went to try and pick up some of the things off the floor. There was a plaster model of Laurel and Hardy, one of my favorites, all in pieces. I picked up the bits and held them, but they can't be mended because half of it is mashed into dust on the ground. It is no good anymore. Nothing's any good and I am no good and Jack hates me.

## Jo

*I don't know what to do.* Ron never phoned me last night. When I left work, I thought, oh, God, I don't want to be on my own, and I knew Mel was staying late at school. There's this project they're doing for the VE Day thing, a big collage all round one room, and Mel's really good at art so she was helping. I wasn't bothered. I knew Gerald was at work, for one, and Sonali's mum said she'd bring them back in the car. I couldn't face Mum so I went round to Karen's.

Of course, because she's such a nosy cow, she starts chatting away about Ron, and inside I'm like, that's the trouble, yeah? only I'm not saying it. What it was, I'd got this feeling sort of building up inside me, really uneasy, that he and Paul shouldn't be going after Gerald. I know it's mad, because when they were talking about it I was well into it, but I just . . . well, it seemed a bit . . . you know, like ganging up or something, like kids at school.

I mean, with Gerald, right, I know I was really wound up about it. I could practically see these horns and tail growing out of him, you know, like he was totally evil, and when I thought about him doing something to Mel, it really upset me . . . but we don't *know*, do we? And with Ron and Paul, when we were in the pub, it wasn't like they were saying, oh, good, we're going to beat this bloke up, but when Ron came round to my flat, he was being so matter-of-fact about it and not telling me what they were going to do. It wasn't like I wanted to know or anything, but he just seemed a bit, sort of . . . hard, and you know how blue eyes can look so cold sometimes. It's 'cause all the rest of the time his eyes look sort of sparkly and nice, but when he said good-bye it was like he wasn't really paying attention to me at all, you know? Oh, it's probably nothing. Anyway . . .

But, like I said, he never phoned me, and when I tried to ring him his mobile was switched off, and that's the only number I've got for him. And then this morning, when I get into work, the car park's full of police cars and it's, like, mayhem. Neville's there, back from his holiday. He's waiting for me outside, and he goes, "Oh, there you are, J.F."

I thought, that's a bit funny, so I check my watch. "I'm not late, am I?"

"No, no, right on time, but there's a bit of bad news, I'm afraid. We've had a break-in."

I couldn't believe it. "You *what?*"

" 'Fraid so. Last night."

I just stood there with my mouth hanging open. I thought, it can't have been *them,* but then Neville goes, "The funny thing is, they didn't take anything. Didn't go near the office, so they can't have been after the computers, and there's no money. To tell you the truth, Jo, I can't imagine what they thought they were going to get. Made a hell of a mess though."

"Was it you who—?"

He nodded. "I thought I'd get in early, first day back and all that. Nipped in for a quick scout round and found the place looking like a bomb had hit it. So I called the precinct and, well, there you have it. Or not, as the case may be."

"Bloody hell."

"My sentiments exactly. Might be a good idea to get in there once the police have finished doing their stuff and make a list of anything broken. Won't be able to replace a lot of it, of course, but the insurance bods will want to know. Nice to be back, eh?" Neville rolled his eyes. "Well, best get on with it, no sense hanging around here." Off he went, and there's me left standing in the middle of the car park, thinking *oh, my God . . .*

It was eleven o'clock before the police let me go into the warehouse, and honestly, you should have seen it. I didn't know where to start. Broken china everywhere. I've got the inventory and I'm poking around trying to work out what's what . . . and all the time I'm thinking, I can't believe Ron and Paul did this, because it was *horrible*. And I kept thinking about Gerald, was he all right, you know? Then after about an hour, Neville comes down. "Bit of news for you, J.F. Apparently G.H. was here last night, and they bashed him about a bit. It seems he had to go to hospital."

"Is he . . . all right?" I could barely get the words out.

"Head wound. Bit of concussion, I expect, that's why he didn't get on the horn to the cop shop. Don't look so worried—there's no permanent damage. Few days' rest and he'll be as right as rain."

"What did they do to him?"

"Bashed him on the head, apparently. Fought like a lion, according to his landlady. I don't know about that, but they certainly buggered off pretty quickly. Anyway, they've stitched him up, but it sounded pretty nasty."

"Were they in a car?"

"God knows. Police haven't mentioned it."

"Was that who you spoke to, his landlady? Not him?"

"Yes. Mrs. Clarke her name is. She's going to phone back later with a progress report."

A couple of hours later he was back, saying Gerald had arrived home safely from the hospital and would I mind going over there with his flask and sandwich box? "He's in quite a state about it. You know what he's like. . . . Anyway, I thought you'd like to see him. Cheer him up a bit." And he gives me this big smile. Well, I couldn't exactly refuse, could I? It would have looked really funny, what with me working for him and everything. So I go, "Yeah, no problem," and Neville tells me to take some money out of petty cash for a taxi, plus a bit more for a box of chocolates, and all the time I'm thinking, what if it's a trap and Gerald's going to get the police onto me or something? What if Ron or Paul mentioned my name? And even if they didn't, if they'd said something about Mel, well, he could have put two and two together—I mean, Gerald might be weird, but he's not stupid. Because Ron never phoned me like he said he would, did he? But of course I couldn't say anything to Neville, so I'm pretending everything's all hunky-dory and he's going, "Give him our best wishes," and I'm, like, "Yeah, right. Will do."


It was okay in the end, because I never even saw him. His landlady was sweet though. Ron called her a walrus, but I thought she looked quite nice—well, for an old person. She said Gerald was asleep, but she invited me in for a cup of tea. I couldn't really refuse. I mean, I'd told her my name, and she didn't go, oh, you're that evil woman and it's all your fault, or anything like that, but I was still really nervous. I thought, she must have told him I was coming, and I kept expecting him to come through the door and have a go at me.

We were sitting in the kitchen. It's funny, because Mrs. Clarke is really *neat*, the same way Gerald is. It was exactly the kind of place I'd imagined Gerald living—not that I spend all my time thinking about him or anything, but it was just so right somehow. Everything was very old-fashioned but looked-after, if you know what I mean. There were all these funny little things, like she had all these pots—with tea, coffee, sugar, rice, and whatever written on them—and they all had these little covers that she'd made herself, you know? Not knitted or anything, but made of tinfoil, all smoothed flat with sharp creases in the corners to make little, sort of, hats.

She saw me looking at them—because you could hardly see the labels—and she said, "Oh, I know where everything is. I put everything back in the same place every time," which was *so* like Gerald. And when she was making the tea it was like it all had to be perfect. You know, just so.

She was getting all excited telling me about it, and I'm, like, steady, girl, but you could see she hadn't really talked to anybody for ages, she was getting so carried away. "Oh," she said, "it was dreadful. I came downstairs for a glass of water, about one o'clock this was, and Mr. Haxton was sitting there, right where you are now"—she's pointing at the chair like she wants me to kiss it or something—"covered in blood. I couldn't get a word out of him, he was that upset. His jersey was torn, and you should have seen his face! He looked like a tiger'd been at him, like you see on these programs, wild animals attacking . . ." I'm sitting there staring at her, trying to imagine Gerald as, like, a wildebeest or something—totally bizarre—so then she goes, "Well, I called a taxicab right away to go to Charing Cross, and of course the driver couldn't speak a word of English and didn't have any idea where we were supposed to be going. It's always the same with these people— illegals, all of them, probably don't even have a proper driving license. Mr. Haxton was ever so pale, sitting there holding his head—the blood had stopped, really, but I'd cut up a few plastic bags and pinned them round his shoulders because I didn't want it getting on everything, you know—but I couldn't take my eyes off this driver for a second in case he went off in the wrong direction, and there's that terrible one-way system they've put in all round Hammersmith Station, frightens the life out of me. . . . We ended up going round three times and he kept jabbering away at me in his funny language, bongo pongo zongo, that's what it sounded like, and I couldn't make head nor tail of it.

"Then he stopped the car under the overpass and turned round to open one of the back doors as if he's just going to throw us out on the road. . . . Well, I'd been a bit nervous going out in the middle of the night like that, especially with this driver, but I said to him, 'You ought to be ashamed of yourself, frightened of an old woman and a wounded man. We're stopping right where we are, and if you want paying, you'll take us to the hospital.' He was muttering away to himself, bongo mongo fongo or something, but he took us in the end. And then when we got there it was disgusting, filthy, drunks everywhere, and the wait! Best part of two hours, and six stitches in his head at the end of it. But do you know, he never flinched. Not *once*. The nurse didn't have to tell him to keep still. I've seen rocks that moved more than he did. But it could have been worse, a *lot* worse. He could have been killed."

"Did Ger—Mr. Haxton tell you how it happened?"

"Well, to be honest, dear, he didn't, not really. Mind you, he was in no fit state when he came in and he didn't say much in the car that I remember. I think he was in a state of shock. When we were at the hospital, he told me two men had attacked him, and I thought he meant they were muggers, but this morning when I rang your . . . what's-his-name . . . he said there'd been a break-in at your work last night and it was thanks to Mr. Haxton that nothing was stolen. Honestly, it makes you scared to walk down the street."

The way she was telling it, it was all like this big *adventure*. I'm sitting there thinking, oh, *shi-i-i-t*, because I wanted to say to her, look, you don't know the half of it, he's a child molester and he's been after my daughter, but at the same time I'm starting to feel sort of queasy. Mind you, the tea wasn't helping. Mrs. Clarke refilled my cup about eight times, even though I'm going, "No, thanks, I'm fine, really . . ." But I'm thinking, suppose I'm wrong, 'cause it was like I was the one that did it to him, you know? I don't mean actually *did* it, but it comes down to the same thing, doesn't it? I was just, like, really confused.

I suppose I was there about half an hour in all, although it felt like a lot longer. I spent most of the afternoon helping Neville sort out the insurance claim, but I can't say my mind was on it. In fact, I had to phone this film company and tell them we couldn't do one of their orders, because they'd asked for this huge dinner service for some banquet scene or something, and most of it was in shards. It was the one thing Neville was seriously pissed off about, because it really was Victorian, and there's just no way we can replace it. He said to me, "I don't know what G.H. is going to say when he finds out—better break it to him gently, eh?" and I'm nodding away, thinking, *just shut up about Gerald, okay?*


Ron was there when I got home—he and Mel were in the kitchen. She was sitting on the counter like I told her not to, chatting away, swinging her legs. Honestly, she's a real little flirt—don't ask me where she gets it from! I could tell from the way she looked at me when I came in that she was trying to figure out if I was going to tell her off or if I wasn't going to say anything because Ron was there.

*Honestly.* It was sweet though; she looked all pink and pleased as punch. "Look, Mum, flowers! Aren't they lovely?"

Ron goes, "One each," and I saw there were these two bunches of red roses on the kitchen table. Proper flowers as well, not something half dead off a truck. But I really wanted to talk to Ron, so I'm just, like, "Oh, yeah, lovely, thanks," and put them in the sink. Then I go to Mel, "Haven't you got homework?" She looked at me a bit . . . you know . . . but she didn't argue, and the minute she was out of the room I turned round to Ron.

"What the hell happened? And don't give me all that shit about it being better if I don't know either, because when I got in this morning, the place was half demolished, there were police everywhere, and *then* I found out Gerald had to go to hospital to get his head stitched up!"

"Did you say anything?"

"What do you think? Course I didn't. Jesus, Ron, you said you were going to warn him—you never said you were going to smash his head in!"

"We never laid a finger on his head. He fell over, that's all."

"What, so he just took one look at you and passed out? Come off it."

"You're joking. He was chucking things at us left, right, and center. It was him that did all the damage, not us—well, most of it. But it's like a maze in there, all those shelves, I can't see how you ever manage to find—"

"Stop changing the subject! What *happened*?"

"Jesus *Christ,* Jo! We were doing you a favor, there's no need to get stroppy." He looked totally pissed off with me and I thought, perhaps I'm overreacting, so I said, "I'm sorry, but I've had a really horrible day, that's all. I had to go and see him, take his lunchbox—"

"His *what*?"

"What he keeps his sandwiches in. His landlady—you were right, by the way—she rang up and told Neville he wanted it because he's not coming in for a few days, so of course I had to take it to his house."

"He shouldn't expect you to run round after Gerald—you should have told him to get lost."

"How could I? Neville's my boss, and anyway, he was just being nice."

"Did you see him?"

"No, thank God. Just his landlady. She was full of it. The way she was telling me, you'd think it was the most exciting thing that ever happened to her."

"Probably was."

"She was sweet though. Gerald's going to be so upset about all that china. I'll have to tell him sooner or later."

"What is the *matter* with you? We said we'd fix Gerald, right? Paul and me. Well, now we have and you're going on like you're sorry for him. I don't believe it! I mean, what do you want him to do, rape your daughter?"

"No, of course not, but—"

"But *nothing*. We've seen to him and he's not going to be coming anywhere near Mel again. I'd bet on it."

"What if he goes to the police?"

"I told you, no chance. Come on, sit down and have a drink. I brought you some wine. It's in the fridge."

"Have you been here long? Before I arrived, I mean."

"I don't know, five minutes, something like that. Why?"

"Just wondered, wine in the fridge and all that."

"Yeah, it's in the door."

I pulled out the bottle of white wine. "This is really cold. It has to have been in here more than a few minutes, Ron."

"Yeah, well, I got it out of the fridge in the shop. Listen, someone at the market told me a great joke this morning—want to hear it?"

"What?" I was rummaging in the drawer for the corkscrew, not really paying attention. "Let me just open this . . . yeah, all right, what is it?"

"Well, there's this bloke, he's been to the pub and he's had quite a few. Then he drives home and it's a bit dodgy, so this policeman pulls him over. 'Excuse me, sir,' he says, 'have you been drinking?' 'Why, officer?' says the bloke. 'Is there a fat bird in the car?' "

"Eh? Oh, yes, very good. There you go." I gave him a glass of wine. I didn't think it was all *that* funny, to be honest, but Ron's laughing to himself, repeating, "Is there a fat bird in the car?"

I mean, I know Ron was right about Gerald and everything, but I wish he'd just told me what happened. I didn't mean to be . . . *aggressive* about it, you know, but even though he was nice after, I felt like he'd had a real go at me, and it was just 'cause I was in a state, you know? I felt really upset about it and I wanted to be on my own for a bit, but he was sitting there and he'd brought flowers and wine and everything, so I couldn't just tell him to piss off, could I?

He stayed the night in the end, and it was okay, but . . . Well, I suppose the thing was, I think he was a bit miffed that I wasn't more *grateful* to them. Don't get me wrong, he wasn't saying, "Look at me, I'm this big hero," or anything, but all the same . . . I mean, he's cuddling me, saying, "It'll be all right now," and I'm thinking, yeah, but *will it*?

## Gerald

*I don't remember getting home.* I must have gone into the kitchen, because I was there when Mrs. Clarke came in. She was in her bathrobe. She said, "Do you know what time it is?" I thought she was going to be angry with me, but then she said, "Oh, Mr. Haxton! What's happened to you?" and her voice was more gentle, so I knew she would not shout at me. But then I found I was crying and I couldn't stop, and I thought she would say I was a crybaby and pathetic, so I put my face in my hands because I couldn't bear it. She went out of the room. I heard her come back and she pushed something across the table, and when I looked down it was her box of tissues with the pink cover on and the braiding around the edges. At first I didn't want to take one because I know they are her special ones she keeps on top of the television, but she said, "Go on, Mr. Haxton, it's all right."

I said, "I'm sorry if I woke you up."

"That doesn't matter," she said, and her voice was kind. "To tell you the truth, I don't sleep so well nowadays as I used to. I suppose that's what happens when you get old." The way she said it was like a little joke, and that made me look up, because I didn't expect anything like that. Then she said, "That's a nasty cut on your face. Why don't you let me have a look at it?" and she soaked some of the tissues in water and dabbed the blood away. "I think you're going to need some stitches in this. We'd better get you to the emergency room. I tell you what. I'll put one of my hankies on it and fix it with a bit of tape." It felt scratchy because of the lace, and I tried to get up but the whole room seemed to lurch and I sat down again. "You're in no fit state to go on your own. I'll ring for a cab, and then I'd better put some clothes on. I can't go anywhere looking like this, can I? Now, don't you try to move until I come back."

The ER was full of people, shouting and rushing around. The bright light hurt my eyes, and the floor was filthy. The plastic chairs weren't much better, and they were most uncomfortable too, because of the bruises on my bottom. Mrs. Clarke gave the chairs a dusting with her handkerchief. She said, "We'd better try not to touch anything. With all this AIDS going about, you never know what you might catch." She bought us some coffee from the machine, but neither of us could drink it.

She tried to make the nurse see me straightaway, but they said it wasn't an emergency and we'd have to wait. Mrs. Clarke said, "Honestly! I'd like to know what *is* an emergency!" But then we saw a stretcher go past with a young man on it in a bad way, and she said, "Well, that's fair enough, I suppose." Which was true because for all we knew, he might have been at death's door. I said, "I'm sorry to be the cause of so much trouble. I'll understand if you want to find someone else for the room."

She said, "I wouldn't dream of it, Mr. Haxton. I know we've had our differences in the past, but we rub along all right, don't we? You know, I don't think I could get used to anyone else." I had my hands in my lap and she leaned over and gave my wrist a little pat. I must confess I was a wee bit shocked when she did that. I can't remember the last time someone did that to me, and it made me feel a bit brighter, so I said, "Please call me Gerald. We've known each other long enough, haven't we?"

"Yes, and you must call me Doreen." Well, of course, I knew that was her name, because I'd seen it on letters, but I'd never . . . well, I suppose it never came up, that's the truth of the matter. She said, "It's silly, really, especially nowadays. You know, Mr.—"

"Gerald!" I said, and she laughed.

"Sorry, Gerald. There's something I've been meaning to say. . . . If I've been a bit, well, short-tempered recently, it's just because with all this business about the war coming up, remembering it all again, you know..."

I said, "Don't I just. I wish they'd forget about the whole thing."

"I know with some people, they like to talk about it, and I've got nothing against that, of course, but it was a bad time for me. I had a sister, you see, a twin. Pam. Robinson. That was my maiden name, you see. Doreen and Pam Robinson. Always together, and always laughing, that's what people used to say about us. We were evacuated, but they put us with different families, and we hated it so much that Mum came to get us. Well, Pam was killed in one of the raids. She'd gone round to my aunt's—it was only a few streets away. It blew all our windows out, and I remember Mum saying, you know, I hope Pam's all right, and then of course when we heard the all-clear we dashed round there and it was half the street—*gone*. And both of them with it. I never stopped thinking about her, never. We moved away after the war, just a few streets, so we were still in touch with a lot of the old neighbors. One of them took me and my mother round to see this woman who'd moved into our house. Mum was asking how she liked it, and she was saying, 'Oh, yes, very nice,' but then she said, 'It's an odd thing, but there's a little girl here,' and when Mum asked what she meant—because she didn't have any children, this woman—she said she thought it was like a ghost, not frightening, just a little girl walking round the house. And I said, 'That's Pam, she's looking for me.' It seemed to me quite an obvious thing, but of course Mum said, 'Don't be morbid.' She didn't mean to be unkind, but I don't think it's something you can understand, necessarily, if you're not a twin. Sorry, are you all right, Mr.—I mean, Gerald?"

"Yes. Yes, I'm quite all right, thank you. What you were saying, about your twin—I do understand, very well. It's just that I've never heard anybody say . . . I suppose you wouldn't expect it, but I'm a twin myself. You see, my brother died when we were born, and . . . well, I feel he's still with me in a way. I talk to him, but it's not . . . it's not as if people would understand that."

"Heavens, I talk to Pam all the time! In my head, of course, not out loud. But I know what you mean, you don't like to say it in case people think you're a bit funny. When I married Victor—Victor Clarke—of course my name changed, and I felt I was going a bit further away from Pam because of that, but I used to say to her, 'I hope you approve.' Because I was lonely, you know. When Victor came along I thought that would all change, and we were very happy. Well, I say I was happy, but there's always been a feeling of something missing inside. I don't mean up here"—she tapped her head and laughed—"although some might say that, but inside me. When you're hungry, you feel empty, don't you, but that's just your stomach. This was all of me, somehow. . . . And then when Victor died, that was dreadful. But that's what I wanted to say, really. All this on the television about the war, saying how it was all marvelous, and when I think about Pam, well, it upsets me."

"Yes, I can understand that. It's extraordinary, because I never thought I'd hear another person saying those things, how I felt. I mean, I didn't think I was the only one in the world, I knew there must be someone who . . . oh, dear, now I'm all in a knot, but I do know, the empty feeling, what you said. Oh, yes, I do know all about that."

"Yes, it's nice to think you're not the only one, isn't it?"

Then the nurse called my name. I said to Doreen, "I shouldn't think I'll be long," but the nurse said, "If your wife would like to come through as well . . ." I liked that, the idea of Doreen being my wife, and it must have tickled her too, because she went a little bit pink. But I thought it best to correct the nurse, in case of any misunderstanding, because I suddenly thought, what if Doreen's there and they ask me to take any of my clothes off? But in fact she said she'd come along too.

When we got to the cubicle, the nurse had a look at the hanky with the bits of tape sticking it to my head and said, "I'll do this as quick as I can, but it might sting a bit." Before I realized what was coming, she gave a tug and the whole thing came off in her hand. "Oh, dear, I am sorry," she said, "but it's taken a piece of your hair with it."

"You want to be careful with that," I said, "I haven't got a lot left."

They both laughed at that, but then the nurse said, "I'm afraid you might have a bit less in a minute, because this looks as if it might need a stitch, and if that's the case we'll have to shave some off."

I thought the doctor would just tell the nurse to stitch me up and that would be that, but he started asking all sorts of questions. I told him I'd fallen over, but he was very insistent, asking if I'd been knocked out and for how long and what sort of surface I fell on. It made me very uncomfortable, because I didn't know what to tell him, and with Doreen being there listening to it all, I got a bit flustered. The other thing was, he could see I was sitting awkwardly on the chair, and he kept asking if I was hurt anywhere else. I said, "It's just a bit of stiffness, I'm not so young as I used to be," and that seemed to satisfy him. I had to have an X ray to see if the skull was fractured, and as the nurse was taking me off down the corridor I heard the doctor say something to Doreen about whether there was an argument, and that bothered me even more, him thinking I'd been involved in some sort of a fight.

The nurse had hold of my arm, and I tried to pull away to get back to the cubicle and hear what the doctor was saying about me, and I think I must have knocked into one of the trolleys, because there was a great clatter and I slipped. Suddenly I was on the floor with this nurse standing over me, saying, "Shall we get you a wheelchair?" Before I'd had a chance to collect myself, another nurse appeared and the two of them sort of manhandled me into this chair. I tried to get up again because my bottom hurt, and my back, but they wouldn't let me, and all of a sudden I was being wheeled off at a great rate. I must have shouted or something because the doctor came flying out and everyone was staring. I said, "Stop it, let go of me, I want to go home," but they took me off to the X ray and banged me down on a couch. It was agony, and I didn't know what they were saying. They were thinking bad things about me, and all the nice time with Doreen might as well not have happened, and everything started up again in my head and I was so frightened, I thought they were going to call the police and that Palfrey would come. To be honest, I'm not quite sure what happened after that, because the next thing I knew my clothes were gone and I was in a bed with just this cotton gown over my shoulders, and the nurse was there with Mrs. Clarke—Doreen—looking at me.

The nurse asked me what my name was. For a moment I thought she must have forgotten it but then I realized it must be a test, because the next thing she asked me was, "Can you remember who the prime minister is?" I'm very pleased to report that I answered both questions correctly! I went to sleep after that, but another nurse woke me up a few hours later and did my blood pressure. She asked me what my name was too.


Doreen was there in the morning to take me home. They said I was okay to go, but I'd have to go to the doctor in ten days' time for the stitches to come out, so that'll be more time away from work because they told me to take a couple of days off and rest as well. I said to Doreen, "You shouldn't have gone to all this trouble," because she'd even rung up Neville at work to say I couldn't come in. There was a bad moment when the nurse said to me, "That's a nasty bruise you've got on your behind." She must have been looking when she took my clothes off.

While we were outside, waiting for the cab, Doreen said, "You didn't trip over, did you?"

"No." It came out of my mouth before I could stop it, and quick as a flash I remembered her talking to the doctor in the cubicle, and I started to panic again.

"The man I spoke to in your office—Neville something?"

"It would have been, yes. Neville Rigby."

"Well, he said they had to call the police. Someone got in last night.

Into the warehouse, was what he said." Doreen stopped and looked at me. I hadn't thought. All the mess. They'd know, of course. I felt sick. I could hardly concentrate on what she was saying. "Neville said he didn't think it was hooligans, not judging by the damage. He said it looked more like there'd been some sort of a fight. He said there was no sign of a break-in, and the door wasn't locked." She looked at me again. She wanted me to tell her, she was giving me the chance, but I couldn't. I knew I couldn't. I knew that even if I tried to explain about the men coming—if I left Melanie out of it altogether—I didn't think I could say it without breaking down, and then . . . and then . . .

Doreen grabbed my elbow. "You've gone white. Come on, let's sit you down." She took me over to the bench and sat down beside me. I shut my eyes. I couldn't look at her.

"Gerald . . . you don't mind if I still call you that, do you?"

"No. No, please do . . . Doreen."

"Good. Well, then. There's a lot I don't know about you, Gerald, and we're none of us perfect, but I've always thought of you as a decent man. Wouldn't have you as my lodger otherwise, would I? You haven't done anything that's . . . well, anything to be ashamed of, have you?"

"N-no. Thank you, Doreen. Thank you for saying that. But—"

"Never mind about 'but.' Did somebody attack you? At the warehouse?"

I nodded with my eyes shut, because I could feel the tears welling up behind the lids.

"Why didn't you tell me? I could have dialed 999. Was that why you were shouting about the police last night?"

"What?"

"When they took you to the X ray, you were shouting something about the police."

"I don't want any police. I don't want them involved."

"Well, I don't see how you can stop it, because they'll want to talk to you, won't they? Why don't you want to see them?"

"They . . . they think . . ."

Doreen sighed. "I'm sorry, I don't mean to pry. You don't have to tell me. Look, that man at your office, he wanted to speak to you, but I told him he couldn't. What's more, I told him you'd give him a ring when you felt up to it and not a moment before. They take advantage of you at that place, I've always thought so."

"That's very kind of you. Doreen, I wanted to ask you, last night, that doctor, what was he saying to you?"

She didn't answer for a moment, and when I looked at her, I saw that she was embarrassed. "It was a bit silly really. I mean, he didn't realize, he thought we were . . . well, husband and wife, and that we'd had an argument, you know, a fight, and that was how you got the—" She gestured toward her head.

"Oh, dear."

"Don't worry, I soon put him straight. Honestly, it makes you wonder what goes on in some of the marriages these days. . . . Let's go home. I'll make you a cup of tea."

"That reminds me—my flask and tupperware, I must have left them in the office."

"There's no need to worry, I'll ring that Neville again. I told him I'd let him know how you were getting on. Heavens, it wouldn't take much for someone to bring them over—I'd say it was the least he could do, considering."

"I suppose you'll have to tell him I was there."

"Well . . . not unless you want me to."

"I suppose we ought to . . . it's really very kind of you, Doreen. I'll pay for the calls, of course. And the cabs."

"We can worry about that later. Now, let's get you home. You know, I've just remembered—I've got a bit of Horlicks left. It's been in the cupboard awhile—come to think of it, I wouldn't mind a drop myself. Can't remember when I last had any. There's the cab, look, and not before time either."

## Tilly

*Nicky died last night.* He's got his cushion in the corner, you see, but he always comes to my bed when I wake up. That's the first thing I see when I open my eyes, his little black nose and the eyes looking up at me, like shiny berries . . . but this morning he didn't. When I saw him all curled up I knew straightaway that something was wrong, so I pressed the button for someone to come, because I can't get out of bed without help, and they told me he'd gone. I've had him since he was a puppy, and he's been a good friend to me, but I can't say I'm sorry, not entirely. He was getting a bit doddery and I didn't want him to suffer. So dying like that, peacefully in his sleep, was the best thing for him.

When they got me out of bed, one of the nurses put him on my lap, and I gave his coat a last little brush. He looked so sweet, just like a puppy again. The nurse and I were both in tears, because she used to give him his food, and she always made a fuss over him. I'm going to miss him ever so much, but that's the thing with dogs, they're only lent to us for a short time. She said, "He was always such a happy little thing."

"He had a good life, didn't he, with me?"

"Course he did. He was very fond of you, anyone could see that."

I said, "I hope he'll be happy in heaven. Do you think I'll see him again?"

"Oh, yes," she said. "I'm sure of it."

"I hope I'll see him again very soon. . . ."

"Oh, no," she said. "I'm sure we'll have you with us for a long time yet." I know she meant to be kind, but she's too young to understand the awfulness of it, being old and having all your friends die and leave you. I don't know what I'd have done without Tiny. They let me sit with Nicky for a while, on my own. Silly, really, but I just wanted to say good-bye. Then Tiny came up to see me at about eleven. He said, "They told me downstairs. I'm ever so sorry, Tilly. . . . How are you doing?"

"Everyone's been very kind. They're going to let me bury him in the garden. Under his favorite tree. I thought I'd put one of his toys in there with him, for company. He never liked being left on his own."

"Oh, darling, don't cry. He won't be on his own, he'll be in heaven, with lots of chums."

"Yes, but not me. Oh, Tiny, I will see him again, won't I? I couldn't bear it if—"

"Of course you will! I tell you what, when I talk to Dennis I'll tell him to look after Nicky, shall I? I talk to him every night before I go to sleep—he'll be delighted, he always liked dogs."

"Did he? Really?"

"Oh, yes, he always wanted one, but we lived in a council flat, you see, and they won't let you have them in there. It was one of the first things he said when we moved into the bungalow—'Now we can have a dog'—and we were going to, but then he got ill."

"Oh, Tiny, you're so kind. . . . I'll miss him so much."

"I know you will, but you've always got me, girl. I know I haven't got a tail to wag, but it's something, isn't it?"

"You haven't got a wet nose either."

"Only when it rains."

"Oh, Tiny . . . would you mind carrying him downstairs for me? He always liked you."

"Course I will." He took Nicky off my lap.

"There's a rug on the end of my bed—tartan—you can wrap him in. And the toy's on the cushion . . . the squeaky bone."

"I've put it between his front paws, look. In case he wants to chew. . . . Now I'll just take him down to the office, then I'm coming right back and we'll get you out of this room, all right?"

Tiny was pushing my chair along the shore, but it wasn't very good because I kept looking down expecting to see Nicky, so after a while he stopped and said, "I tell you what, why don't you come back to my place and I'll rustle up a spot of lunch?"

"Well, if it's not too much trouble . . ."

"No trouble at all! Only take us five minutes to troll round there—you've never seen where I live, have you?"

"No."

"We bought it together, Dennis and me. First home we ever owned—the only home, as it turned out."

"What did Dennis do?"

"Librarian. Worked in the V&A when I first met him. Cataloging. 1961, that was."

"Were you still dancing?"

"No, I was backstage by that time. Wardrobe—panto—that sort of thing. Oh, have a vada . . . over there, the kids in the playground, aren't they lovely?"

We were passing a school and there was a group of little girls, skipping with a rope, chanting. It reminded me of Vera. "You don't see that much anymore, do you?"

"No, it's a shame. You hardly ever see children out playing. When I was young, we could go wherever we wanted. It was a proper childhood, wasn't it?"

"Oh, I don't know. It's tempting to look back and think the sun was always shining, isn't it? But when I think about some of the things that happened, and there was the war. . . . My niece, Vera, she used to play skipping games with her pals, they had this little song they used to sing: *On the mountain stands a lady/ Who she is I do not know/ All she wants is gold and silver/ All she wants is a nice young man.*"

Tiny said, "Don't we all, dear?" which made us both giggle. "Dennis hated me saying things like that. He loathed anything camp. He'd say to me, 'Stop it, Daniel, you sound like a great poof,' so I'd say, 'But, darling, I *am*.' And then I'd start camping it up just to annoy him. He used to go absolutely *mad*."

"Is that your real name, Daniel?"

"Yes. Daniel Sidney, would you believe? Dreadful, isn't it? Dennis was the only one who used it."

"You should worry. Mine's Matilda Gladys."

"You don't look much like a Gladys to me."

"I'm relieved to hear it. How did you come to be called Tiny?"

"It was when I was in the navy. My first ship. Full of men, all missing their girlfriends. I never came across much prejudice. 'You remind me of my girl,' that's what they used to say to me, all these big, burly chaps, and there might be a few kisses, or a bit of—you know—but it was sweet, really, very innocent. They were ever so protective of me, because there was a lot of swearing, you see, every other word was four letters, but if I came along, it would be, 'Oi, you watch your mouth in front of Tiny!' Mind you, it wasn't special treatment, I fought for my country as well as the next man, and I've always been proud of that. Oh, yes, I was always in action, one way or the other. There were some terrible things though. There was this one time when we were in a convoy, and there was an oil tanker—one of ours—and it must have been hit by more than one torpedo, because it just blew apart. This was at night, so the whole sky was lit up like Christmas, flames everywhere, and we were like sitting ducks for the Germans. We managed to rescue about twenty men all told. They were drenched in diesel and their skin looked like . . . well, bacon, fried bacon, that's the best way I can describe it, because of these terrible burns they had. Quite a lot of them died. That's where I got my name though. I think I was lucky—well, I certainly *was* lucky to come out unscathed at the end of it, but it was really more to do with people's attitudes. Because I've never pretended to be anything other than what I am. Well, if I tried to be this great butch omi, people would have seen through it straightaway, wouldn't they? Just be yourself, that's what my mother always used to say. Mind you, if I *had* been the great butch omi, I think it would have been a different story."

"Why do you say that?" All the time he had been talking, I had Gerald in the back of my mind. About how he was different and people didn't like him for it, whereas with Tiny, everyone seemed to adore him. Personality plays a big part, mind you, but it's not everything.

"Well, what I think is, people don't like to feel threatened, do they? I mean, with me, I can't remember any moment when I realized that I'm the way I am, because I've always known it. But what could I do? It wasn't legal to be what I was, not then. Though as I say, I've never pretended to be anything else, right from when I was at school. I was tarting around in my little shorts and people used to laugh about it, or perhaps they felt sorry for me. But if you *are* different, then it can have a funny effect on people. I've seen that with some of my chums, persecuted, they were. Dennis had the same trouble, that's why he kept quiet about it. All the years he spent in those libraries, none of the people he worked with had any idea he was coming home to me every night. Here we are." He stopped in front of a pretty little cottage with leaded windows.

"Tiny, it's *beautiful*."

"Yes, it is rather nice, isn't it? Let's get you inside. Now, could you go for an omelette? I do a lovely Arnold Bennett. Truly bona."

"It's sweet of you to go to all this trouble."

"Nonsense! I'll have to concentrate a bit though, so we'll put your chair in the doorway and you can talk to me while I'm cooking. Dry sherry, do you?"

"Lovely."

"Now then, what shall we talk about?"

"Well, as a matter of fact . . ."

"Yes, flower?"

"There's something I want to ask you."

"Anything you like, darling. Feel free."

"It's about Gerald, really."

"Gerald your nephew?"

"Yes. Tiny . . . I'm not going to be here forever—well, none of us are—but now that Nicky's gone . . . well, I don't know how long I've got, that's all, so what I wanted to ask you, when I'm gone, will you look after him?"

Tiny raised his eyebrows. "Well, dear, from what you've told me about him, it doesn't exactly sound as if I'd be his cup of tea."

"It's just . . . you know when I got upset the other day, and you said you wouldn't hate me, whatever I'd done? Well, if I tell you—"

"Listen, Tilly, if there's one thing I've learned in my life, it's not to make judgments about other people, and that's the truth. Tell me anything you like, and I promise you, the roof's not going to come off—although it might if I don't see to what's in this pan. Just give me a minute and you can tell me whatever you like."

So we sat down to lunch, and I told him all about Vera and Johnny Treece, and how she died and the GI was hanged, and Arthur going away like that and the effect it had on Gerald, and he looked straight at me and said, "You don't have to tell me if you don't want to, but there's more, isn't there?" And before I knew it I was crying again, for Nicky and Gerald and Vera and Arthur and Joe and my baby and then for the whole world, it seemed. "Oh, dear, I'm making such a fool of myself—must be all that sherry you've given me. But I should have looked after them better, Tiny—Gerald and Vera. And Arthur. I failed them. All of them."

"No, you didn't. Don't say that, girl. Don't even think it."

"But I *did*. I'll tell you the rest, Tiny. I've never told anyone—I promised Arthur—but if I tell you, you must swear that you won't tell

Gerald. If you see him, after—you know, if you talk to him—you won't tell him."

Tiny thought for a moment, then he got up and fetched a photograph from the mantelpiece and laid it on the table.

"That's Dennis, isn't it?"

"Yes. Whatever you want to tell me, it's between you, and me, and him." He laid his hand flat on the frame. "There. It won't leave this room. You have my word."

After a few minutes stumbling through the damp, gloomy passages, they came to a cave with a dry, sandy floor. "Let's sit down for a minute and think what to do," said Tom. "There must be a way out of here, otherwise those men wouldn't—" He broke off, for at that moment Scruff pricked up his ears and began growling.

"Can you hear something, boy?" said Peter.

"Well, he's got jolly good ears," said Jill. "I can't hear anything."

"Wait a minute!" said Tom. "What was that?"

Then they all heard it, a low, menacing roar. The children's hearts began to beat fast.

"What a terrific row!" said Jill. "It must be the monster. The farmer's wife told us about it, remember?"

"Monster!" said Peter scornfully. "That's a bit much, even for a girl. There aren't any such things."

"Well, whatever it is," said Tom, "it's coming from over there. Better keep hold of Scruff's collar, Jill."

But it was too late! Quick as a flash, the excited dog bounded forward in the direction of the noise. Ignoring the children's shouts, he began running down the dark, smelly tunnel underneath the rock as fast as his legs could carry him.

Jill's face was white. "Tom," she said, "supposing the monster—or whatever it is—supposing it hurts him? It sounds awfully fierce."

"We'd better follow him," said Tom, his heart sinking. "Come on!"

They raced down the tunnel toward the noise, which was growing louder and louder. Suddenly, Tom, who was in front, stopped. "There's something blocking the way!" he shouted. "It feels like a big rock." At his feet, Scruff was whining and scratching, thumping the children's legs with his wagging tail.

"What's happening?" shouted Jill. "I can't see a thing!"

"Wait a minute, I'll switch on my torch," said Peter.

"You might have thought of that before," grumbled Jill. She took a step backward and banged into him. There was a sudden clatter. "What was that?"

"The torch. I've dropped it!"

"You idiot!" hissed Jill.

"It's all right, I've got it," said Tom. "I don't think it's broken. Let's try—" and he switched it on just in time for the children to see Scruff's tail disappearing through a crack in the base of the huge stone slab that was blocking their path.

"Oh, no!" shouted Jill. "He'll be hurt, I know he will!" and she started pounding on the rock with her fists. "Tom! Peter! We've got to rescue him!" Suddenly, the roaring noise stopped, and there was a queer clicking sound. Then the children heard the whirr of machinery, and the slab began to slide back, very slowly, into a groove in the tunnel wall. They found themselves looking into a little room.

"What a find!" said Tom. Jill was so glad to see Scruff that she fell on her knees and hugged him.

"Well," said Peter, "I've never heard of a monster that makes clicking noises before, have you, Tom? And I've certainly never seen one that looks like this!"

There was a table in one corner with a strange machine on top of it. "That's a funny-looking thing," said Peter. "I wonder what it is."

"It's a recording machine," said Tom. "I'm sure of that. Those men must have set it up to frighten away the villagers. They didn't want anybody coming here and interfering with their dirty work."

"We've got to find a way out," said Jill.

"Yes," said Tom, "and quickly too, before—hullo, what's that?"

There was another whirr of machinery, and the three children whirled round and stared in horror as the slab began to slide back *into place. They rushed toward it, but it was too late—it was shut fast, and they were trapped inside the room.*

*The children groaned. "Now we're in a fix!" said Peter. "What on earth are we going to do?"*

*"I say, Tom," said Jill in a small voice, "my feet are wet."*

*"Honestly, Jill," said Peter, "we can't waste time worrying about your feet now."*

*"No, she's right," said Tom. "My feet are wet too, and they were quite dry a moment ago. What—"*

*"Look!" shouted Jill. "Over there! The crack in the wall! There's water pouring through it!"*

*She was right. Gray-green seawater was rushing into the room through an opening in the rock. In another moment, it would be lapping around their ankles, and then their knees, and then— Tom was no coward, but at that moment he felt very frightened indeed.*

**Tom to the Rescue,** 1948

## Gerald

*I missed* Starlight Express *tonight.* The first time in four-and-a-half years. I so wanted to make it five—that would be one for the record books, five years with the same show, but it won't happen now. With all that's been going on, I clean forgot what day it was, and when I realized and looked at my watch, it was too late.

What I don't understand is, if Jo got those men to hurt me, why did she come round with the chocolates? Doreen said they had quite a nice chat. There was no cause to try and keep me away from Melanie, no need. I thought of saying that to Jo, that I'm her friend, I'll look after her, I even thought of trying to explain about Vera . . . but it wouldn't be any good. I know what she'd say, you see. Because everyone's the same nowadays, they see sex in everything. It's the first thing they think of— abandoning themselves to any sort of disgusting impulse. Well, you won't catch me going down that road—I've seen where it ends. Filth, that's all it is. Filthy minds.

Palfrey's the worst of the lot, and this has got his name written all over it. I've worked it out: him knowing Paul Cosworth and Jo knowing Paul as well because of Channing & Mason—that's the connection. Has to be. No wonder he covered his face up; he's a disgrace to his uniform. Too busy knocking innocent people about and ruining property to catch any criminals. Oh, yes, *they* can do what they like . . . making me miss my show like that. Keeping me away from Melanie. And spoiling everything for me at work, because that's all ruined. When I think of how I used to look forward to Monday morning, seeing everybody after the weekend—I always thought I was one of the lucky ones in that respect, because it's not everybody who can say that, is it? But that's all gone out the window.

Those two days I had off—I was supposed to be recovering, that's what the doctor said. It was to get my strength back, and it might have been very pleasant, with Doreen being so kind to me, but all the time I was worrying about when I had to go back and what might happen. That first morning was a walk into the lion's den, all right, with no Jack there to help me. I thought my chat with Doreen in the hospital was bound to improve matters in that department, because he likes me to get on with people, but he's not returned. I've tried telling myself it's because I told Doreen about him—breaking the confidence—but I know it's not that. It's all this other business, he doesn't like it. I didn't cause it, that's what I've told him, but he's not listening. He liked Melanie, I know he did, and I thought we were in it together. I thought he'd want to help me.

It was all very difficult. Jo wasn't there, but Neville came over from his office. I didn't know what to expect, but he was very jovial. "Ah, G.H. Good to have you back on board. How are you feeling?"

"I can manage, thank you."

"Oh, of course. Actually, it's rather more a question of whether *we* can manage without *you*. This past couple of days . . ." He shook his head. "When this VE Day anniversary is over, I, for one, will be breathing a huge sigh of relief. You wouldn't believe the orders we've had. Still, at the end of the day, it's all money in the bank, isn't it? But you're to take it easy—after all, it isn't every day someone gets injured in the line of duty. Your landlady tells me you were the hero of the hour."

"Well, I don't know where she got that from."

"Nothing like modesty, eh, G.H.? Fancy a cup of coffee?"

"No thank you, I've got my flask."

"Of course, I was forgetting. Well, Jo's at the dentist this morning, in case you were wondering. She'll be in about half-eleven. And I'm on my way to a meeting. Will you be all right holding the fort for a couple of hours?"

"Fine, thank you."

"Jolly good! I'd better be off." Then he looked at my head where they'd shaved the hair round the stitches and said, "You know, some people would pay good money for a haircut like that."

"More fool them, then."

He looked a bit taken aback when I said that, but he said, "Yes, indeed . . . you're quite right. Just a joke. Oh, I almost forgot. The police should be sending someone over for a word about the break-in. Sometime in the next couple of days, they said."

That gave me a nasty jolt. "I've got nothing to tell them. I don't remember anything. It's because of my head."

"They still want to talk to you. Hear it from the horse's mouth, as it were. You needn't worry—I doubt they'll keep you away from work for more than a couple of minutes. Now, I can see you're raring to go, so I'll leave you to it. Jo's marked the urgent stuff with yellow stickies. It's all there on the left, look."

"Oh . . . yes. Thank you."

"Cheerio, then. And remember, don't go mad!"

I looked at the great pile of stuff Jo had left me and shuffled through it a few times, but I couldn't seem to make a start. In any case, both the lines kept ringing at once, and I had people bombarding me with questions. I couldn't concentrate on anything and my head was starting to hurt, so after about half an hour I thought I'd go down to the warehouse to see if it was properly cleared up, but by the time I got to the bottom of the stairs I was in a real panic, sweating, heart pounding. I thought I was going to collapse. We've got a display at the bottom of the stairs with all the ventriloquist dolls sitting on garden furniture, with crockery on the table and papier-mâché food to make it look like a tea party, so I took one of them off its chair and sat down.

All I meant to do was close my eyes for a moment, but then I heard footsteps, and when I opened them again John from the loading bay was standing right in front of me. He didn't say anything, but it gave me quite a fright, seeing him so close, because he's got a nasty, bullying way about him—never misses the chance for a rude remark—and there he was, staring at me. Then he called over his shoulder, "Over here!" and two of the others came up and they all stood there looking down at me. I didn't like the look of them at all. I tried to push back the chair to get away, but it was wedged up against the stairs. John leaned down toward me. "Gerald, mate—"

"I'm not your mate! If I was, you wouldn't be laughing at me, would you?"

"We're not laughing at you, are we?" He turned to the others. They both shook their heads. "We just came to see how you were, that's all."

"Don't think I don't know . . . I know what you say about me."

"Gerald! We're not saying anything. We was worried about you—" He looked at the others again. "Isn't that right?" They nodded. "We wouldn't laugh, we're really disturbed about what happened."

"Then perhaps you'll stand back and let me get back up the stairs."

"Do you want a hand? You don't look too good."

"I can manage on my own, thank you."

As I made my way back up the stairs I heard one of them say, "Poor old sod, they really had a go at him, didn't they?"

I went and sat at my desk again. I could hear them downstairs, and I could tell they were mucking about with the dummies, because one of them was saying, "Gottle of geer? Gottle of geer?" and I wanted to go and lean over the banisters and tell them to stop, but I couldn't find the energy. I suppose it was all very unfortunate, but opening my eyes and seeing them standing over me like that, I really thought— That was when I heard Jo's voice. She must have come in through the loading bay, because I heard her say, "Watch it, that thing's valuable." Then there was a bit of giggling—at my expense, no doubt—before one of the men said, "He's upstairs," and then, "Aren't you going to go and say hello to him?"

I didn't know what would happen. My mouth was dry and I had a horrible queasy feeling in my stomach. I could hear her coming up—I can see the top of the stairs from my desk, but I didn't want her to think I was watching for her, so I pulled some of the paperwork toward me and pretended that I hadn't heard her come in. Then I heard her say, "How are you, Gerald?" Without raising my head I could see her standing in the office doorway, or rather, I could see the skirt and legs but not the rest. Not her face. I thought of what I wanted to tell her about not harming Melanie, and how I'd never be able to make her understand, and tears came flooding into my eyes without any warning. I bent down as if I were looking for something in one of the desk drawers, so she wouldn't see. Then she said, "Well, I'd better go and start filling those orders," and I heard her clattering off down the stairs again.

Then the police rang. It wasn't Palfrey, it was some woman. Bossy. I told her I couldn't remember anything, but she insisted on coming to see me anyway. Of course once I'd agreed—not that I had any choice in the matter—she was all sweetness and light. "I won't take much of your time, Mr. Haxton. Just one or two questions." I know their game. They think I'm a soft touch, I'll answer all the questions the way they want just because it's a woman asking. Well, two can play at that game. I told her they had a gun. I said they were after the contents of the safe and when I told them it wasn't in the warehouse, that's when they hit me.

Palfrey can just put that in his pipe and smoke it. If he thinks I'll go running into his trap by telling the police about Melanie, then he's got another think coming, hasn't he?

## Jo

*I can't believe this.* It's like a nightmare. You read these stories in the papers, but I never thought it could happen to us, not for a minute. It's Mel. She's just, like, *gone*. Disappeared.

At first I thought I must have got the days mixed up, that she was staying on at school to work on that art thing, but when I phone the school it just rings and rings, and then this man answers—he's the caretaker or something—and he says, "Oh, no, there's no one here." I said, "Are you sure?" and he goes, "Positive. I'm all on my own." So then I thought, well, where can she have got to, and I phone Mum to see if she's round there. Of course the minute I said, "I don't know where she is," Mum says, "Right, get on to the police, now!" and I'm, like, "It's okay, she's just late back from school, that's all." In the end I managed to get her to chill out a bit, and I could hear Colin in the background going, "Calm down, Polly, it's all right," 'cause that's my mum's name. Next thing, I ring up Sonali. I'm thinking, Mel's forgotten what day it is, the dozy mare, and she's gone back with her. So I phone there and I get her mum and she's, like, "No, she's not here," and I'm thinking, *what?* I go, "Can I speak to Sonali?" and she comes on the line and says she didn't walk home from school with her. I say, "Why not?" because they always come home from school together, and Sonali told me Mel wanted to go down the shops. When I asked why, she goes, "Oh . . . she wanted to buy a present." She was hesitating a bit, so I thought, well, that's funny, and I'm racking my brains trying to think of who's got a birthday soon, but I couldn't come up with anything. Then I'm thinking, what do I do? So I rang Ron, not that I thought he'd know where she was or anything, just for a chat, because really I just wanted someone to say, you know, you're worrying about nothing, it's cool, or whatever. But his mobile was off.

At first I was just a bit pissed off with her. I kept thinking, what is she playing at? But then when it got later and later and she still didn't come home, I started getting scared. Thing is, I've always said to her, right, it's not like I want to stop you having fun, I just need to know where you are, yeah? And she's always been really good about it. I mean, she's not like some kids where the parents ask them where they're going and they're just, like, up yours, and go off and do whatever they want. I'm not trying to make out she's perfect, but *on my life,* she's not like that.

Then Sonali phones at about half-ten and she goes, "Can I speak to Mel, please?"

"She's not back yet! Sonali, did she say anything else about where she was going? Because I'm getting really worried."

"Well . . ."

"Listen, you're not going to get in any trouble, I swear it, but I just need to know where she is, okay?"

So then Sonali goes, "Well, I don't really know, not like a name or anything . . ."

I said, "What, you mean she went off with someone? After school?"

"Yeah, but she's done it a couple of times, and—look, I don't know, really."

"What, recently?"

"It's been, like, the last week, really."

"So is it a boyfriend, or what?"

"I don't think . . . well, not exactly."

"What do you mean, *not exactly*?"

"Well . . . she keeps mentioning this one bloke. I don't know who it is or anything, and when I ask her she just goes, 'Oh, no one you know,' and I said to her, I don't believe you, because if it's one of the boys from school, then I'll know him, won't I? Or at least who he is. But then she said it wasn't someone from school and she went all secretive about it."

"But she definitely said it was a man, did she?"

"Yeah. But that's all I know, really. Look, I'm sorry if I didn't tell you before, but it was difficult, because when you rang I thought, Mel's probably on her way home right now, you know? And I didn't want to tell on her or anything."

"It's okay, Sonali. I'm not angry with you, and I'm not going to be angry with her. I just want her safely home, that's all." I thought I was going to cry, so I was trying to catch my breath when she said, "Don't worry, I'm sure she's all right."

"Yeah, well . . . 'night, Sonali."

The minute I got off the phone, it rang. "Mel? Is that you?"

"No, it's Ron. Are you all right?"

"It's Mel. She hasn't come home."

"Bit late, isn't it? What's she up to?"

"I don't bloody *know*, do I? That's the problem! I'm going out of my mind with worry."

"Relax, Jo, she's a big girl. She's probably out with some friends, that's all."

"She's not a big girl, she's *twelve years old*! And in any case, I've tried her friends."

"What, all of them?"

"Well, no, but I rang Sonali—"

"Yeah, but it's not like that's the only friend she's got, is it? Why don't you ring a few of the others?"

"Well, I could, but she'd have told me, wouldn't she, if she was going off with them?"

"Not necessarily. They might have sneaked in to see a film or something."

"I haven't got any of their numbers."

"Look in Mel's address book. It'll be in her room, won't it?"

"I don't know."

"Go and look. I'll hang on."

So I rush into Mel's room and I'm pulling out all these drawers, turning everything over, but I can't find it.

"It's not there. I can't ring directory inquiries, I don't know any of their surnames."

"What about Mel's friend—the best friend?"

"Sonali?"

"Yeah. Won't she have their numbers?"

"She might. . . ."

"Well, then, ring her back and ask her."

I look at my watch and it's five to eleven, but I thought, this is an emergency, so I get on the phone and this time her dad answers. When I explained he said he'd go and get her address book and look up the names for me. Sonali had Abby's number and Tara's and Chanelle's, but when I rang up they all said Mel wasn't there. I had this same conversation three times—with the parents—and they're going, "You should phone the police," and, "Is anybody there with you?" and all like that, really concerned, you know, but I was, like, "I'm fine," because I just wanted a bit of time to go over it in my mind and make sure Mel hadn't told me something that I'd forgotten. Calling the police, that's like saying something is really wrong, isn't it, and I didn't want to do that if . . . I'm sitting there with all this going round and round in my head, and at the same time I keep seeing these pictures of Mel being dragged off into the bushes by some horrible man and . . . I just couldn't think straight.

Well, by then it was close on midnight, and Ron said to ring him back whatever time it was, so I did, and I go, "I've got to call the police." Then he goes—and I just could not *believe* this—he goes, "You're blowing it out of proportion." I said, "In what way?" I mean, she's my daughter, isn't she? It's not like I've lost . . . I don't know, a *goldfish* or something.

So then he's, like, "Come on, Jo, you're going really over the top about all of it."

"I'm not going over the top. I am really, *really* worried about her. Oh, God, Ron, you don't think . . ."

"What?"

"Well, with Gerald . . . What's if it's, like, a revenge thing? What if he's taken her off somewhere and won't let me have her back because of what you and Paul did to him?"

"I told you, we didn't—"

"For God's sake, Ron, he had to go to hospital! When I saw him at work—I told Neville I had a dentist appointment first thing, because I didn't know if I could handle seeing him, but I had to go in later—he looked terrible. And he was just . . . really subdued, wouldn't look me in the face. Not that I gave him much chance, I couldn't be in the same room as him, you know that. Mind you, he's still recovering, so he probably wouldn't be able to get his act together enough to—"

"Wait a minute. You said he banged his head, didn't you?"

"Yes. I told you, he had stitches."

"Well, it could have had an effect on him, couldn't it? Sent him a bit . . . you know."

"Well, his landlady told me he was in a real state when he got home, but that doesn't mean . . . He told the police you had a gun, Ron."

"*What?*"

"A gun. He said you'd threatened him with it. I wasn't supposed to be listening, but the door was open and I was on the stairs, so I heard. Did you?"

"What, have a gun? No, we didn't. He's off his head. I bet that's it—he's lost it."

"But listen, what Sonali said about Mel going off to meet someone and talking about them and all that—it's hardly going to be *Gerald*, is it?"

"Mel said she was meeting someone? But—"

"I didn't tell you, did I? Well, Sonali said there was some bloke she thought Mel was going to meet and she didn't know who it was because she was being really secretive about him."

"Did she say anything else?"

"No, not really, just that Mel told her it was no one she knew, that's all."

"Could be anyone . . . if there *is* a bloke."

"What do you mean, if?"

"Well, she could have made it up, couldn't she? You know, wanting to look cool in front of her mates, grown up and that."

"Mel's not like that, Ron. She really isn't."

"Jo, you've got to ask yourself, how well do you really know her? I mean, kids don't tell their parents everything—I know I didn't."

"I did."

"Did you though? When you had Mel . . . did your mother know you'd been having sex, before?"

"Well, of course she— Oh, I see what you mean. No, she didn't, but what's that got—"

"Well, then."

"Well, then, *nothing*. What are you telling me, that she's pregnant?"

"No."

"Then what *are* you telling me, Ron? One moment you're saying it's Gerald, the next moment you're saying she's gone off with some man— listen, I've had enough of this. I'm calling the police."

I was just about to ring them when Mum phoned. "You've been on the phone all evening; I couldn't get through. Is she back?"

"No, she's still—"

"Have you called the police?"

"No, I was—"

"Right, that is *it*! I'm putting the phone down, then *I'll* ring them, and then I'm coming straight over, all right?"

* * *

I remember looking at my watch and thinking, half past midnight, over seven-and-a-half hours since she should have been home. It was like that was all time meant, not time to go to bed or time to have supper or anything like that. It was just time when Mel wasn't here.

I got a call from the police station about ten minutes after that. This WPC introduced herself and then she says, "We've had a call from a Mrs. Farrell about a Melanie Farrell; apparently she's not come home today. . . ."

I go, "That's right. She should have been home after school, but she never arrived."

The policewoman says, "Mrs. Farrell gave us your number—she's your mother, is she?"

"Yes."

"And you're Melanie Farrell's mother, are you?"

"That's right."

"What's your name?"

"Jo. Joanne Farrell."

"Well, perhaps you can tell me what's happened, can you?"

Well, even though I'm in such a state, I'm thinking, oh, please, patronize me a little bit more, why don't you? But I start telling her what's happened and she keeps interrupting, asking if we've had a row. I go, "No," and she goes, "What about yesterday?"

"No."

"Earlier in the week?"

"No! Look, we haven't fallen out! Can't you take no for an answer, or something?"

And she's all, like, "Well, if you're sure, but I have to ask, because that's often the cause of it, kids going missing."

"Right, but I can't remember the last time we had an argument. This morning she seemed really happy, and just . . . settled, like life was great, you know?"

"Well, perhaps that's why—has she got a new boyfriend?"

"She's only twelve."

"Doesn't mean anything these days, I'm afraid."

I said, "It does in this house!"

Then she had the nerve to say, "Well, perhaps that's why she's gone behind your back."

I nearly told her where to stick it, but then I remembered what Sonali told me, so I said, "Well, much as I hate to say it . . ." and I explained what she'd said, and she trots out the line about kids don't always tell their parents, blah, blah, blah. It was like she'd got it all settled in her own mind, but she obviously had this list of questions she'd been told to ask, because then she went, "Does Melanie's father live with you?"

"I haven't seen Mel's dad since she was four months old."

"What about Melanie? Does she see him?"

"You've got to be joking!"

"He's not been in touch at all?"

"We don't even know where he is."

"Do you have a partner living with you?"

"No."

Then she goes, "Are you in a relationship at the moment?"

"I'm seeing someone, yes."

"But he's not living there?"

"No. I told you that, didn't I?" All I'm thinking is, never mind asking me all this rubbish, what about getting out there and looking for her?

"So you're a one-parent family, then?"

"Yes!" I felt like saying, what planet are you from? Don't they have one-parent families there?

"Did you go out tonight, with your partner?"

"No, I didn't. In any case, I wouldn't leave her by herself. I'd never do that."

She starts trying to reassure me. "Most children who go missing are found in a very short space of time . . ." or whatever, and then she runs through all the suggestions: Have you tried ringing round her friends, did she take anything from her room, and all the rest of it, and I'm going done that, done that. In the end she says, "Well, it's not a lot to go on. You'll need to give me a description, and we'll put it out to all the cars, but I don't think there's much else we can do right at the moment." So I said, "Wait a minute, I haven't finished yet." And I told her about Gerald. All of it, Ron and Paul, and the lot. That got her attention.

I felt bad about it because it was like betraying them, really. After all, they were only trying to help, but I thought, if that's got something to do with it, well, it's worth it, even if it means that me and Ron split up because of it. I didn't say they'd beaten Gerald up or anything, just that they'd had a word with him. I mean, it's not like I actually know what happened, so it wasn't like I was lying to the woman, was it? She took down all the names, then she said, "This Mr. . . . Haxton, you said he's known to the police?" So I explained about how they've had him in for flashing at schoolkids and everything, and she tells me they'll look into it, and in the meantime, if Melanie comes home, would I phone the station immediately and let them know? Then she tells me to try and get some sleep!

All that was Wednesday—it's Thursday night now and she's still not back. Colin's been great. He rang work for me and he's been all round the streets looking for her. Mum's been really good, getting meals—not that I've eaten anything. That policewoman's been round here; she's not as bad as I thought, actually, to be fair. She keeps telling me they're doing all they can. They've been to the school and all the rest of it and they've talked to Sonali. I've had her on the phone twice in tears, poor kid, convinced it's her fault. I keep trying to tell her it's rubbish, 'cause it is, but then I'm thinking, whose fault is it?

I always come back with the same answer—mine. I mean, if I'd been a bit more *together*, you know? Instead of thinking about Ron all the time, and then that business with him and Paul and Gerald. I know it was like I was doing it for her, but still . . .

Paul rang this afternoon. He said he'd called to talk to me about some order and Neville told him what happened. He sounded really choked. "I can't imagine what you must be feeling; if it was one of mine . . ." and all this, and I'm just crying and crying. He said, "Did you tell the police about Gerald?"

I said, "Yes, I'm sorry, I didn't mean to get you into trouble, but—"

"Don't be daft! You've done exactly the right thing. Listen, I'm going to give my friend Steve Palfrey a call, okay?"

"Steve . . . who?"

"The copper, remember? He was the one who told me about Gerald in the first place."

"But what about—"

"What, that business at the warehouse? I can square it with him, no problem. He hates nonces as much as I do."

"Do you think it is something to do with Gerald, then?"

"Well, he's the obvious one, isn't he? I'd go round to his house, but—"

"No, don't. I mean, you know he had to go to hospital, don't you? And Mel's friend said she was talking about a man she was going to meet like she fancied him or something, so that's not going to be Gerald, is it?"

"Don't forget, Jo, people like him can be very cunning—they've got lots of tricks. I'm sure your Mel is a sensible girl, but she's only young."

"But I've told her not to talk to strangers, and . . . well, anyway, she'd have recognized him, wouldn't she? When she told me she thought someone was following her, she gave a really good description—that's why I thought of Gerald in the first place."

"But they can write letters. They can do all sorts of things, these people."

"Yeah, but . . . well, when I've asked this policewoman what they're doing about Gerald, she just keeps telling me they're looking into it and not to jump to conclusions and all this, you know? It's like she doesn't believe me."

"Listen, I'm getting straight on to Steve, all right? I'll have a word with Neville too. I know it's easy to say try not to worry, but you've got to be strong for Mel, right? It's early. I'm sure you'll get her back safe and sound."

"Paul . . . anything you can do . . . I just want her back so much."

"Course you do. We all do. You leave it to me."

It's like I'm going out of my mind—telling myself all different things. One minute this could have happened, next minute it's something else, and all this horrible stuff about child molesters, pictures in my mind that I try to block out because it's not doing any good but you can't, you just *can't*. I keep looking at my watch the whole time, and each time it's, like, that's another hour gone, and she could be *anywhere*. I can't eat, I can't sleep, I can't do anything. I just want my baby back.

## Tilly

*I reached across the table* to take Tiny's hand, and I suddenly had this very peculiar feeling, a pain shooting up into my chest. I heard his voice, very sharp. "What's wrong, sweetheart?"

For a minute it was as if everything had sort of stopped, but then all the pain and funny sensation subsided, and I felt all right again. "Nothing to worry about—just a spot of indigestion."

"It's Arnold Bennett, giving you a funny turn."

"Yes, it must be."

"What about a tablet? Or . . . I know! Milk of magnesia. That always does the trick for me."

"No, don't get up. No point shutting the stable door after the horse has bolted, is there?"

"Well, if you're quite sure . . ."

"Don't worry, I'm not going to peg out on you. Not yet, anyway. What I was saying, before . . . It's not that I don't trust you, Tiny, because I do—it's just the thought of telling anyone, really. I don't want Arthur's ghost to haunt me."

"That's not going to happen, girl. I told you, it stays in this room."

"Here goes, then. Where did I get to?"

"Let's see . . . you said the GI was hanged, and Gerald's father went off and never came back."

"That's right. Well, I'd had this trouble over a soldier, gone and got myself pregnant. I had to get rid of the baby and it affected me a great deal, especially with what happened to Vera, because it happened at around the same time, you see. Almost like . . . like the slaughter of the innocents, so *horrible,* and I'd let it all happen, I can't tell you . . ."

"Come on, let's get your hanky out, have a mop-up, and I'll pull my chair round next to yours, like this, see, so I can hold your hand. That's better, isn't it? Now, you just take all the time you want."

"It's no use my shedding tears over it, I know that, it's not going to bring them back, not her, not Joe, not—"

"Joe? Was that your soldier?"

"Yes, but he'd been killed, so that was why—"

"You don't have to explain yourself to me, Tilly. It must have been dreadful, all by yourself. I wish I'd known you then."

"I wouldn't have been much fun. You see, when Arthur told me Vera'd been pregnant, it was like the same thing happening all over again. He thought it was the American's baby, they all did. They thought that was why, that she'd told him and he didn't want to marry her, so they'd had a fight. The police found her purse with his things. He was arrested a couple of weeks after she was killed, and then there was the trial. He never confessed though. Never. I didn't go to the trial—well, Marjorie'd told me to keep away, and besides, I didn't want to. I knew it was going to be a travesty before it happened. We all did. Well, when I say 'all' I don't mean the police, although a lot of the evidence was pretty sketchy, secondhand— what they call circumstantial. People saying they thought they'd seen him, that sort of thing. Treece was one of them. Said he'd been in his garden and seen an American soldier going into the woods. He could see the woods from his garden, all right, but it was a downright lie."

"How did you know?"

"Oh, I knew all right. That's what I meant, we all did. Marjorie and Treece—and Arthur too, of course—they cooked it up between them, what they were going to say. And I stood by and did *nothing.*"

"Was that why Marjorie told you to keep away?"

"No, that was before. I'd written to her, you see, after Arthur told me. I was in no fit state to go anywhere, so I wrote her a letter saying how sorry I was and telling her I'd been ill. I didn't tell her why, although Arthur knew, of course, but I told her I'd come up the next week, and if there was anything I could do . . . A few days later I got back this furious letter saying how dare I take Arthur's side against her? It was absolutely vitriolic, said I was her enemy and that I'd always been jealous of her and a lot more like that. I can't remember if she actually said it was her against the world, but that was certainly the implication, and she made it quite plain that she didn't want me to come anywhere near her. I remember something about how John Treece had let her down, but I don't think she mentioned Vera's name once. It was the most astonishing outburst of . . . well, *hatred,* really, right out of the blue. It upset me so much I think I read it only once before I tore it up, and I remember I even went off down the road looking for somewhere to throw it away because I didn't want the pieces in the flat.

"I couldn't understand it at all. It crossed my mind that she might have had it out with Arthur about our affair, because she'd have been justified, but she never brought it up once, and I remember being struck by the fact that there wasn't anything like that in the letter. She called me a turncoat and all this sort of thing, but there was nothing you could call a direct reference, and Marjorie wasn't usually one to mince words when she was accusing somebody of something, so I was baffled. And upset, of course, because I wanted so much to help and she turned me down in this very cruel way with no real explanation. I couldn't see what it had to do with Vera, but the tone of this thing was so absolute that I really felt I couldn't telephone, so I waited for Arthur to get in touch with me. He did, after a few days, to tell me that the police had arrested this American, Eddie Mayo. 'He's been in trouble before, apparently. With his CO, not with them. Stealing from other men on the base.'

" 'Is he a pilot?'

" 'Ground staff. They think he's a bit limited—mentally, I mean. Makes up stupid stories to try and impress people, that sort of thing. Sounds just the type to take up with an underage girl. I tell you, Tilly, I wish I could get my hands on him, just for five minutes. . . .'

" 'They're sure about it, are they?'

" 'Pretty certain. The bastard was supposed to be taking her to a dance at the base, but he obviously persuaded her to go into the woods with him instead. He swore she never turned up, of course. I told Marjorie it wasn't appropriate, that Vera was too young for all that social stuff, especially with Americans involved, but she wouldn't listen. Too busy being infatuated with that bloody John Treece.'

"I said, 'Are you sure?'

" 'She's besotted with him! You must have seen it.'

" 'Yes, but how do you know he feels the same way about her?'

" 'You don't have to spare my feelings, Tilly.'

" 'Believe me, I'm not. There's something I've got to tell you, Arthur. Something I should have told you a long time ago.'

"So I told him about Treece and Vera. Oh, Tiny . . . I can't even *begin* to tell you how many times I've gone over that conversation in my mind and wished I'd kept my mouth shut. I should never have told him. Well, I should have told him when I first found out what was going on, because if I had, Vera might still be alive today. But I shouldn't have told him *then*. After all, it wouldn't have saved Eddie Mayo if I hadn't. I was thinking I'd undo some of the damage, but all I did was cause more. I'm not saying ignorance is always bliss, but believe me, in this case . . ."

"But you couldn't have known all that when you told him, could you? You can't blame yourself for everything."

"Please don't be kind to me, Tiny, I can't bear it. What happened, you see . . . well, I told Arthur about Vera and John Treece, and there was this awful silence on the other end. I was shouting into the receiver for him to say something, because I was terrified that he'd rushed off to murder the man. Then he said, 'Did Marjorie know?'

" 'I don't think she *knew*, but she was jealous of the time Vera spent with him. I don't know if she put two-and-two together, but I certainly didn't tell her, if that's what you mean.'

"He started to say something, just a few words: 'That was why—' Then he stopped. In the end, he just said, 'My God.' That was all. *'My God.'* Then I heard the receiver go down.

"I didn't hear from Arthur for about a week after that. One night he turned up at the flat—I was still living with Millicent at that time, and we were both asleep. She was the one who heard the noise. I didn't know anything about it until she came and woke me and told me there was a man waiting for me in the sitting room. I must have been in a very deep sleep not to have heard him. Millicent said he was pounding on the door with his fists and the woman from the floor above had stuck her head over the banisters and hissed, 'Do you *mind*?' There's a certain moment before you're completely awake, isn't there, and you feel quite happy until some horrible realization comes and spoils it."

Tiny nodded. "Don't I know it? I get that every morning, with Dennis. I wake up feeling wonderful, then I remember he isn't here anymore."

"Yes, that's what I mean. I could have sworn Millie said *Joe* was waiting for me, and I'd forgotten he was dead, just like you said. Not to mention wishful thinking, of course. So I leapt out of bed and rushed over to the mirror and started trying to get my hair into some sort of order where I'd slept on it, when I suddenly saw Arthur's reflection in the glass. He was leaning against the bedroom doorway, watching me. He was as immaculate as ever, but the look on his face . . . He must have seen the look on mine too, through the mirror, because he said, 'Did you think I was your latest boyfriend?'

"I let go of the comb and turned round to face him. I could feel myself blushing, and I couldn't think what to say. 'No, no . . . I was a bit confused. I've only just woken up.'

" 'Sorry to disappoint you,' he said. I don't think I've ever heard anyone sound so bitter.

" 'Would you like a cup of tea? A drink? I don't know what we've got, but I could—'

" 'No, thank you.'

" 'Are you quite sure? Because I wouldn't mind something. Let's go through to the kitchen, shall we?' Without thinking, I turned back to the mirror to have a last poke at my hair.

" 'No need for that, is there? Since you're not expecting company. Perhaps you'll join me when you're ready.' And he turned on his heel and I heard him walking down the passage to the kitchen.

"Well, I knew Arthur was going to tear a strip off me, and I could see why he felt entitled to do it. My heart was pounding and it was several minutes before I could bring myself to follow him, so I was killing time trying to put on lipstick, but my hand was shaking so much that it missed my mouth and left a stain on my chin when I tried to scrub it off again. I remember turning away from the mirror and looking back again over my shoulder and seeing a lined face and blowsy hair and thinking, it's all starting to go. . . .

"When I got into the kitchen, Arthur was already sitting at the table. He'd found a bottle of something brown and poured me a glass. He didn't say anything, just nodded at it. I sat down opposite and cupped both my hands round the drink so he wouldn't be able to tell what a state I was in. He stared down at the table for what must have been a couple of minutes—although it felt like hours—while I waited for him to say something, and then all he said was, 'Aren't you going to drink it?'

" 'Give me a chance, I've only just woken up. Look, if there's something you want, you know—'

"He started talking as if I hadn't spoken. 'When you were fiddling with your hair back there, you reminded me so much of Marjorie. You've got a lot in common, haven't you? Funny how I've never seen it until now. How you must despise me, the pair of you.'

" 'Stop it, Arthur.'

" 'Both with your secrets, while poor, stupid Arthur doesn't know anything. You must think I'm half-witted!'

" 'Stop it!'

" 'Do you know, that's what Marjorie said. Those exact words.'

" 'You're frightening me . . . what's the matter with you?'

" 'Do you need a reminder?'

" 'I didn't mean that. You came to tell me something, didn't you?'

" 'Yes. Do you remember the night we first . . . in the summer house at Broad Acres? We said if we ever needed help, we'd tell each other. You said I was to come to you if I needed anything . . . or is that something you say to all your lovers?'

" 'Please, Arthur . . .'

" 'Well, is it? Do I have to join a queue? Hand over some coupons?'

" 'Listen, I know you're angry, and I know *why* you're angry, but you're not playing fair!'

" 'Aren't I?'

" 'No! I've never pretended I was a . . . a plaster saint, but I don't make promises if I'm not prepared to keep them!'

" 'You wouldn't let me keep mine—you didn't come to me when you needed money, did you?'

" 'I told you, it wasn't—'

" '*It wasn't mine.* Yes, I know. And I told you that didn't matter. You didn't trust me.'

" 'I'm sorry. I've said I'm sorry. It's just that most men—'

" 'I'm not *most men*! Tilly, I thought we were friends, you and I. And now . . .' He stopped. 'I don't know what to do. If I can't trust you, I honestly can't see how I can come through this . . .'

" 'You *can* trust me. Whatever's gone on between the two of us, we're a family, Arthur, and we've got to look after each other. God knows, I haven't done very well in the past, but we've got to put it behind us— not that it's going to be easy, with Marjorie saying she never wants to speak to me again, but we've got to try.'

" 'When did she say that?'

" 'She didn't say it, she wrote me a letter. Last week. She called me a turncoat and said I always took your side against her. I don't know what's going on and I can't help you if you won't tell me what happened.'

" 'God knows, I didn't want to come here and have a go at you, Tilly. It was just seeing you like that, it made me realize how much . . . It's no good.' He shook his head. 'I'll tell you.' "

## Gerald

*It's almost dark now,* and it's getting chilly. I want to go home, but I can't. The police have been in, you see. I rang Doreen from a phone booth and she told me what happened. They said it didn't matter if I wasn't there, because they had a search warrant. They've been all through my room, and Doreen said they took some of my things away. Theft by another name, that's what it is. She said she saw them putting my scrapbook into one of their bags, and now I don't suppose I'll ever see it again. It's persecution, spreading lies about people and going through my private things without asking, just coming in and sniffing round like a lot of dogs. Doreen said she's had the vacuum out twice since they left, but it's still not right.

When they look at the scrapbook you can bet they'll make something dirty out of that, because what they're doing is looking for an excuse to get me into trouble. Doreen knows I haven't done anything wrong. She said she told them to leave me alone, but she might as well have said it to a brick wall for all the notice they took. I asked her if she knew what their names were—she couldn't remember, but she said they were a nasty-looking bunch and that she's going to make a complaint. But one thing's for certain: Palfrey was in on it. The idea of him nosing around in my things, fingering everything, and all the time thinking his dirty thoughts, it's made my stomach all upset. I didn't get any supper so I bought this chocolate instead, but now I can't even eat that. And I rushed out of the house without a sweater—no hope of going back for it now, of course—so I'm cold as well. I thought it couldn't get any worse, but now I'm stuck out here on this bench and they're looking for me.

But I think I've chosen a good spot here, because I've been keeping an eye out and there's been nothing like a policeman yet. I saw a black-and-white, but I'd got my *Daily Mail* out of the bag already and I put it up in front of my face in plenty of time. Those undercover tricks I've learned in the past couple of months are coming in handy. It did occur to me that I might be better off buying one of the larger newspapers, but they can be difficult to fold and it's easy to knock into people when you spread them out—I've had that happen to me on the tube several times, and it attracts attention. Ideally, I'd like something to put over my head too, because I've noticed people looking at the stitched part. The doctor said to let air get at it, so that's another consideration, but . . . it's too much to think about all this at once.

I've been watching the people go past. First it was all the smart ones on their way home from the office, then quite a few in the opposite direction. Going out for the evening, I suppose—in fact, I noticed a couple of the same faces, wearing casual clothes, of course. Then there were all different sorts going in both directions; it was hard to keep track. I did wonder if I should stop someone and ask about a bed for the night, but it's best to be on the safe side, and they all seem to be in such a hurry. One of them came up to me, as a matter of fact. It was a group of youngish chaps—they walked past and I thought they'd gone, but then one of them doubled back. That made me nervous, because they'd seemed a bit boisterous and I thought they might turn nasty, but all he said was, "You all right there?" He didn't look like a policeman, more like a student, but you have to consider it might be some sort of trap. I thought it was best to answer, so I said, "Yes, I'm very well, thank you."

"You sure?"

"Yes, thank you for asking."

He backed away then, but I could see him shaking his head as he went back to the others. I wondered if I should try to make a run for it, but they just carried on walking. I thought I heard one of them say something about "care in the community"—not very nice, but I suppose it was the scar. I thought I'd handled the situation rather well, but I could see it was time to move on. I don't mind admitting it's still something of a problem, sitting down, what with the bruise on my bottom and the cold making me stiff. I wanted to ring Doreen again, in case she was worried about me, but I thought with all this business about Melanie, the police might be there.

They said I'd been pestering her. It wasn't Palfrey who came, he's too clever for that, it was the same woman who asked me about the men at the warehouse. I found I could not manage at work at all—not just my head but the worry of being there with Jo all the time and wondering what they were saying about me. Then Jo didn't come to work and Neville came into my office and told me that Melanie had gone missing from home and the police are involved. I didn't know what to think, except that if I'd been there to look after her it wouldn't have happened.

I told Neville I didn't feel well and I was going home. I thought he might object, but he just said to have a rest and he would see me in the morning. So then I got home and I was lying on my bed when I heard the bell, so I got up and opened my door to listen because my room is just at the top of the stairs and you can hear. I couldn't see who it was but Doreen said, "Oh, you'd better come in," so I thought she had a visitor. Then she came up and told me it was the police, wanting to speak to me. She said, "They told me it was just a few questions. It'll be more about the break-in, I expect." I had to sit down on the bed again so she said, "I'll tell them you're feeling poorly and you can't see them."

I said, "I don't think it'll do any good," but she went back down the stairs. When I looked over the banister I could see this policewoman in the hall. She was saying to Doreen, "We need to speak to him urgently." So Doreen came back up to me and I thought I'd better go down, otherwise she would be angry, and the woman might come up to my room and I didn't want that.

Doreen said we could go into her sitting room and she would make some tea. There was a policeman with the policewoman, but she did all the talking, wouldn't let him get a word in edgewise. She kept asking questions and wouldn't give me a chance to think. At first she said, "It's just a few things we need to clear up," but then she started asking if I knew Melanie Farrell. I said, "Well, I know she is missing because I was told," and she asked who told me, and when did they tell me, and why did I come home early, and how did I know Melanie if I'd never met her. I said, "Well, I know who she is, I know her by sight," but she carried on with when was the first time I saw her and had I ever followed her, and I started to get confused again. It was upsetting me so that I couldn't think straight. Then she started talking about the men at the warehouse, saying how I'd told her they'd had a gun and asking if I saw the gun and did the men threaten to shoot me, and I got all my words jumbled up. So when she said, "They told you to keep away from Melanie, didn't they?" I said, "Yes," which I did not mean to do but she got it out of me and kept on and on and in the end I don't know what I said. I tried to tell her it is all lies and I have not done anything wrong, but she wouldn't believe me and the man was there all the time looking at me in that nasty way. I saw that the door was open, and I was worried that Doreen would hear and what she'd think, so I said, "You mustn't speak so loud," and the woman said, "Why's that?" I said, "I don't want my landlady to hear what you are saying, she wouldn't like it."

It didn't make any difference. She kept asking if I knew where Melanie was, and then the other one joined in, saying it's serious and I have to tell them. I said, "I know it is serious, and if I knew anything I would tell you, but I don't. Anyway, you should not be bothering me, because I would not hurt her."

The man said, "Why do you think she is hurt?"

I said, "Well, she might be if she's gone missing." That is true, but then they started again, asking me if I had hurt her and why had I been following her. I said, "I'm not going to sit here and be accused, you have no right to do that." Doreen came in with the tea and she told them to leave me alone as well. She said, "Mr. Haxton hasn't done anything wrong, and you should be doing your job catching criminals, not coming here pestering him with questions." They said they would need to come back and speak to me again and they wanted to speak to her too. Then they told me not to go anywhere. I know what it means—they will try and incriminate me and Palfrey is behind it.

I had to tell Doreen afterward that I would never hurt Melanie, because she asked me what was going on and why did the police come. I tried to explain, but it was so difficult—the worst of it is, I have had it all before with these people when it was Vera and the other thing that happened before when I was in National Service. I didn't tell Doreen about it. When Aunt Tilly came to see me in hospital afterward, I could not tell her, because it was caused by the sergeant shouting at me the whole time, right up to my ear with disgusting language. He said, "The best part of you ran down your mother's leg." He meant Jack, because that is the best part of me and he's dead. You can't keep it out of your mind when that happens and it comes back and back, always the same and it can't be stopped except by one way—if I am dead as well. Then I will be with Jack, and that sergeant can shout until his head falls off but I won't hear him. I just wanted it to stop. But it didn't work. They found me and cut the rope and then I had to go to hospital.

Aunt Tilly said, "Why did you do it?" but I told her, "I'm not going to talk about it, so leave me alone." She said Dad would come and see me. I wanted to see him because I hadn't for five years at least, although by that time I had stopped counting. But he never did come, and when I came out Aunt Tilly said there had been a car crash and he'd died, so after that I had no hope of seeing him again.

They are lucky to be with Jack—Vera and Dad—but not me, I couldn't do it. Aunt Tilly said I could live with her for a bit and she would look after me and it would be all right again. I didn't really believe it, but I thought I must grit my teeth and try because that's what Jack would do. But what is the point if I did it all just so this could happen to me?

After the police left the house I told Doreen I would go out for a walk. I knew they would come back, and I was right. She told me they came and took all my things from my room. I will go and tell Aunt Tilly and perhaps she'll let me live with her again at the seaside. I can get a bus to Liverpool Street and the train to get to Frinton, and that is what I will do.

## Tilly

"*Arthur loosened his tie* and reached into his pocket for his cigarettes. 'Pour me a glass of that, will you? You know, Tilly, all this . . . it's made me realize what a crashing hypocrite I've been.'

" 'Why do you say that?'

" 'It's the thing I've always admired most about you, Tilly, your attitude toward life. *Carpe diem,* to hell with the consequences. Not that any of us has got a choice about it at the moment, but . . . it's one thing when it's your mistress, but when it's your daughter it takes on a different complexion. I'm sorry if that sounds, well . . .'

" 'It's all right, Arthur.'

" 'When you told me, I didn't want to believe it. I couldn't believe that she—with Treece, of all people. I kept thinking, why should Vera be like you? After all, you're not her mother, but then I realized, with the two of us, and Marjorie going about like a . . . a cat in heat . . . well, she must have learned by our example. I'm not blaming you, Tilly, it was more . . . trying to find a reason for it, get it straight in my mind. That chap, the one whose baby it was . . . did you love him?'

" 'Yes.'

" 'I'm glad. Not glad that— Look, it's none of my business, just that I'm glad that there was some love somewhere in all this mess. . . . Do you think Vera loved Treece?'

" 'I don't know. Perhaps she thought she did. Or she liked the attention. . . . Love's a funny thing, isn't it? But Vera loved you. I'm sure of that. Gerald loves you too, you know.'

"Arthur buried his head in his hands. 'Gerald . . . I can't even look him in the face! I can't stay with them, Tilly, I just can't . . . and knowing I've got to leave him with Marjorie . . .'

"I reached across the table and pulled his hands away from his face. He looked so desperate, almost as if he was beyond help. All I could do was listen. 'Arthur, what happened? I don't understand.'

" 'After you told me—about Vera—I went round to see Treece. I didn't know what I was going to do. I wanted to kill him, put my hands round his throat and throttle him, it was all I could think of. But when I got there . . . He was in his studio. Drunk. He'd been drinking, sitting there, surrounded by all those ridiculous daubs he's so proud of. I don't think he'd been sober for a week. That wretched wife of his tried to stop me, said he was working and couldn't be disturbed, but I went in. He backed away when he saw me. He must have caught the easel with his foot, because suddenly I was on top of him, on the floor, and he was flat on his back with his head on this canvas. I was pummeling him and he was trying to protect his face with his hands, fingers covered in paint, and it was on my trousers, my arms. Then, in the middle of it all, it was as if—as if I suddenly *found* myself for a moment, and I could see the two of us as if I'd stepped outside my own body. If I were a religious man, I'd say it was an *intervention.* I saw it so clearly, that face of his, lying on the canvas, and beside him these two great flat painted eyes, and I could see it was Marjorie—he'd painted her not as a human being but as a monster, a great brutish thing. But it wasn't the picture that made me stop hitting him, it wasn't because of that. It was this *clarity,* knowing I mustn't kill him, as if the thought had been . . . *parachuted* into my mind and obliterated everything else, and I knew that whatever else I did, I had to hang on to it. I know it must sound quite mad, but there's no other way I can describe it.'

" 'So what did you do?'

" 'I picked myself up off the floor, and then I helped him to his feet. He gave me a rag to wipe the paint off, and we both stood there cleaning our hands like a couple of garage mechanics. He said, "Did Marjorie tell you?"

" ' "She didn't have to."

" ' "I've been thinking, all week, wondering when you'd come. I didn't think you'd go to the police."

" ' "I'm giving you a chance to put your side of the story first, but that's exactly what I intend to do."

" ' "I don't think you will, you know." He was quite matter-of-fact, no triumph in his voice. "Not once you've heard what I've got to say."

" ' "I'm listening." '

"Arthur said the words came shooting out of Treece's mouth as if he couldn't wait to get rid of them.

" ' "Vera was supposed to be meeting some American boy at a dance that night. I'd been out painting and I met her coming through the woods. She didn't take much persuading not to go. In fact, she said she wanted to stay with me instead. So we went to the hut because I had some beer there. I suppose we'd been there for a couple of hours when Marjorie came bursting in without any warning. We weren't—that is, when she came in, we were talking, but Vera hadn't put her dress back on yet, and when Marjorie saw her lying on the blanket in her slip, she went berserk. She dragged her outside—by her hair, I think, because I saw Vera put her hands up to her head to try to stop her. I went after them and Marjorie was shouting at her, calling her a whore. She'd obviously had quite a bit to drink, because she wasn't very steady on her feet. She was stumbling round the clearing, taking Vera with her, because she had hold of her hair. I managed to pull Vera away and I told her she ought to go back into the hut and get dressed, but she wouldn't. She started telling Marjorie that she was going to come and live with me after the war, we were going to France to paint. I told Marjorie I'd never said anything of the kind, that Vera was making it up, but she wouldn't listen to me. She was yelling that Vera was nothing but a filthy little tart. She said, 'I took you into my family out of the kindness of my heart, and this is how you repay me.' Vera shouted at her, 'You haven't got a heart. You only wanted me because you thought you couldn't have children of your own and you just wanted a child to show off in front of everyone.' Marjorie went as white as chalk. She said to me, 'Of course you know that she's pregnant, don't you? It's that American she was supposed to be going to the dance with. She knows he's not going to marry her, so she thinks she can trap you.' Then Vera told me it was my child, and Marjorie called her a liar. I didn't know what to do, they were both shouting at once. I said, 'For God's sake, I've already got enough children, I don't want any more.' Marjorie told Vera she'd have to get rid of it, and Vera said no. Marjorie said she'd already made the arrangements and Vera wasn't going to bring disgrace on her family, and Vera practically spat at her, 'You don't care about your family, only about yourself—all those mummies and daddies wouldn't let their precious kiddies near your books if they knew what sort of person you really are.'

" ' "Marjorie was on one side of the clearing, Vera on the other, and I was between them, trying to keep them apart. Marjorie suddenly dashed past me and lunged at Vera, who sort of twisted away. She must have been caught off balance, because she took a step to the side to steady herself and tripped on one of the roots. I heard her fall, but I didn't see because I made a grab for Marjorie and caught her round the waist, and the next time I looked at Vera, she was kneeling on the ground, holding her hands up to her mouth. I could see that there was blood on her chin and the front of her slip, so I think she must have knocked a tooth out when she fell. She started to get to her feet. I must have loosened my grip on Marjorie for a moment, because she jabbed her elbow backward into my stomach. It hurt like hell and I fell over backward, and the next thing I knew, Marjorie was racing past me with a wooden stake in her hand. I don't know where it came from, but it looked like part of a fence. Vera must have heard her, because she started to run, and I saw her look back over her shoulder and then Marjorie was right behind her, blocking my view. She raised the stake above Vera's head and brought it down. Vera cried out once and I saw her fall. I wanted to get to her, but I couldn't—I was on my hands and knees. Then Marjorie hit her again—twice, I think. I don't know, they were under the trees and the branches were in the way. . . . Vera was dead by the time I reached her." '

"Arthur said, ' "She did that? *Marjorie?*"

" ' "Yes. I'm telling you the truth."

" ' "No . . . you're lying. You killed my daughter yourself." Even as I said it, I didn't believe it. All the time Treece was talking, I'd been remembering the row we'd had that night and how Marjorie had stormed out and the dog had come back on his own. She had been drinking, just like he'd said, more than usual. I'd gone up to bed, but I saw her skirt in the morning with earth on it, and dirt in the bathroom sink. She must have washed her hands. She told me she'd fallen over in the woods. Ruined a pair of nylons. That didn't surprise me at the time because she hadn't been very steady when she left, but when Treece told me, it all made sense.

" ' "As God is my witness, Haxton," he said, "I'm telling you the truth."

" ' "Was that what you were planning to do—take Vera to live with you in France?"

" ' "No. I swear I'd never mentioned anything about living together. I don't know where she got the idea. It was a fantasy, a daydream. You know what girls are like at that age. . . ."

" ' "Not half as well as you do, apparently. You seem to be quite an expert."

" ' "I didn't mean—look, Haxton, you've got to believe me: I didn't know she was pregnant either, not until that night."

" ' "I see."

" ' "I've got babies crawling out of the woodwork. I'm a married man."

" ' "That didn't stop you seducing my daughter."

" ' "My wife—Sinty—she's got no idea about any of this. God knows, she doesn't have an easy life with me, but this would kill her. Please, Haxton . . . Arthur . . ."

" ' "I want to know what happened after you realized what had happened to Vera. What did you do?"

" ' "I picked her up. Wrapped her in a blanket. I took her to the hut. Marjorie said we should leave her there. Until later. She said we should go back home—to our separate homes, that is—and she asked me if I'd come back, and . . ."

" ' "Bury her."

" ' "Yes."

" ' "And you agreed?"

" ' "I had no choice. Marjorie said I'd be held responsible. She was so calm. I argued with her, said we should go to the police and say it was an accident. I pleaded with her, *begged* her, but she wouldn't listen. I couldn't make her see . . . She said that if I didn't agree to bury Vera, she'd go to the police and tell them everything. She said I'd hang for it. I knew nobody would take my word against hers, especially if she told the police about . . . told them that we . . . She said, 'Who do you think they will listen to when I tell them you corrupted my child?' And she was right. I knew she was right. What else could I have done? She said I'd be safe enough now they've stopped the patrols, nobody would see. So I told her I'd do it. God knows, I barely knew what I was saying or doing, I was in such a state of shock. I came back here. There's a separate door to the studio and I often work at night. Sinty knows I don't like to be disturbed, so I knew she wouldn't come in. I suppose I must have had quite a few drinks. I couldn't stop shaking. I went back into the woods about midnight. I don't remember much about the actual burying part. I can't have done a very good job of it, because—"

" ' "Because *my son* found her body."

" ' "Yes, I know that. I'm sorry."

" ' "What else?"

" ' "Well, afterward, I knew there was a trash can behind the hut for burning things, so I made a fire and burned the wooden stake that Marjorie . . . that she'd *used*. It had blood on it. Then I threw in the dress that Vera was wearing, because I didn't know what else to do with it, and the blanket that I'd wrapped her in. It slipped off, you see, while I was carrying her out, and I thought it might have stains on it, where it had been round her head, so I put that in too. It took a long time. Look, Haxton, about the burying . . . I tried to be . . . careful with her. I did the best I could. I was fond of Vera, you know. Very fond of her. On the way back, coming back to the house, I said a prayer." Do you know, Tilly? He actually began to cry. In front of me. I know it sounds monstrous, but I almost thought that he expected my thanks, expected me . . . to *absolve* him. For what he'd done. Oh, God, Tilly, I can't even begin . . . I can't . . .'

"I didn't know what to say. Arthur sat staring at me, his teeth clenched and his body held rigid, trying not to break down. After a few moments, he said, 'I went back. Confronted Marjorie. Told her what Treece had told me. She wouldn't hear it—spun me some story about how they'd fallen out and he was lying, making it all up. She was so adamant I think I'd have believed her if I hadn't heard his story first. When I said, how could she, she attacked me, said it was my fault. Tilly, she said it was because of *us* that she and Treece—as if it had nothing to do with Vera at all. I felt as if I was going mad, I couldn't make her see . . . Did you tell her, Tilly? Did you tell her about us?'

" 'No, Arthur. But don't you remember, last year when you threw the drawing into the fire? She saw us looking at each other and that was when she knew. I couldn't understand why she didn't say anything, but I knew she was infatuated with Treece, we both did. She must have convinced herself that he felt the same way about her, and then finding the two of them in the woods like that . . .'

" 'I didn't know she knew.'

" 'I didn't mention it because I didn't want to cause any more trouble between the two of you. And it wasn't as if the two of us were, you know . . .'

" 'But it doesn't make any *sense*! She's got it all upside down in her mind.'

" 'But Marjorie's *like that*, Arthur. Do you remember—at the beginning of the war we had a conversation and you said she wasn't touched by things? I was telling you what happened to my father, and you said she didn't seem to be any part of it?' Arthur nodded. 'Well, it's true. She'll believe whatever she wants to believe, and that's where the truth is, as far as she's concerned. It's like her stories—that's what exists.'

" 'But *this*—'

" 'I know! But if it's something she doesn't like, she'll ignore it. That's what she did with us—ignored it—until we became . . . part of her story. Can't you see that?'

" 'I suppose that's right. You know, she's convinced herself—God knows how—that it was the American, Mayo—that *he* killed Vera, that it had nothing to do with Treece at all. I can't go to the police, Tilly. You do see that, don't you? For Gerald's sake.'

" 'Yes . . . but what about Mayo? If he—'

" 'Don't you think I haven't thought about that? I've been round and round in *circles*. There's nothing we can do.'

" 'No . . . I see that. But . . . he's somebody's son too, Arthur.'

" '*I know that!* But I can't, not without involving Marjorie, and then Gerald . . . What it would do to him . . . Tilly, we *can't*.' Arthur stared at me. He looked completely defeated.

" 'No . . . you're right. We can't.'

" 'You won't—'

" 'No. I won't. For Gerald's sake.'

"I wouldn't say I was religious, any more than Arthur was, but if there is such a place as hell, then I know what it's like to be there.

Those few minutes, staring at each other, with that . . . *knowledge* hanging there between us, taking that decision. That's what it felt like. Descending into hell.

"Arthur said, 'I'm not going back to Broad Acres. Marjorie knows that. It was the one thing I did manage to get through to her, that I wasn't coming back.'

"He left soon after that. I tried to persuade him to stay, at least until the morning, but he wouldn't. Said he couldn't bear to be near anybody. I was glad, really, because I had the same feeling. I only ever saw him a couple of times after that—it was too difficult, really. He and Marjorie were divorced after the war, but he never married again. I don't think he could get close to anyone after that—not that I'm one to talk. I'd go and see Gerald, of course, from time to time. Even managed to be civil to Marjorie for the few minutes whenever we did see each other. Arthur never saw Gerald again."

Tiny stared at me, shaking his head. "Oh, Tilly . . . oh, *darling* . . . I don't know what to say."

"I—we—did a terrible thing."

"Yes . . . but it was too big, too much . . ."

"I shouldn't have told you. I'm sorry."

"No, it's all right . . . it's all right."

"I just . . . well, why I told you: It was for Gerald, you see. He's always struggled. As if he were born with a sign on his back—Kick Me As You Pass. After everything that happened . . . he tried to commit suicide once. When he was doing his National Service. I went to see him in hospital—they'd given him something to calm him down, and I couldn't get a lot of sense out of him, but he kept saying to me, 'There's no point in my being here.' I think it was the bullying, it became too much. I knew a visit from his father would have meant the world to him, so I wrote Arthur a letter, begging him to go, and he said he would. He never did though. He died a few days later—car crash. Only a handful of people at his funeral. He'd cut himself off, you see. Marjorie wasn't there. She'd gone to see Gerald in the hospital. That wasn't a success, because Marjorie never wanted the kind of son Gerald was. She only wanted one who'd be like that character of hers, Tom Tyler—officer material. I didn't tell Gerald about his father until he came out. The army didn't want him back, so I took him home with me. I told him Arthur'd promised to visit him, but I don't think he believed me. He's always been so alone, Tiny. I haven't been much use to him, God knows, but at least it's been something, and when I go . . . I know it's a lot to ask . . ."

"If I can help him, I will. If he'll let me."

"He doesn't have to know I asked you. He doesn't like people inter-fering, but all the same . . . At least I'd know someone was looking after him. A guardian angel."

"I'll do my best."

"Oh, Tiny, thank you."

"That's what friends are for, girl."

"What I said . . ."

"I told you, that's between you, me, and him." He nodded at Dennis's photograph. "Gerald won't hear it from me, and that's a promise."

"What would you have done? If you'd been in my shoes."

"I think . . ." Tiny looked down for a moment at our hands—he was still holding mine, and he gave it a little squeeze. "I don't know, girl. I honestly don't know."

After a while he said, "It's all been a bit much for one day, hasn't it? How about a cup of tea before I take you back? You look as if you could do with a rest." We cheered up a bit after that—it could have been the brandy, of course, having it with the tea, but mainly it was the weight off my mind. Putting the burden down. Christian in *Pilgrim's Progress*—wasn't he the one with the bundle on his back? I knew Tiny was shocked by what I'd told him, but what he'd said before, about not making judgments, it was absolutely true. There aren't many people around like that, I can tell you. Most of all, I knew I could trust him. I've often wondered if Catholics get that from confessing. A clean slate.

Mind you, there can't be too many priests around who can do a decent Nellie Wallace impression. On the way back he was wheeling me down the beach, both of us singing our heads off: *My mother said, Always look under the bed, Before you blow the candle out, To see if there's a man about, I always do, But you can make a bet, That it's never been my luck to find a man there yet!*

The wind blew most of it straight out to sea, but we got our share of funny looks from the old folks out on their walks. Other old folks, I should say.

"They'll think you've been at the gin," said Tiny.

"I'll tell them you kidnapped me. Those ones there, sitting on that bench, look . . ."

"That one on the end! She even looks like Nellie Wallace."

"Maybe she *is* Nellie Wallace."

"Don't be daft, Nellie Wallace died years ago. That palone she's with though . . . she's pushed the boat out—have a vada at that frock."

"It's a bit fur-coat-and-no-knickers, if you ask me."

"Ooh, don't . . . I don't like to think of it."

"Better change the subject, then. Don't want to put you off your dinner."

"Oh, it will, put me right off. I know, here's a joke for you. This chap goes to his doctor with bum trouble: 'Ooh, I've got the hemorrhoids, Doctor, they're giving me trouble like you wouldn't believe,' and the doctor says, 'Well, that's easily remedied, just take two of these'—and he holds up this box of suppositories—'stick them in the back passage every night, and I guarantee you'll be as right as rain in two weeks.' Well, two weeks later this bloke returns, in a terrible state. 'Doctor, it's my piles, like the hanging gardens of Babylon, they are, and that treatment you gave me was no good at all.' 'Well,' says the doctor, 'did you follow my instructions?' 'Oh, yes, Doctor, I took two of those things every night and put them in the back passage, under the mat, but for all the difference it's made I might as well have stuck them up my arse!' "

Well, it was a nice day, really, in spite of poor little Nicky. But I never wanted him to get old and miserable, and he's gone to a better place, I'm sure of that. They're going to bury him tomorrow, under the tree, and they'll put in some nice bulbs there, to come up in the spring. I feel easier in my mind, better than I have for a long time.

One of the nurses put Nicky's photo on my bedside table so I can see him when I wake up in the morning. That was kind. Lying here, I can just turn my head and see his little face. I can hear them outside, putting up the bunting for that VE thing. Seems odd to be celebrating something like that, but if it's what people want, who am I to argue? If you've had no wars in your lifetime, then you're fortunate. There've been two wars in mine. They both changed things for me, and not for the better either. When you stop and think about it, we've done pretty well since 1945—fifty years and we haven't had another one. Let's hope it continues—not for me, of course, because I won't be here to mind one way or the other, but for you and your children.

## Jo

*It's been three days.* Seventy-two hours. She's been missing for *seventy-two hours.* The police have been on to Gerald, and now he's disappeared too. They told me we shouldn't have taken the law into our own hands. I'm trying to explain it wasn't like that and Mum's there listening, and she's going, "That's all very well, but we don't see you lot doing much to protect people's kids. If she'd come and told you, you'd have gone, well, come back when he's murdered her, then we might do something." They kept telling me how they could have cautioned him and all the rest of it, and Mum's going, "Oh, right, that's a big help." I'd told her about Gerald and the flashing, you see, how they'd had him in before. I gave them Ron's mobile number, and they said, "What about an address?" so I go, "I haven't got one," and Mum says, "Tell me you're joking!" and I'm going, "No, I never had it, he's always come round here." Mum goes to me, "I can't believe you could be so stupid," and the police are trying to calm her down, saying they can trace it. I said, "What are you going to do?" I mean, I don't know how it works, whether they could charge him and Paul with damage to property or actual bodily harm or whatever, just by themselves, without Channing & Mason or Gerald. I always thought if someone beats you up, then it's up to you to press charges, right? Anyway, I didn't know if that was true, so I'm asking all these questions, and they're all, like, "We'll sort that out later." They've started asking me how long I've known Ron and do we get on well and has he been here much and has he met Mel and all this other stuff, and I'm going, "How's this going to help?" But I did my best answering the questions and I got my diary out to show them. Mind you, I've got to say, I'm pissed off at Ron, because he never got in touch with me. Not that I've thought about it much, because all I'm thinking about at the moment—every minute of the day—is Mel. But, I mean, I'm going through hell and I could do with some support. I keep having these long conversations with the police, telling me they're doing this, that, and the other, and they've been all through Mel's room looking at her stuff, and all I'm thinking is, *just get out there and find her.*

It's like my mum said: They spend all this money protecting people like Gerald, when they should be putting them where they belong, behind bars. Because it *is* him. They know it is. When they searched his room, they found this scrapbook full of pictures of Mel. They think he's got this . . . obsession with her, because she looks like his sister who Paul told us about in the pub, the one who was murdered. They asked me if he'd ever talked about her—the sister. He hasn't, but he must have been thinking about her all the time, brooding. The police said if it *is* that, it doesn't necessarily mean he's going to hurt Mel, because it's, like, he wants to get his sister back or something. Mum's going, "Is that supposed to make her feel better?" But all I could think was, at least it means she's not dead.

It makes me sick though, when I think of all the days I've spent sitting opposite him in that office, working. If he's laid a finger on her, I'm going to kill him. That's a promise. Fussing with his stupid lunch box. I can't believe I even took it round to him! And all the time he was thinking what he was going to do to Mel. If he *has* hurt her, then he is going to be *dead.* I don't care what anyone says: If he's done . . . *anything* to my baby, that's what he deserves.

They told me they're going to release his name. They've taken photos from me for the papers. Colin showed me all the headlines: HAVE YOU

SEEN THIS GIRL? I couldn't bear to read them. I couldn't concentrate, and, anyway, it's like I've read it all before, only it's somebody else's kid. You see the parents on TV and they're saying, we want you back, and all this, and you can see they're hoping and just . . . praying that the child's still alive. And you're sitting there feeling really sorry for them because it's like hoping against hope, you know, and at the same time you're thinking, thank God it's not my kid. Every time, when I used to see something like that, I'd have to go and check that Mel was all right. I'd go into her room and give her a hug, and she'd be all, like, "Mu-um, get off!" and I'd think, I'm going to look after her, make sure she's safe.

But I didn't, did I?

Mum gave me this note from the local church. She said it came through the door—it was this woman saying they're all praying for Mel. I've never even been in there, but I just thought, that's something I can do, at any rate, say a prayer. So I did—it was just like, please, God, let her be safe and come back to me. I wanted to say the proper one, Our Father—we used to say it in assembly, just gabble it off—but I couldn't remember all the words. In the end I just made some stuff up about God looking after us and everything. I don't know what I said, really. If you'd asked me last week if I believed in God, I'd have said I don't know, and I *don't,* not really, but it's something.

Colin just brought the radio in because they had something on about Gerald, with a description, and saying they want to interview him because of Mel, and if anyone thinks they've seen him can they please come forward. They've asked me to make a statement too, to go on the news, but I thought, if he hears it, what with Ron and Paul having a go at him, he might go mad or something, and then . . .

The phone just rang. Mum's been answering it, in case it's, like, a weirdo or something. But every time, *every time,* I'm thinking, please, please, let it be Mel, because that's all I want, to hear her voice again.

## Gerald

*It was nice on the train.* There was a girl in the car, she couldn't have been more than five or six, and she was singing "Hark! the Herald Angels Sing," or that was how she started off, with the right words and tune, but after that she was making it up as she went along. The mother said to her, "That's a Christmas song. Don't you know any about the spring?" But the little girl said, "No, I like this one," and carried on singing. It reminded me of us when we were children: *Hark! the Herald Angels Sing / Mrs. Simpson's pinched our King.* I remember the village boys singing that in church. Not me though—I was standing next to Mother, and anything like that would have been most frowned upon.

Funny, that's the only time I remember being inside that church, although we must have gone sometimes. I remember my mother telling me that everyone in England was christened, it was how you became a Christian. Eric said to me he hadn't been christened; neither had his brothers. I didn't believe him and we had quite an argument over it. It bothered me for days. Looking back, I don't know why . . . but when his mother came to see them, I asked her if it was true. We were in the kitchen with Mrs. Paddick, having tea, and when I asked her she said to Eric, "What have you been saying? Of course you were." I was watching her to see if she touched her hair at the back, because that was what *my* mother always did when she wasn't telling the truth. She didn't, but I remember thinking it must be made up because she sounded embarrassed. Eric asked, "Where was I?"

"Where was you what?"

"When I was christened."

"In a church, silly. You were only a baby, you wouldn't remember." And she leaned over and gave him a little push on his arm. Then Eric said, "Why didn't you bring Blackie?" That was his dog; he'd been telling me about him for days, boasting that he was better than our dog, Sammy. I didn't believe that any dog could be better than Sammy, because he was the best in the world, and we'd quarreled about that too.

Mrs. Watkins said, "Don't be silly, I couldn't bring him on the train."

Eric said, "You promised I could see him," and she said, "I never did anything of the kind." Then she turned to Mrs. Paddick. "He was so terrified of the raids, poor thing, I didn't know what to do for the best."

Eric said, "What do you mean? What's happened to him?"

"Nothing's happened to him, he's fine." She spoke to Mrs. Paddick again. "He was eating me out of house and home."

Vera said, "Why can't he come here and live with us? We could look after him for you."

"Oh, that won't be necessary, dear, he's fine where he is."

We all knew something had happened to Blackie, and there she was, lying about it. Eric wouldn't talk about it. When I said, "What's happened to your dog?" he told me to shut up and leave him alone. Vera kept asking Mother to write to Mrs. Watkins and say Blackie could come and live with us. Mother wouldn't, of course, and Vera was upset for days afterward. Looking back, of course, I can see that Mrs. Watkins had had the dog put to sleep and didn't want to tell Eric, and Mother knew it, but at the time I didn't realize that. I just couldn't understand why grown-ups told lies all the time.

I didn't like having to change at Colchester—one or two people gave me odd looks, but I think I got away with it all right. As we got closer to

Frinton I realized I don't know the name of the place where Aunt Tilly lives—that is, I do know, because it's written in my address book, but now I suppose the police have got hold of that along with all my other things. I can't understand why I didn't think of it before. I don't like all this rushing off with no preparation. Normally, when I go to see Aunt Tilly I've got it all sorted out weeks in advance so it's properly organized, but now I can't plan anything.

When I got off the train I didn't know what to do, so I went and sat on a bench, but it was too much to try and think about it all and my head was hurting. There were some taxis and I watched them, coming and taking people away from my train and then the next one and another one after that. I wanted to get one but I couldn't think of any name to give the driver, even a road name, and I didn't have very much money left so I thought it would be better to walk. I asked a man to point me in the right direction to the sea, because that's where it is near. He offered me a lift, but I refused because I thought he might start asking questions.

I'd hoped that I might recognize the place where Aunt Tilly lives, but the part where I thought it was seemed to be just a lot of flats—King's House and Queen's House and North House and South House—so that was all wrong. I went down another road because that seemed better, from what I could see from the corner, but it was all small houses. I looked at the names to see if there was anything I could recognize, but it was all Scottish names with Glen- at the beginning—Glencoe and Glenmore. That struck me as funny, to have these little houses with names like that, when they should be castles with big lakes and rivers instead of just a pond with a gnome doing the fishing.

It kept me going for a while, thinking about that, but when I got to the end it was nothing but a row of shops. I wandered about a bit more. I don't know where I went, really, I couldn't recognize any of it. I looked into the shop windows. One had china dogs, all the different breeds. I thought it would be nice to buy one for Doreen as a present because of all the trouble, but in fact I don't know if she likes dogs and then I would have even less money. Besides, the shop was closed, so I couldn't do that. But looking at those dogs made me think about Sammy and Vera again, and Aunt Tilly, because one of them was a little poodle, black like Nicky.

I didn't hear the man come up behind me. He gave me quite a start. "Good evening. I apologize if I startled you."

I said, "Not at all," and waited for him to move on, but he didn't. It was getting dark by this time, and we were standing between two street lamps, so I couldn't see him very well, but I had the impression he was quite effeminate. His hair looked as if it had been dyed and he was wearing a very jazzy cravat round his neck, fastened with a big silver thing—not a proper tiepin, more like a woman's brooch. I was afraid he might proposition me, because I've heard this is what they do, but he didn't say anything, just looked into the window. There were a lot of ornaments, but they had this one big crab in the middle, an ugly, floppy thing made of bright green flannel. I don't know what it was doing there, because all the other things were quite tasteful, to my way of thinking.

The man said, "They've got some lovely things in here, haven't they?" Which confirmed my suspicion about him, because it was the sort of thing a woman would say, but I felt I was required to make conversation, so I pointed to the crab and said, "That's a stupid thing. Who would want that?"

"Well," he said, "it takes all sorts, doesn't it?"

I wanted to say something about "I know what sort you are," because there was something not quite right about the way he'd said it—suggestive—but I didn't want any trouble so I said I'd lost my bearings and could he tell me the way to the beach. He gave me directions and said good night. When I saw him move away I realized why I hadn't heard him—he was light on his feet like a dancer.

It crossed my mind, walking back to the seafront, that I could have asked him if he knew Aunt Tilly—you do get a lot of *them* in the theater—but then I thought it wasn't very likely, with Frinton not being such a small place. I certainly wasn't prepared to go after him to find out!

By the time I got back to the Esplanade I felt as if I couldn't walk another step. It was very quiet—most of the flats had their lights off—and nobody bothered me when I went across the grass and down the path that leads to the beach. There's a narrow road behind it with a row of bathing huts, and my first thought was to spend the night in one of those, because it was getting quite nippy, but they were all padlocked so I sat down on a bench instead. I must have fallen asleep immediately, because I don't remember anything about it, and when I woke up I felt clammy and cold at the same time, very uncomfortable. I couldn't think where I was at first, but then I remembered the china dog I'd wanted to buy for Doreen and the little man who talked to me and not knowing where Aunt Tilly was, and then it all came back with a big jerk about Melanie and my room being searched. I must say I had it in my mind to walk out into the sea and never come back.

It was Jack who stopped me. When I gave him the signal in my head, he didn't answer me, and I thought, if I can't be with him, there's no point in doing it. That's the one thing that's kept me going as I've gotten older, you see, thinking that he's waiting for me. When I tried to commit suicide before, when I thought about it afterward, I came to the conclusion that I'd been jumping the gun, that Jack wanted me to stay put, because with only one of us having the chance of a life we had to make proper use of it. But I wish . . . I just wish . . . that it had been him who got the chance, and not me.

I thought I'd better get up quickly, before anyone came along and started asking questions. I checked my pockets, just in case, but the money was still there, and I've got a special five-pound note I keep in my jacket, in a plastic bag with a seal, in case there's an emergency. I wanted to go back and have another look at the china dogs, but when I got back up to the Esplanade, I felt so light-headed I had to sit down.

I suppose I must have nodded off again for an hour or two, because the next thing I noticed, there were people and cars everywhere.

I was about to get up when I saw the man again, the little chap with the cravat, walking straight toward the bench where I was sitting. I tried to get up, but my head was spinning and I couldn't seem to pull myself upright. He was waving at me, shouting something, and before I knew it he was sitting right beside me with his hand on my arm. I said, "What do you want?"

"You're Gerald, aren't you? Gerald Haxton?"

"No . . . my name's John . . . John . . ." My mind went blank. I couldn't think of any other name with him holding on to me like that.

"You needn't be afraid of me, you know. I wondered, when I saw you last night. You must forgive me, I should have said something. I've been calling myself names ever since."

"How . . . how do you know?"

"Tilly. She told me about you. Showed me a photograph. I never forget a face, and there I was, twittering on like a great fool."

I felt as if I were in a terrible nightmare, this little man clutching on to me, chattering into my face like a monkey, and nothing I could do but sit there. I couldn't get away from him or call out, because it would attract attention and I couldn't risk that. "I'd be grateful if you didn't touch me. I don't like it."

"Sorry." He let go of my arm and moved down the bench. "Carried away. I'm just so relieved to have found you. *Made contact.* When I got there this morning and they told me . . ."

"Got where? Who told you? What are you talking about, made contact with me? I don't understand. You're not—not some sort of policeman, are you?"

He raised his eyebrows. "Do I look like a policeman?"

"Well, no, but you said someone told you about me."

"They told me about *Tilly.* At the home. And as soon as I heard, well, I put two and two together, and . . . oh, dear, you don't know, do you?"

He moved toward me again and put out his hand. I shifted as far up the bench as I could, away from him. "Oh. Sorry." He put his hands up in a sort of flutter and moved back again. "Sorry, sorry. Didn't think. Oh, dear, I am making a mess of this, aren't I? It's just . . . I'm upset, that's all, with it happening so quickly like that when just yesterday . . . I should have known, really, if I'd only stopped to think."

"What's happened? What are you talking about?"

"Gerald . . . my name's Tiny. I was a friend of Tilly's, from the home. I play the piano there sometimes, for the old folk, and—"

"That's why I'm here, to see her, but I don't know where she is. I couldn't get my bearings. If you could show me how to get there, then I could . . . I need to see her, you see, talk to her. There's something—"

"Gerald. I'm sorry . . . Tilly's dead. She died last night. When I went to see her this morning, they told me. They said it was very peaceful, in her sleep."

"She can't . . . she can't be . . . I don't believe you. You're trying to stop me . . . keep me from seeing her. It isn't true."

"I'm sorry, I'm so sorry . . . I wouldn't lie to you about something like that. Why would I lie to you?"

"I don't know . . . I don't know about anything anymore."

"We'd had such a lovely afternoon. We . . . When I brought her back, in her chair, we were singing . . . Nellie Wallace . . . and we saw the children, all playing . . ."

"Stop . . . stop it! I can't think . . . I'm hungry, and . . . What am I going to do?"

He took a bar of Cadbury's out of his pocket and held it out to me. "Eat this. Plenty of sugar, good for shock."

"But it's yours."

"Yes, and now I'm giving it to you."

"But I can't just take . . . I'll give you some money for it."

"You can put that away, for a start. I wouldn't dream of it. It's the least I can do. Take it."

So I ate the chocolate, with this little man talking all the time. "If I'd only asked you last night . . . I could have given you a bed . . . and you with that great *gash* on your head. Did you find a room?" I had a mouthful, so I shook my head.

"But . . . where on earth did you sleep?"

"I . . . down there."

"On the *beach*? Oh, you poor man!"

I ate the last piece and folded the wrapper to put in my pocket. "Do you know if there's a place where I can get a cup of tea? I'm very thirsty."

"Of course, you must be. There's a café down the end there. It doesn't open until ten, but they're nice people. I'm sure they'll rustle up something for you if I ask them. Shall we give it a go?"

"Yes, please, I'd appreciate that."

It was a little white kiosk with a few tables outside. The hatch was down when we arrived, but the little man trotted round to the back and returned almost immediately with two teas in foam cups. "Here we are. Do you take sugar?"

"No, thank you."

"Me neither. Gave it up during the war."

I tried to give him some money for the tea, but he wouldn't let me. It made me uncomfortable, to tell you the truth. I don't like to feel beholden to anyone, especially someone like that because you never know when they're going to take advantage. While we were drinking the tea, the kiosk man rolled up the hatch and started laying things out on the counter. He had the radio going, but it wasn't music, just talking, news and weather. I said, "I'm glad it's not pop music, I can't bear all that racket."

The little man nodded. "It's just *noise*, isn't it? There don't seem to be any tunes anymore. Mind you, they wouldn't allow anything like that here—don't want to lower the tone."

I'd noticed the man putting out a box of Penguin bars. They're my favorite, and I was just wondering whether it would be a good idea to buy one in case I felt peckish later on when the man on the radio said, *The police have taken the unusual step of releasing the name of a man they want to interview in connection with the disappearance last Wednesday of twelve-year-old Melanie Farrell, last seen in the Shepherd's Bush area of London. Gerald Haxton, believed to be . . .*

I didn't hear any more. I froze. I wanted to get up, to run, but I couldn't move. The little man was staring at me. "That was you . . . what they said on the radio. It was your name."

"I didn't do it." Even forcing the words out of my mouth, I could only manage to whisper. "I haven't done anything wrong."

"Why do they want to talk to you?"

"I haven't done anything. I haven't. I just—she was my *friend!*"

"The girl who disappeared? You knew her?"

"Melanie. Yes. I only followed her. I haven't got anything to do with it—they're trying to blame me—"

"They just want to talk to you, that's all. What do they call it . . . eliminate you from their inquiries. Look, why don't I come with you? It'll probably take only a few minutes, you know what they're like."

"Oh, I know what the police are like, all right."

"But if you haven't done anything . . ."

"That's not what they think. They came and searched my room, took my things away . . . all my belongings."

The little man put out his hand. "Why don't you come back to my house?"

"No!"

I tried to get up, but it's never easy with those molded plastic chairs— I got stuck and I had to twist round and struggle with the wretched thing, and I kept thinking the police would arrive at any moment. The little man stood up too, and said, "If you come back with me, then we can decide what to do for the best."

"Stop pestering me! Leave me alone!"

He took a step toward me, but I was still trying to push the chair off, so I couldn't get away. "You've got to trust someone."

"Well, I don't trust you. You're trying to trick me, I know your type, preying on people like . . . like . . ." The chair fell off, backward. He was blocking my way between the tables. They were only made of plastic so it was easy to push past. I heard him shouting after me, "Stop!" as I ran off down the road.

I went as fast as I could. I kept expecting to hear police sirens come after me, or at least footsteps, but there was nothing. By the time I got past the houses I had a terrible stitch in my right side, so I went into a field and sat down behind a hedge to catch my breath. I heard a couple of cars going past, but still no footsteps, and I thought if the little man had run after me he would have caught up with me by now, because I don't have much speed.

The important thing is to keep on the move, keep away from people. Nice spring day, I will say that—with my luck it ought to be coming down like cats and dogs. Difficult walking through the fields though. They don't clear the footpaths properly; there's stinging nettles and thistles and things slowing you up all the time. I saw a woman with a collie in the distance, but she didn't come close.

After a while—a couple of hours, I think—I found myself on a golf course. One of the players shouted at me, but he was quite a way away, so I kept my head down and carried on. They don't like you walking on the greens or whatever those flat bits are, but it was difficult skirting round them and each one looked the same as the next, so I just concentrated on going in a straight line. Then I came to a big pond or lake or something, so I had to give up that idea, but that brought me into the woods. I thought it was just a narrow strip of trees, but I must have taken the wrong turn, because I found myself in the middle of a thick forest with no idea how to get out. There were no proper paths, or signs, just branches everywhere you turned. One of them nearly took my eye out. Eventually, I came up to a chain-link fence, so I followed that along until I came back onto the road again. Then some idiot in a van nearly ran me over. Writing on the side . . . going too fast for me to see. Talking on his phone at the same time. They shouldn't allow that, phones in cars. It's downright dangerous. I fell right into the ditch and tore my jacket on a bramble. Have to put a patch on it now. Nobody mends things anymore, just buy new every time, and they don't last. . . . Maniac.

I started to see houses after a while, then a parade of shops, and I got worried in case it was going to take me right into the middle of a town. I guessed it was probably Clacton because I thought that was the direction I'd been going, but I didn't want to ask anyone in case the broadcast had mentioned anything about my appearance that they might remember. In any case, I saw a sign for Clacton Dry Cleaners after that, so I knew I was right. Seeing the supermarket next to it reminded me how hungry I was—should have bought the Penguin bar while I had the chance. There was a drinking fountain there too, and I was so hot and thirsty I decided to use it. I wouldn't normally—you don't know what sort of germs you might pick up—but it was a case of needs must. Children everywhere—one pair chasing each other up and down nearly knocked me off my feet—but no adults, so it seemed safe enough. There should have been adults, mind you, keeping an eye on them, especially with the way things are at the moment . . . but I suppose it was my good fortune, because if they'd been about I couldn't have taken the risk.

I followed the signs to the beach and walked all the way along with my head down, as if I were looking for shells and things. You see a lot of people doing that, beachcombing, and no one gives them a second look. I thought that was a stroke of genius, much better than trying to thread my way through the town with all the people staring at me. I was congratulating myself on getting so far without being stopped, but it was starting to get dark and the tide was coming in, and I knew the beach wasn't going to go on forever, so I thought, where do I go now?

It was my feet that were bothering me most. I'm not used to so much walking, and I knew they weren't going to carry me much farther—the last half mile or so had been almost impossible. I looked for a place to sit down. There was a concrete wall separating the beach from the road, and I noticed a couple of little sailboats near it, which would be some cover at least, so I went and sat down between them and took my shoes off. Nasty blisters on both heels. Never had them as big as that, even in the army. Great balloon of white flesh, all dragged down where it had rubbed against the shoe. The one on the other foot had burst—fluid all over the sock, and of course I had to go and drop it so it was all covered with wet sand and I couldn't put it back on again. I couldn't manage to fit my shoes back on either. I left them behind the boat in the end, with the socks inside. Too much to carry.

It's been a long time since I've walked barefoot. It's a bit chilly, but I wouldn't say it is unpleasant, although it's probably a good thing that I can barely see what I'm walking *on* now. I found an opening in the wall, steps up to the road. More light here. Have to be careful though—glass. Road's a mess, tarmac breaking up. Funny little seaside houses. Look like beach huts, but they're too big for that. Wooden verandas, falling down, half of them, windows rotting away—shacks, almost. *It's only a shanty in old shantytown . . . There's a tumbledown shack by an old railroad track . . .* No, I've left a bit out. Was it The Crazy Gang? It's no good, I can't remember. Half of these places look as if one puff of wind would blow them over. That one at the end . . . imagine putting stone cladding on a thing like that! No wonder it's all coming off. Nasty-looking, like scabs. Not many people about. Lot of windows boarded up, bars across doors. Like it's all been abandoned. Few doors open though. Watching TV. Not nice, everyone looking in at you. That one's got a name. Can't make it out— O.O.K.A.R.E.S. Have to think about that one. Sounds Red Indian to me.

Better see where I am. Road name, that's a start. Alvis Avenue. And this is . . . Humber . . . Riley . . . Sunbeam . . . All cars! There's a café up ahead. Lit up, so it must be still open. Better not get too close though.

What's that on the blackboard? PIE + MASH + LIQOUR. That's not how you spell it, they've got the letters the wrong way round. I didn't know anyone ate those things anymore. Wonder if they do Penguin bars. There's a man coming out. Got a rubbish bag. Shouldn't be dragging it like that—got a hole in the bottom, bits going all over the road, making a mess. Not very nice at all.

He's seen me. Shouting something. Can't make it out. Get away from here, *fast* . . . Keep running, don't slow down, don't . . . got to slow down. Gravel. Hurting my feet. Not chasing me though. *Why won't they leave me alone?*

It's like a dream. More roads, more car names. Wolseley. That was a nice car. My father had one. Go up here. On concrete blocks, some of these houses, from what I can make out. No one here, just a lot of weeds between the cracks. One here with a name—T. H. Y. S. L. D. O.—This'll do. No one here. Funny name for a holiday home. You'd think they'd have picked something like *Sans Souci*, wouldn't you? Perhaps they don't know any French. Not that I can remember much myself. No glass in this window. No bar on the door either. Just left. Gone. Something soft here, I can feel it. Mattress? This'll do for me, at any rate. Settle down for the night. It's just come to me what the name of that other house was—Oo Kares. Who Cares, see? Good question.

I wouldn't hurt her. Never hurt . . . I only touched her fingers, her arm . . . under the leaves. Pretty white shoulder, dirt on it, tried to brush it off but more came from my fingers, made it worse. The strap of her underwear hanging down and you could see . . . I wanted to touch her . . .

## Jo

*Mum said, "It's Ron.* For you."

I didn't know what to say. I picked it up and went, "Hello?"

"It's Ron. Who was that?"

"My mum. Did the police—"

"What police? They're bloody useless. I know where he is."

"What?"

"A mate of mine saw him. Got a pie-and-mash shop. He'd heard it on the radio, and he says he's sure it was Gerald. I'd told him about Mel and that—before—so he rang me up."

"Where?"

"I'm going after him."

"Ron, if you know, you've got to tell me, so the police—"

"Bollocks to the police. I'm going after him."

"Wait, Ron—"

"I can't, I've got to go."

"Stop, wait, I—"

"I'm going now."

Then he put the phone down.

I was straight on the phone to the police. Told them about the pie-and-mash shop—there can't be *that* many of them. They told me they'd get straight onto it, whatever that means. Everyone keeps saying to me, don't give up hope, and I'm not, but some of the things I've been thinking, about what might have happened to her . . . I try and block it out of my mind, because it's like Mum says, it's not doing any good, but all the same . . . But you don't know, I mean, unless it's happening to *you*, you can't know what it feels like. There's just no words to describe it.

One good thing though. Our policewoman—liaison officer or whatever she's called; Marion, her name is—she told me they've had another call about Gerald. Some friend of his, apparently, so now they know where he's gone. Well, they know the *area*, that's what she said. Essex coast. Mum had a look at Colin's road atlas, and she turned round and said to Marion, "Well, it's a bloody big area, from what I can see."

I said, "But he doesn't have a car, does he? I mean, as far as I know, he can't drive."

"There's always trains though."

"Yeah, but someone's *got* to see them . . . right? She's had her photo on the news and in every single paper, and all it needs is one person . . ."

Colin said, "Jo's right. Someone's bound to recognize her."

Mum said, "I know, but this bloke, the one who phoned, he never said anything about Mel, did he? About her being with Gerald, I mean."

Marion said, "That may not be significant . . . we don't know yet."

I said, "What about Ron? Have you spoken to him?"

"They've been trying to get hold of him. I'm sure you'll be told if there are any developments."

That was it, really, because then Mum started talking about all the letters I've had, messages of support and all that. After Marion had gone, I said to Mum, "There's something we're not being told . . ." because all the time we'd been talking, that was what was going round in my head. I mean, I don't know if I'm being paranoid or whatever, but it was like I could sense something funny was going on that they're not telling us. But all the time, you're just living from one minute to the next, you know? Nothing's *normal* anymore, because . . . well, how can it be?

I said to Mum, "They couldn't have found Mel and they're not telling us, could they?" and she's, like, "Knock it off!" But she said it really sort of quickly, *too quick,* and I suddenly thought, Mum and Colin think she's dead but they're not telling me. I just ran out of the room. I couldn't bear to be in there with them if they were pretending, but I couldn't bring myself to ask. I heard Mum calling after me, and Colin going, "No, leave her be."

I went to sit in Mel's room. I do that all the time now, because it's, like, being nearer to her if I'm in there, looking at her things. I was thinking we might redecorate it when she comes back . . . get some paint. We could do it together. I was going to ask Colin to go down the shops, get some charts. I always wanted a gold and silver room when I was little, but knowing her she'd probably want something a bit more grown-up, like blue. I was looking through her clothes the other day, and I'd never noticed before how many blue things she's got.

Even if it's just me and no one else, I've got to believe they'll find her. Believe she's all right. I've been round and round in circles with it all, and that's the one thing I know I've got to hang on to. I can't give up hope.

## Gerald

*I did not do it*, I didn't, I didn't. *Not my fault, not my fault.* Light outside. Mattress . . . *not my room.* Nasty smell. People. Outside. Lots of people, making a noise. Woke me up. Don't like it. Shouting . . . shouting bad things . . . Tried hands over my ears, it didn't work. People coming to get me. Why do they want to hurt me? I haven't done anything wrong. Don't like the noise. Breaking wood. What are they doing? Jack? I didn't do anything wrong. Jack, make them stop it, *please.* . . . They're smashing the house. The back, get to the back, more people, I can hear them, at the sides, dragging something, corrugated iron. I can't think, Jack, help me to think. . . .

Voices. Hundreds, all shouting at me. "Per-*vert!* Per-*vert!* Per-*vert!*" Banging the sides of the house with sticks.

"Leave our kids alone!"

Keep on the floor, hands and knees . . .

"What have you done with her, you evil bastard?"

Sick, going to be sick . . . *help me* . . .

"Come out!"

*I haven't done anything wrong* . . .

"We'll tear the house down if we have to!"

My head, that voice, in my head, recognize . . . from the warehouse. Likes playing children's games, that's what he said. I remember the voice . . . tearing the house apart . . .

*I never meant to hurt her.*

"Per-*vert*! Per-*vert*! Per-*vert*!"

Something shattered now . . . Coming from the back, they're breaking the windows at the back, get away from the glass . . . Someone said a
crowbar, get the crowbar, smash the door . . .

Right inside my head, this banging, can't think, everything coming
sideways toward me, they're breaking the door down . . .

She was my *friend* . . .

Got to stand up, get upright. It's going, the door. I can see it falling,
coming toward me. Back, get back . . .

Dust. Can't see for the dust. But no noise now. Go forward. Bright
light. From the doorway. *Go toward the light.*

Hold on to the door frame. Nothing below my feet. Don't look
down. Where the veranda was . . . just wooden planks, lying in the dirt.
They tore it up. Look at them all. How many? White blur. Faces in a
semicircle, going out and out, all the way down the road . . .

"Bastard!" A single voice, from the back. The rubbish man. From the
café. Then a stone flying over my shoulder, landing somewhere behind
me with a clatter. Now a man in the middle, stepping forward, something in his hand—wooden spar. Must have come from the veranda.
Nail still fixed to the end . . . Watch his face, not the nail, don't look at
the nail. Eyes, hard blue eyes, coming toward me, it's all I can see. . . .

Everything has stopped. I cannot move. Only the eyes, locking mine.
*He knows where she is.*

Then the noise again, coming closer, sirens. Cars in the street, the
lights flash on, off, on, off, and people scatter and ripple, open and close
again around the cars. I can see it all over the man's shoulder and he has
gone back, back, wooden boards bang up and down where he steps on
them. Now the little man is here in front of me, his arms move up and
down. He is talking but I can't hear what he's saying. Why is he here? I
have to speak to him . . . tell him I didn't do it, it wasn't me. Tell him . . .
Aunt Tilly . . . *Jack* . . .

"Well done," said the inspector. "Mr. Porter and his friends are safe in jail. We've been after those men for a long time, but now they'll be brought to justice—thanks to you."

The children blushed with pleasure. "You've been remarkably clever," said the inspector. "You should think about joining the police when you're older," he told Tom. "People like you are just the sort we want."

In no time at all, the police car had arrived at Myrtle Cottage. The inspector shook hands with each of them. "Good-bye. I expect you've got a fine spread waiting for you. You certainly deserve it!"

It was a very jolly tea. Mrs. Peak had baked new scones for them and made a big plum pie. There was even a big, meaty bone for Scruff. All four ate hungrily, until everything was finished up. "That was delicious," said Peter. "I wish I could eat it all over again."

"What a shame it's the last day of the holidays," said Tom. "We've had a fine time, haven't we?"

Just then, Mrs. Johnson came into the kitchen. "I've just been talking to the inspector," she said. "He's very pleased with you all, but really, you mustn't do these dangerous things. It might have all ended very differently."

"But it didn't," said Jill, "and we've had the most wonderful adventure—haven't we, Scruff?"

Thump went the dog's tail on the floor, thump-THUMP!

"You see, Aunt Fenella?" said Tom. "Scruff agrees with us."

"We'll have lots more adventures together, won't we, old boy?" said Jill, patting his head. Scruff looked up at his mistress. What a silly question! Of course they would! "Woof!" he said happily. "Woof, WOOF!"

**Tom's Island Adventure**, 1941

## Gerald

*Everything is white.* Except straight ahead, a big square, pale green, divided into little squares. Something round, dark, in the middle. I'm not in my room. My room doesn't have those things.

The little man's here again. He's got something in his hands. Flowers. He's putting them in a vase. Can't see his face.

Behind the squares . . . the dark object is moving, turning . . . into a face. It's ducking down now, opening the door. I can see . . . uniform. Policeman! Coming into the room. My hand banging against rails, no rails on my bed—a prison bed would have rails and a policeman. But I didn't do it, wasn't me, not me, I didn't—

"He knows." The little man is beside me, looking down. "We all do."

"I didn't do it."

The policeman at the foot of the bed is saying something now. "It's all right, we know all about it, you're all right."

"Why am I here?"

"Hospital." The little man is speaking now. "You're in hospital. You're quite safe."

Something on my arm. Touching . . . "Sorry." The little man took his hand away. "I forgot."

"Doesn't matter."

"Do you remember me? Tiny."

"Yes. At the place, I saw you. You were there, with the police."

"That's right."

"I didn't do it, I—"

"We know you didn't do it, Mr. Haxton. You mustn't worry. It's all sorted out." It's the policeman talking. "The doctor'll want to see you." He started to go toward the door.

"Wait . . . the girl . . . Melanie . . . I—"

"She's here too."

"Is she . . ."

"She's alive, yes. She's in a bad way, I'm afraid, but she's still very much with us."

"I didn't—"

"Gerald . . ." The little man pulled a handkerchief out of his pocket. "Here, let me wipe your eyes . . . that's better."

"What's your name?"

"Tiny." He turned to look at the policeman. "Daniel Sidney McManus to you, dear."

The policeman turned and left. "Get a load of him!" The little man laughed. "Gone off in a huff. Can I get you something?"

"I'm thirsty."

"I don't know if you're allowed anything until the doctor's seen you. They left some ice cubes though. Would you like one? Here, open your mouth."

"Um . . . thank you. Where's Palfrey?"

"Never heard of him, dear. Is he a friend of yours? I could—"

"No!"

"Steady, don't want you choking, do we?"

"No . . . he's not my friend, but I thought . . . what's your name again?"

"Tiny. Don't worry, you'll get there in the end. Here's the doctor coming. I'll just nip outside for a moment."

The doctor didn't stay long. He had a look at me and said they'd keep me in overnight, because of my head, but I should be able to go home in the morning. "You've got some bumps and bruises, and we'll give you something for those. Better try and keep it quiet for the next few days, eh? No party-going."

That made me smile. "Not much chance of that."

"Well, I won't keep you—I can see you've got visitors."

It was the little man again—Tiny—waving at me through the glass. "All done? Can we come in now?" Mrs. Clarke was behind him, with a lovely bunch of chrysanthemums. "Look, more flowers! Lovely! I'll pop them in water, shall I?"

Mrs. Clarke gave them to him. "You do that. I'm going to talk to Gerald." She sat down beside me. "Now, then. Was that the doctor?"

"Yes."

"He looked like a nice man. Not bad in here, is it? Clean." She patted my hand. "Better than that other place, at any rate. And you've got a room all to yourself, haven't you? Very nice."

"Yes, it's a lot better . . . You'll have to forgive me, Mrs. Clarke—"

"It's Doreen, remember?" She laughed. "I wouldn't blame you if you didn't remember, after what you've been through. I heard all about it, from that one" —she nodded toward Tiny—"and as soon as they let you go, you're coming home and I'll take care of you. Dreadful, the whole business! I told them, I kept telling them, I knew it was nothing to do with you, but they kept coming back and back with more and more questions. I told them I had no idea where you were, and then *he* phoned up—" She nodded at Tiny again. "Oh, it was quite a to-do, I can tell you."

"What happened? I don't understand. I was in that house, I remember that. Then there were all those people outside."

"And then *we* arrived!" Tiny sat down on the end of the bed. "Not on your feet, am I? You should have seen it," he said to Doreen. "Like the Seventh Cavalry, we were! Rushing in . . . And Gerald here standing there, in front of all that crowd—it was like *High Noon*."

"But how did you—"

"*Well.* After we'd heard everything on the radio and you'd rushed off like that, I didn't know what to do. But I had a note from your aunt Tilly. They'd given it to me in the morning, when I'd been . . . you know. You remember that, don't you? Aunt Tilly?"

"Yes, you told me. I'm sorry if I seemed . . . well, if I didn't believe you."

"I don't think I said it very well. As I said, she was a good friend of mine, and I was upset, but she'd told me . . . well, she'd told me to look you up, if you know what I mean. Anyway, I had this note in my pocket, so I opened it, and she'd said some things . . . one of them was your address, you see, and the telephone number. So I rang up and got Doreen, and we talked about it, and neither of us thought . . . you know, that you were *involved* at all. But we were worried, we thought you wouldn't be *safe*—well, you saw the type of people involved. So she said she'd get in touch with the police, and I did the same at my end, you see? And of course we didn't know where you were, so I got into my car and headed off in the direction you'd gone. I thought you'd probably walked down the coast, so I parked in Clacton and spent *ages* looking for you, but it was like trying to find the Invisible Man. Nobody'd noticed you. . . . You did walk that way, didn't you?"

I nodded. "Down the beach."

"That's what I did! The following morning, of course, not then. I hadn't been able to sleep a wink. All night I was thinking, where could he have got to, and then I had another look at the map, and there it was: Jaywick Sands."

"Was that where I was?"

"Yes, dear, just down from Clacton."

"I didn't know."

"I'm not surprised. It's a funny place." Tiny turned to Doreen. "Used to be popular, from what I hear, but now . . ." He rolled his eyes. "Shame, really, it could be quite nice if they'd only tart it up a bit . . . but it's got a bit of an *atmosphere,* if you know what I mean. All those huts moldering away, empty, half of them. That was what gave me the idea—a place to hide, you see? I remembered you said you'd slept on the beach at Frinton, so I thought I'd better walk down from Clacton and check that you hadn't nodded off in a boat or something. I left the car, and by the time I got to Jaywick, there was this *mob*. I got there at the same time as the police."

"But how did they know?"

"*Them!* They didn't know anything! Didn't know who you were until I told them, and then they got onto the London lot and came back shrugging their shoulders and saying it was all a mistake and it wasn't you they wanted at all. Well, I was *furious*. I said to them, 'What are you going to do, stand there and watch him get murdered?' They got very huffy about it, I can tell you."

"But that man—the one who—"

"Don't worry about him! He's where he ought to be, behind bars."

"But how . . . how—"

"How did they know it was him? Well, from what they told me afterward, they'd been to his house, you see? It was Melanie's mother—"

"Jo," said Doreen. "From your work. The one who came to see me. After the . . . in the warehouse. I told you, remember?"

"Yes, that's right," said Tiny. "Jo. She'd phoned them because it was this chap she'd been seeing, they were trying to contact him, and then he'd phoned her, you see, said he knew where you were."

"*He* knew where I was?"

"It turned out he had a mate down at Jaywick. He's got a café, and he'd seen you. Well, of course, this Ron—"

"Is that his name?"

"Yes, they told me. Ron Russell. Anyway, he'd told his mate all about Jo and Melanie and you, how you were a stalker and he was worried you'd got the girl and all the rest of it. So the minute this man sees you, he rushes inside and picks up the phone. Russell gives him some line about not calling the police, because you'd only get off with a fine and a slapped wrist, and then he drives like the hounds of hell to Jaywick and the two of them charge round the place telling everyone there's a pederast on the loose. Of course, the neighbors thought the worst, what with it being on the news and everything . . . you can't blame them, can you? Half of them were convinced you had Melanie in there with you, and they were all worried about their children. But the police in London, you see, they'd had the name Ron Russell come up on their computer. It turns out that he's been questioned before, same sort of offense, and it was actually his *wife*—well, she was his wife at the time, this was about five years ago—who'd spoken to them, but there wasn't enough evidence. The other thing was, it involved this woman he'd been seeing on the side—the girl was *her* daughter, just like Jo and Melanie. What with the marriage going down the tubes, the police thought the wife might have acted, well, out of revenge, you know. So that was all forgotten, and they pulled in this other man for it."

"What happened to him?"

"Prison. He kept saying he hadn't done it and nobody thought to question him, because he was a bit . . . well, a bit *simple,* and he lived with his mother. Apparently the girl's body was found near their house. Of course they don't *know,* but . . . He died. In prison. About a year ago, they said. They're thinking they'll look into it again, because the man's family's had this campaign going, and now, with this arrest . . ."

Doreen said, "It just goes to show—they're very cunning, these people, they've got it all worked out—"

Tiny interrupted her. "No, but the *van,* you see . . . Once all those people realized that it wasn't you at all but this man instead, and once they knew they couldn't give him a going-over because the police had him in the handcuffs, a whole posse of them rushed off down the road and started attacking this van, which he'd parked right at the end of the road. They had bars, iron bars, some of them. The ones they were using to smash up that house you were in. The police went off to stop them because they were breaking the windows, and then they wrenched one of the back doors off and they saw—wrapped in a piece of canvas, they thought—there she was! Well, I'd stayed with you, because you were passed out by that time, out cold you were. I thought you'd never get up again. I was kneeling beside you, *willing* you to open your eyes, all the time thinking about Tilly, and what she—well, anyway, I could see all this . . . *rumpus,* and then the ambulance came. I saw when they carried her past. Her face, such a *mess,* and I thought, history repeating—"

"History? You mean . . . with Vera?"

"Yes, dear. Tilly, your aunt, she told me. And I thought . . . that was why I was so keen to get the police involved. Anyway, never mind all that. The poor child looked more dead than alive, but I kept thinking there might be a chance . . ."

"That policeman, what he said—"

"Yes, she's going to pull through!" Tiny turned to Doreen. "We asked, didn't we? And they told us. She's going to be all right. The effects, of course . . ."

"It doesn't bear thinking about," said Doreen. "Poor little thing. How can you trust anybody these days?"

"Quite right," said Tiny. "But you're responsible, in a way, Gerald, for saving her . . . because you led the police to him, really. He was going to make it look as if it was you. I mean, it's like these people going on TV all upset, saying bring my child back, when all the time they've done it themselves. And the girl's mother, Jo, she phoned the police, didn't she? So she must have thought something strange was going on with the boyfriend. But that was difficult too . . . for the police, I mean, because sometimes they're condoning it, aren't they? Or turning a blind eye— the mothers, I mean."

"Evil," said Doreen. "Pure evil, that's what it is. No two ways about it."

"But there's something we wanted to say to you, Gerald, didn't we, Doreen? I think the police . . . well, they might want to have a word with you about it." Tiny looked at Doreen and then at me. "The thing is, you mustn't follow people around. We know you didn't mean any harm, but a young girl like that, it could be very frightening, and . . . well, you mustn't do it again."

"I know. I'm sorry I did it. She looked like Vera, you see, and I was lonely."

Tiny leaned forward. "I know, but you've got us now. Hasn't he, Doreen?"

## Jo

*When they told us,* I can't tell you. I can't even start . . . The police-woman, Marion, she came in with this huge smile, and I just *screamed.* She didn't even have to say anything, she's just hugging me, going, "It's all right, it's all right . . ." Then she's all, trying to tell me what happened, but I can't take any of it in. So we go to the hospital, and there's all the reporters outside, all these faces. I tried to say some-thing, but I couldn't get the words out, I just burst into tears. I felt like, all I want is to see her. They're asking loads of questions, but that was the only thing I could think of. The hospital staff though, they've been so great; they gave us this room and everything. We're in there, and Mum's hugging me, and it's, like, *"Oh, my God . . ."*

It was really dark when they took me in there, but I could see her poor face, one eye swelled up like a football and really bruised. I knew that Ron . . . I knew . . . he raped her, because Marion told me before I went in, and that when they found her she had her hands tied behind her back. Marion said they think she must have put up quite a fight. I was imagining what it was like for her, you know, thinking she was hav-ing this secret meeting with Ron and it was just a bit of a laugh, and then he suddenly turned on her and—or maybe he was up-front about it, trying it on and she was thinking, okay, because she was, like, flat-tered or whatever, but then he went too far and he wouldn't stop. He'd suffocated the other girl, put a plastic bag over her head. Another five minutes and that could have been Mel, 'cause he was going to do it and blame Gerald. We'd all have believed it, wouldn't we?

When I saw her, she was really sort of woozy. I didn't know if she could see me or not, or if she even knew I was there. I kept thinking, you've got to be really *calm,* but of course I start crying again, and I'm going, "Oh, Mel, I love you, I'm really sorry, I love you . . ." and I can hear Mum behind me, "If I ever get my hands on that bastard," and all this, but I'm just, "You're alive, I can't believe it, I love you so much . . ." And then Mel, she turns her head so she's looking at me, and she says, "Hello, Mum." I could barely hear her, but the tone was, like, so *normal,* you know? I felt like my heart was going to burst . . . like everything inside me . . . it's no good, I can't explain, it's just, when I heard her voice . . .

It's so hard to believe Ron could do something like that. Taking Mel, then pretending he's helping me, when all the time . . . And when I saw them in the kitchen together and I'm, like, oh, it's great they're getting on so well, you know? There's me thinking we're going to have this relationship and everything—I mean, *I just let him into my life.* I did think something was funny, but it was over the business with Gerald, that's the really stupid thing. Because people say, trust your intuition, right? But I was wrong about Gerald, wasn't I? It's like Mum says, he may be a bit mad, but he's not *bad* mad. Whereas Ron . . . I mean, how can someone *do* that? I just can't get my head round it. But thinking about it, it's really because of Gerald that Mel is still alive. I've got to have a proper talk to him about it, say thank you and everything. They said he was, like, following her because he was lonely. I don't really get it, to tell you the truth.

Marion said she'll go over everything again, because I wasn't really taking it all in, only bits. But I can't deal with any of it, not at the moment. Mel's the only thing I care about right now. I've been sitting here, just looking at her and thinking, you're safe. Because that's all that matters, really. Everything else can wait.

## Gerald

*I must have fallen asleep after that,* because it was dark when I woke up. I switched on the bedside light and saw that someone had left a card on top of the little cabinet. It was from my show, *Starlight Express. Come back soon,* it said. They'd all signed it. Some of the writing! I had quite a time trying to work out all the names. Of course, I've got all my signed programs, but this is . . . wonderful. So kind of them to think of me. When I get my things back, I'll have to give it pride of place. That's going to take quite a bit of doing, sorting them all out. Still, it's something to look forward to—makes a change. Funny, that's what I thought when . . . well, when all this started. I never meant to do anything wrong. Sometimes things happen that you don't mean . . . but the main thing is that Melanie's going to be all right. Tiny said because of me. I hope that she and Jo . . . I suppose we'll have to see.

It's nice here. Peaceful. One of the nurses just popped her head round the door. Jamaican. Beautiful smile. Said I should try and get some sleep.

Better turn the light off now. Put the card back up here first. I can look at it again in the morning.

Perhaps I could ask Doreen if she'd like to come out with me one evening. We could have a bite to eat. I've seen a place that might be suitable. A little bistro. Italian. Nothing fancy, just . . . can't be sure about the food though, all that garlic. I could go by myself, of course, first— just to make sure it's all right. . . . Yes, I'd like that.

## About the Author

Laura Wilson lives with her partner and a basset hound in North Essex and London. A former editor and author of children's books, her first novel, *A Little Death,* was shortlisted for the Crime Writers' Association Ellis Peters Historical Dagger Award and was also recently nominated for an Anthony Award. She is currently at work on her fourth suspense novel, which Delacorte will publish in 2003.